A HYPHENATED LIFE

SYLVIA BARNARD

 FriesenPress

One Printers Way
Altona, MB R0G 0B0
Canada

www.friesenpress.com

Copyright © 2024 by Sylvia Barnard
First Edition — 2024

Edited by The Indy Editor; Maggy Morris

All rights reserved.

No part of this publication may be reproduced in any form, or by any means, electronic or mechanical, including photocopying, recording, or any information browsing, storage, or retrieval system, without permission in writing from FriesenPress.

ISBN
978-1-03-831222-8 (Hardcover)
978-1-03-831221-1 (Paperback)
978-1-03-831223-5 (eBook)

1. FICTION, COMING OF AGE

Distributed to the trade by The Ingram Book Company

Dedicated to my Parents

TABLE OF CONTENTS

Chapter One - 1963: Family Visit 1

Chapter Two - 1963: Arrested Progress.....................7

Chapter Three - 1963: Trapped 15

Chapter Four - 1963: Cousins and Friends..............27

Chapter Five - 1963: Too Canadian........................43

Chapter Six - 1963: Auf Wiedersehen, Germany.....55

Chapter Seven - 1951: Time to Go..........................67

Chapter Eight - 1951:
Welcome to the New World 81

Chapter Nine - 1951: Making a Home 95

Chapter Ten - 1963: Ontario.................................107

Chapter Eleven - 1963: A Place to Stand...............117

Chapter Twelve - 1964: Pen pals............................129

Chapter Thirteen - 1965: Too German..................139

Chapter Fourteen - 1965: Friends 153

Chapter Fifteen - 1966:
Facing Uncomfortable Truths................................165

Chapter Sixteen - 1967: The Good Girl 179

Chapter Seventeen - 1968: Innocence Lost............185

Chapter Eighteen - 1969: The Final Schuss 197

Chapter Nineteen - 1969: Creative Defiance 207

Chapter Twenty - 1969: Crossing the Line 219

Chapter Twenty-One - 1970: Choices 231

Chapter Twenty-Two - 1970:
Mini-skirts, Jeans, and Rouladen 247

Chapter Twenty-Three - 1971:
Just an Ordinary Girl 261

Chapter Twenty-Four 1972:
Home for Christmas 275

Chapter Twenty-Five - 1972:
From Heaven to Hell...285

Chapter Twenty-Six -1973:
Belonging to Herself..293

Chapter Twenty-Seven - 2000:
The Good Mother 301

Epilogue - 2003..315

Author Afterword - Legacy 323

Acknowledgements..329

CHAPTER ONE - 1963

Family Visit

Marta's hands pleated and un-pleated her full skirt as her eleven-year-old daughter, Angelika, stared at the planes taxiing in and out of the airport. This would be Marta's first time back to Germany since she and Kurt had emigrated twelve years ago. What changes would her family see in her and she in them?

Marta couldn't wait to introduce Angelika to her mother. Angelika was polite, obedient, and helpful. Her mother would see that Marta was fulfilling her duties of teaching her daughter to cook, clean, sew, and knit, so she'd be ready to run her own household when she married. Marta didn't argue when Kurt took Angelika hunting and fishing, taught her basic carpentry skills, and taught her to ski and skate. Marta respected Kurt's way of bonding with his daughter, since she hadn't been able to give him a son. Although these activities hadn't been suitable for girls when she was growing up, today's women were agitating for an equality with men in the workplace and in the home. While Marta was happy keeping her home and caring for her husband and daughter, she wanted Angelika to be ready to take advantage of all the opportunities that might open up for her.

Angelika flopped down into the seat beside her mother. "Are we boarding soon?"

Two women in Lufthansa uniforms were setting up at the desk that guarded the entry to the catwalk.

"I think so," Marta said.

"How long does it take to get there?"

"The flight to Frankfurt takes seven hours, then we have to change planes and fly another hour to Berlin."

"What's the first thing you want to do when we get to Oma's?"

Marta swallowed around the lump clogging her throat. "Hug her." She looked away to compose herself.

"Will we be able to see the ground when we're flying? Jacques Boudreau said we'll be so high we'll only see clouds."

"I've never been on a plane, but that does sound right."

"Jacques said his dad told him you have to stay strapped in your seat. I can't go seven hours without going to the bathroom." Angelika's brow furrowed.

"Who is this Jacques and how does he know about planes?"

"A boy in my class." Angelika shrugged. "I think his dad works at the airport in Val d'Or."

Marta patted her knee. "I'm sure they have toilets on the plane."

"I wish Papa was coming with us."

"Me too." Marta squeezed her daughter's hand. "But he has to find a job and a house for us."

Angelika gave a sniff. "Why do we have to move, anyway? I don't want to leave my friends." She slouched into the chair, arms crossed over her chest.

Marta sighed. "We've been through this already. The mine is closing. We can't live in Beaupré-sur-Lac without work for Papa. Besides, most of your friends are moving, too, so even if we stayed, it wouldn't be the same."

Angelika humphed.

Marta hugged her daughter. "How about some chocolate for the trip? Will that help?" She handed Angelika a quarter. "A Coconut bar for me, please, and you can have your usual Milky Way." She watched Angelika skip across the large hall to the confectionary.

When her daughter returned with two Dairy Milk Bars, Marta asked, "What's this?"

"They didn't have anything else," Angelika muttered.

The boarding call came over the speaker before Marta could ask further questions.

* * *

July 3, 1963

Chère Journal,

I can't believe we're on a plane! And not just any plane. A Lufthansa jet! Mama and Papa thought it would be a good time for me and her to visit Germany and go to Oma's eightieth birthday party while Papa's looking for a job and a house in Ontario. I get to meet my aunts, uncles, and cousins. I hope they'll like me. Mama showed me pictures of them. All her sisters look a lot like her, but not like her at the same time.

The airport was not a very nice place. Mama gave me money for chocolate. When I asked the man behind the counter for a Coconut bar and a Milky Way, he told me I had to say it in English. When I tried, he laughed at me, and called me a maudite immigrante. The other man gave me two Dairy Milk bars. I grabbed them and ran back to Mama. I told her Dairy Milk was all they had because I didn't want her to think I did something wrong like when Sister Marie-Claire told her about the time I hit Robert in the arm because he kept pulling my hair when no one was looking. Mama made me apologize to Robert and I couldn't play with Victoria for a whole week. She said I must have done something to upset Robert because he wouldn't just pull my hair for no reason.

Moving to Ontario is going to be scary. I know French from school, and we speak German at home. How will I make friends without English? I'll die if I have to start over in grade one instead of going into grade six. Everyone will think I'm stupid.

I wish I could talk to Mama about my feelings. She says she doesn't want to see me crying anymore. She says moving is part of life, like when she and Papa left their families and came across the ocean so I could be born into a better life. She says I'll make friends in the new place.

I see the stewardess is serving supper to the people at the front of the plane, so I have to stop writing. It looks as if they are getting miniature metal knives, forks, and spoons. Mama's going to put them in her purse for sure after we eat. So embarrassing. She's always putting free stuff in her purse. She says we should never waste anything.

Talk to you later.

Angelika

P.S. Jacques was right. When I look out the window, all I see is clouds.

* * *

Since the plane wasn't full, the stewardess offered all the children the chance to spread out as night fell. Marta brushed Angelika's long blond hair off her face as she settled her across the three seats behind her. *She's her father's daughter*, Marta thought. Tall, long-legged, with Kurt's crystal-blue eyes that made Marta's heart beat faster. The only thing she had from her was the Hoffman nose—Marta smiled—and her stubbornness.

Marta reclined her seat as the cabin crew dimmed the lights. Angelika was having a tough time dealing with the move. Hopefully, this trip would be a good distraction. With luck, Kurt would find a job in Ontario, and they'd be in a house there before school started. Marta understood how cruel children could be. She'd never forget the feeling when classmates turned their backs as she walked by, murmuring derogatory slurs and threats under their breath when her father was revealed as a communist.

CHAPTER TWO - 1963

Arrested Progress

Twelve years, and it's as bad as it was the last time I was here, Marta thought, as she led her daughter along the cobblestoned Hauptstrasse in her hometown of Mücheln. They lugged their suitcases past the row of three-storey, dingy grey-brick buildings housing the butcher, the apothecary, a shoe store, a general grocery store, and the post office. Quick glances through the open doorways revealed sparsely stocked shelves. Lace curtains in the open windows of the upper-floor apartments stirred half-heartedly in the desultory breeze. The building façades bore pockmarks where they'd been assaulted by bullets during the war. Occasional windows were still boarded-up, their glass having been shattered during the bombings. Marta drew her mouth tight. *All this time and they still haven't repaired the windows?*

"Mama, I think this is the bakery." Angelika drew in a deep sniff. "It doesn't smell very bakey, but I see a cake. Should we buy something to take to Oma?" Angelika was through the door, leaving Marta no choice but to follow. Inside, she found her staring at the one tiny cake, six cookies, and four slices of marble pound cake. Behind the counter, the bins that used to overflow with six different kinds of buns held a few sad rolls.

"Mama, where is everything?" Angelika whispered.

Marta shook her head at Angelika. *How do you explain oppression and exploitation disguised as socialism to an eleven-year-old who has never experienced either?* Instead of trying, Marta purchased the last four slices of marble pound cake and six butter cookies and left an extra five marks as payment.

Back on the narrow sidewalk, Angelika asked, "That lady wasn't very friendly when I went in. And why did her eyes go into narrow slits when she saw you?"

"We probably just caught her at a bad time," said Marta. Her daughter didn't need to know that the woman in the bakery was Karin, one of her closest friends at school. They'd always spent time together whenever Marta came back from Hamburg where she worked before the war, but Karin clearly hadn't wanted to acknowledge Marta today. She resolved to make time to go back and talk to Karin in a few days.

When the commercial section ended, so did the cobblestones and sidewalks. Marta's throat tightened. This was the hill where her youngest sister, Hildegard, had been crushed by the milk wagon. Hildegard and her friends had been rushing to the town square for the celebration of the end of the war when the horse reared at the sound of firecrackers. The fully loaded wagon had broken from the harness and careened backward down the hill, plunging into the crowd of teenagers. Hildegard had been only sixteen. Marta hadn't been granted a travel visa to enter the East Zone from

Hamburg for the funeral. She hadn't anticipated a sleet-storm of memories when she'd planned this trip home.

Dust kicked up from their feet as mother and daughter trudged along the dirt road. A feeling of impending abandonment hung like a blanket over the residential streets.

"Mama, how much farther?" Angelika stopped to brush her hair from her face. Her eyes narrowed at the layer of dirt coating her palm.

"Just two more houses." Marta pointed ahead to the right with her chin and kept walking toward a two-storey stuccoed house. The formerly glorious yellow paint was dingy under a coating of fine brown coal dust.

Marta paused at the weathered gate. A few flakes of white paint clung to the grey fence boards that segregated the land behind it from the road.

"Is this the house Opa built? Where you grew up?" Angelika asked.

Instead of answering, Marta took a deep breath, squared her shoulders, and pushed through the gate. Angelika followed her along the cracked stone pathway between the house and the side yard. Green foliage spilled over dark earth in ten rectangular gardens. Beyond the gardens stood a dozen trees, some with ripe fruit, others still dropping white blossoms.

The trees are a little bigger, but it's all so much the same.

They came around the back of the house to the sight of ducks swimming on the tiny pond behind the orchard. Angelica jumped sideways when three white geese rushed out of the lopsided chicken coop. She backed away as the birds hissed and spit at her legs.

The screen door squeaked, then slapped, slapped, slapped against its frame. A petite woman, hair the colour of a November sky drawn tightly into a bun at her neck, squinted through faded-blue eyes. "Gertrude, Frieda, *genug*!" She squinted at the intruders on her pathway while wiping her hands on the flowered yellow apron covering her full-length black skirt. "Marta?"

Marta stood statue-still. Angelika's eyes flicked between the two women, the younger a straighter, smoother version of the elder.

"Mutti!" Marta's voice quavered as if it was one word shy of breaking. She dropped the suitcases and flung herself into her mother's arms.

* * *

July 4, 1963

Chère Journal,

I'm writing this from upstairs in Oma's house. I'm supposed to be sleeping, but I have so much to tell you!

Oma's house has a kitchen with a huge wooden table and benches. At supper this evening, I imagined Mama's brothers and sisters as they must have passed food up and down the table. I know their faces from photos. I laughed out loud thinking about how they probably all talked at once, teasing each other. Mama shook her head when I told her my image. She said when their father was home, the kids weren't allowed to talk at the table unless they were asked a question.

There's a narrow bedroom behind the kitchen where Oma sleeps, and a living room behind big double doors. Mama says the kids were only allowed in the gute Stube on Sunday afternoons after church and at Christmas. Upstairs, there's a big room with slanty ceilings and low walls. The chimney goes up the middle. Mama says there used to be a curtain dividing the room in half. The boys slept on one side, the girls on the other. This is where Mama and I sleep.

The sun was rising when our plane landed in Berlin this morning. The airport was very modern. We took a bus through the city. The buildings near the airport looked new with walls of glass just like the ones in Montreal. We passed lots of apartment buildings and stone houses all joined together. Mama explained we were in West Berlin. The city was divided in half after Germany lost the war.

At the border between the two parts of the city, a high brick wall went in both directions for as far as I could see. A strip of sand and broken pavement that looked like a road ran in front and barbed wire was rolled against the bottom and on the top of the wall. Mean-looking men holding big guns met our bus. They made everyone get off and signalled with their guns that we had to walk through the gate. Mama's shoulders jerked up when one of the men yelled at a lady behind us because she wasn't carrying her own suitcases.

When Mama showed our passports at the booth, she didn't say anything to the man until he asked whether we had coffee, soap, chocolate, or cigarettes. I thought my heart was going to jump out of my chest when Mama said no. Our extra suitcase was crammed with all that stuff, plus clothes I've outgrown to give to my cousins. But, when Mama put her arm around my shoulders, I knew to keep quiet. She smiled at the man, then reached into her shoulder bag and handed him something wrapped in brown paper. I caught a whiff of coffee. He pointed for us to walk right through, down the tunnel, and onto the train.

From the train, East Berlin looked drab and dirty. There were piles of stone, broken brick, and twisted pieces of metal blocking the sidewalks and most of the side streets. Mama said that was something called rubble, left over from the war. I wonder why they haven't cleaned it up yet. The war was a long time ago.

In Mücheln, we walked from the station to Oma's house. In the town I saw a mother with her two daughters climbing over the rubble to get to the shops. The little girl stopped suddenly, pulling on her mother's arm. "Look Mutti, eine Puppe!" The dirt-smeared face of a rag doll peeked out of a pile of grey stone where the little girl pointed. Her mother told the girl to leave it, then jerked her away. "But I don't have any dolls, Mutti. Bitte, Mutti." The little one continued snivelling as they walked on. The older girl, who looked about my age, paused to study the doll. Her dress hung from her boney shoulders. She glanced at her mother's back, nudged a few stones with her foot, then quick as a blink, she grabbed the doll and tucked it under her sweater. When she caught up to her mother, I saw the older girl open her sweater to show her little sister the doll, holding her finger across her lips to signal the little one should stay quiet. It was like the sun was suddenly brighter when the little one smiled. Mama called to me to catch up so I didn't see what happened next.

As we walked I imagined the girls washing the doll when they got home. Maybe the older girl would even make some clothes for it from scraps of material. I had a big box of dolls and their clothes at home that I didn't play with anymore. Wish I could have brought them to give away. I would love to have brought smiles to some little girls.

A few blocks further, we stopped at the bakery. It was almost empty, but we did get a few things. The lady behind the counter gave Mama funny looks, as if she knew her but was mad at her. They didn't say anything to each other.

My feet kept tipping sideways walking on the cobblestones. Everything is a grey-brown colour here, the buildings, the road, even the sun trying to peak through the gritty air. Mama says it's the coal dust. It even gets into your skin, so I have to remember to scrub hard each night.

When we got to Oma's, tears started running down Mama's cheeks. I've never seen her cry before.

I hear Mama coming up the stairs. I'll continue tomorrow.

Angelika

CHAPTER THREE - 1963

Trapped

"Hi, Mama." Angelika came into the kitchen, carrying a basket of eggs over her arm. "Oma showed me how to collect the eggs. Feel! Some of them are still warm. She's making me boiled eggs and toast, and she says I can have a piece of chocolate-running-through cake."

Marta turned from the ancient cast-iron wood stove, coffee cup in hand. "It's called marble cake, and you are *not* having it for breakfast." Marta rolled her eyes at her mother as she settled at the table. Watching the grey and blond heads lean together over the egg basket, Marta knew she'd be losing every battle.

Over breakfast, her mother asked, "Still remember how to catch a chicken? I want to make potato salad and chicken for lunch. These old legs aren't as fast as they used to be."

"It's been years, but sure, Mutti."

"The brown ones are young and fat."

Angelika stuffed the last morsel of marble cake into her mouth then followed Marta through the door. Once outside, Angelika whispered, "We aren't really going to catch one of those, are we?" She pointed to the chicken coop.

Marta motioned for her daughter to stay where she was. "Watch." She entered the pen and stood stock-still while the chickens pecked around her. When one of the brown ones came within arm's reach, she pounced like a panther and came up clutching a squawking brown mass of flapping feathers against her chest.

Angelika squealed.

Marta flipped the chicken upside down by its legs with one hand and grabbed the axe with the other. "You might want to look away," she called to Angelika before she flung the chicken onto the stump. The axe came down. *Whack!* The headless chicken ran several circles before dropping lifeless to the ground.

Angelika was breathing rapidly, her eyes wide.

Marta passed the chicken to her mother, wiped her hands on a rag hanging on the fence, then pulled her daughter into her arms. "It's okay, *Schatzi*. Take slow, deep breaths."

"You should have told her to stay inside. Poor child. She didn't need to see that."

"I was younger than her when you had me catching and holding them for you," Marta said glaring at her mother over Angelika's head.

Angelika pulled back, wrinkling her nose at the rank chicken smell that clung to Marta's shirt. "How could you do that?" Her voice quivered, as if she were looking at a sinister stranger.

"*Ach*, Angelika," the old woman said from the warped outdoor table where she was already dipping the chicken in a pot of hot water. "With eleven children and their father away in the war, everyone had to learn early how to help in our family." Her fingers moved with machine-like speed from the bottom to the top, feathers floating on the air as she plucked the bird. "Animals must die if we are to survive. Your mama made sure the bird didn't suffer."

Angelika turned her attention to the remaining chickens calmly continuing their pecking as if nothing had transpired. Meanwhile, Marta asked her mother to list the groceries she and Angelika would be picking up on their way back from the police station.

"Oma, why aren't the chickens scared they might be next?"

"Chickens aren't very smart, but they understand that there is no point in worrying about what might come when there's nothing you can do about it. They are just happy to live from peck to peck."

Angelika trailed behind her grandmother as she puttered around the yard. The old woman's gravelly voice identifying the vegetable plants Angelika didn't recognize in the neat rectangular gardens drifted to Marta as she entered the house to change her clothes.

A few moments later, Marta emerged, wearing a faded, blue dress. "Come, Angelika," she called.

Angelika rushed to take her mother's hand. "Mama, why are you wearing that old dress?"

Marta pulled to straighten the skirt. "The people here don't have very much. It's better if we don't stand out too much."

"Why are we going to the police station?"

"We have to have our visas stamped within twenty-four hours of our arrival."

"Why?"

Marta stopped and pulled her daughter to the side of the road. She cast furtive glances to ensure no one was nearby. "Angelika, look at me." She caught her breath as she locked onto the blue eyes that sparkled just like Kurt's. She missed him. "The government here has many rules to keep people under control. They don't welcome outsiders visiting for too long, and they want to know where we are all the time." She paused as two women about her age walked by. "*Guten Tag*," she said to them.

"*Tag*," one of them responded. The other sniffed, nose in the air.

Marta heard them whisper something about *Ausländer* and fancy clothes as they continued down the road.

"Why did they call us foreigners, Mama? They weren't very nice whispering about us."

"I know you have questions, but it's better that you ask me when we're alone, okay?"

Angelika's lips drew downward. "Are we in danger?"

Marta gave a reassuring smile. "No, sweetheart, as long as we follow their rules, we'll have a wonderful visit." She turned and kept her arm around the girl's shoulder as they continued on their way.

"There it is. *Polizeiwache*," Angelika read aloud.

Unlike the crumbling shop buildings, someone had repaired the crevices created by mortar shells and bullets, restoring the grey brick facade of the police station to a splotchy imitation of its former glory.

Marta took Angelika's hand as they mounted the concrete stairs. "Now, let me do the talking, okay?"

She tapped the bell on the scarred wooden counter.

"*Ja, bitte.*" The weary voice preceded the appearance of a man's head and olive-green-clad shoulders at the window behind the counter. He looked at the visitors with flat eyes, then inhaled sharply. "Marta?" he choked out.

"Franz?" Marta's voice quavered. Her grip on Angelika's hand tightened.

Angelika tried to pull free. "Ow, Mama. You're hurting me."

The spell between the two adults shattered, and the officer shook out his shoulders. "Can I help you?" His voice was all business, with a fierce edge.

Marta shoved their passports toward the open slot at the bottom of the window. "We are here on a visit and need our visas stamped." Her voice was flat, but her heart roared in her ears.

"Canada. Hmph." Franz opened the passports, scrutinizing the visa page at length. When he flipped to the photo in each, he darted his eyes between the two people in front of him and their photos, as if searching for a blemish that would expose them as spies.

Marta shifted her weight from foot to foot, sighing a few times while they waited. When he flipped back to the visa pages again, she broke the silence. "So, police. What happened with the music?" *Damn,* she thought. *What am I doing? He's going to think I care.* She felt the heat from a tide of red rising up her neck.

Franz kept his gaze glued to the passports. "After the bombing, people in Hamburg weren't in the mood for music...and you were gone." He shrugged and reached for his stamp. "I came back home to help my mother and sisters." He grimaced. "And got trapped." Looking over his shoulder to the empty office, he dropped his voice. "These days, you don't dare to even whisper the truth to your children while the government yells lies. It's better if you play the game, let them think you're with them. So police made sense." *Stamp. Stamp.* He handed the passports back across the counter. "The coffee here is terrible. Maybe we can get together for a glass of wine before you leave?" He raised his eyebrows.

Marta slid the passports into her purse. "What would wine bring us?" She held his gaze for several seconds, then turned and, head held high, strode to the door.

"*Auf Wiedersehen,*" Angelika called.

Angelika heard the man's half-whispered response, "Oh, I think we might see each other again," just as the door closed behind them.

Wine? The nerve, Marta fumed. *After that terrible day when the neighbours had to help me to the hospital because he was with her. All his promises drunk away in the bars while I nursed baby Kristof and tried to rock the courage to live into him.*

"Mama, what did he mean about being trapped?" Angelika was panting from jogging to keep up.

"What did I say about questions?" Marta didn't slow her pace. *Trapped was a good description for this country—a population trapped in a morass of whispers and sideways glances, where neighbours sold out neighbours for a fresh pig roast, and friends denied friends for one of Judas's thirty pieces of silver.*

Franz trapped while she lived free and happy in Canada. Why didn't she feel vindicated?

Marta didn't break her silence until they arrived at her mother's gate. "Angelika, go play with the ducks," she said in the tone of voice that told her daughter not to argue. Angelika wandered toward the pond.

Marta let the screen door slam behind her. "Why didn't you tell me?" Her voice shook with controlled anger.

"Tell you what?" Her mother's shoulders rose tightly.

"Mutti, look at me."

Her mother turned from the stove and met Marta's eyes.

"There are probably only two or three police officers in this village." Marta stood in the middle of the kitchen, hands balled into fists at her side. "You knew I'd run into Franz. You didn't think advance warning would have been nice?" Marta's voice rose in tone and volume with each word.

"*Na, ja*. I didn't think it would matter to you after the divorce and so many years." Her mother turned back to the stove. "I need to put the potatoes on." She slid the pot across the stove's surface.

Marta took a few deep breaths. "I suppose you feel I deserved it, after your warnings."

Her mother stopped what she was doing but remained facing the wall above the stove. "*Nein*, Marta. I knew you'd do whatever you wanted. You had a tough childhood. You wanted to get away, see the world." She had tears in her eyes as she turned to her daughter. "And my heart ached when I heard you lost little Kristof. I know what it is like to lose a child, and I wish you never had to feel that pain."

Marta rushed into her mother's arms. "There's a hole in my heart—"her voice broke with a sob"—that even Angelika can't close."

Mother and daughter held onto each other until the wave of pain receded.

Marta was the first to break the embrace. "It would have been nice to know." Her voice had returned to a calmer tone.

Her mother took a deep breath. "Franz was broken when he came back from Hamburg. He couldn't make it *with* you supporting him, and when you left, he almost drank himself to death." She raised her hand as Marta opened her mouth to speak. "I didn't feel sorry for him. He deserved no less for everything that happened, but maybe it helps you to know he didn't come away free."

"*Danke*, Mutti." Marta felt closer to her mother than she ever had.

"He married Karin. They have two kids. She took over the bakery from her parents."

Marta caught her breath. "Karin?" No wonder she looked worn out. It explained her attitude when they bought the cake.

"*Ja*. Franz plays with his four-piece band in the square every Thursday evening." Her mother was back at the stove. "On the radio, all we hear is propaganda about our good life and the evils of the corrupt West. With the churches closed, it's nice to have a little music in our lives."

"He was an incredible trumpet player," Marta said. *Forgiveness is letting go*, she thought. For years, she'd lied about the pain, denied it, hidden from it. Maybe it was time to forgive him and herself. "Maybe…" She held her breath, "No, never mind." She wasn't ready yet.

Her mother was turning the pieces of chicken sizzling and popping in the hot oil of the frying pan when Angelika came into the kitchen.

* * *

July 5, 1963

Chère Journal,

This house has no bathroom, just an outhouse. There's a roof from the back porch, so you never have to get wet if it's raining when you have to go.

Instead of a fridge, Oma has an icebox in the shed behind the kitchen. It has a shelf on the top where you put a big ice block. The inside is covered with tin and so are the shelves where she keeps food. She keeps all the drinks like lemonade, milk, and an orange soda called Fanta in the spooky cellar because, she says, ice-cold drinks give you cramps. Every meal, I have to get the drinks. The wooden staircase sways. There's no handrail, and you have to be careful because the second step from the bottom is broken. Then there are the cobwebs. Mama gave me a broom to brush them away, but every time I go down, I feel all sticky. I love milk at home, but the milk here has a film on the top that smells sour. I think I'm just going to drink water from now on.

Mama killed a chicken today. I almost barfed when she chopped off its head with the axe. Guess I should have looked away like she said. I didn't know Mama could do that. Oma said chickens don't worry about things they can't control. I think she feels people should be more like chickens.

Oma and I walked through her yard while I waited for Mama to change her clothes. Near the back were gardens overflowing with purple and pink flowers. Some were snapdragons and gladioluses like Mama has. When I asked her why she wastes two gardens to grow flowers when vegetables are hard to buy, Oma leaned her right ear toward two wooden boxes at the very back of the yard. A low hum. Bees were flying in and out.

Oma grinned, showing her three yellow teeth, one on the top and two on the bottom, when she said that the flowers are for the bees. Life can't only be the business of vegetables, she said. We need a honey sweetness to give us the courage to keep going.

Oma hardly ever smiles, and her face is very wrinkled, but she's very strong. I think she's had a hard life with thirteen children and two dead husbands from the wars. I'm glad she has the bees. She deserves some honey in her life.

We went to the police station today to have our visas stamped. Mama and the police officer knew each other. When we got back, I heard Mama yell that Oma should have warned her that the man named Franz was back. Back from where? I couldn't hear much from my hiding place. Did Franz and Mama know each other before Mama met Papa? When I asked Oma while we were alone, she told me it wasn't her story to tell. Maybe one of my aunts will tell me at the reunion.

Angelika

CHAPTER FOUR - 1963

Cousins and Friends

July 10, 1963

Chère Journal,

Today is Oma's birthday. I can't wait to meet everybody.

This week, we picked cherries and plums. Then we baked six round Kirsch Torte, just like the ones Mama and I make at home. Oma let me cut the pits out of the cherries. It took a long time, and my fingers were purple, but I was careful and didn't cut myself once. When we made four Pflaum Kuchen, Oma sliced the plums while I pressed them into the dough on the huge cookie sheets. We cooked the extra fruit and ladled it into jars. Then, Oma put the jars in a big metal tub of water in the backyard. My job was to keep the water boiling by feeding the fire. We put twenty jars of preserves in the cellar, ten of each.

Mama was supposed to kill more chickens, but instead, she bought six. We went by bus to two other towns to find enough. She said Oma needed to save her chickens for eggs and meat for herself, but I think she bought them because she didn't really like killing chickens. In one of the towns, a farmer was selling carrots on the side of the road. He had a yellow sign on his wagon that said he was permitted to sell them, but when we tried to buy some, he said he couldn't sell to us because we didn't have an identity card. Then he beckoned, and Mama followed him around to the front of the wagon. He pulled a heavy package out from under his seat and unwrapped the paper. When we got home, I saw it was a huge pork roast. Oma said we paid way too much for it, but mostly she was scared because it's against the law to buy food from farmers unless they have a permit. We couldn't cook it in the outdoor oven because the neighbours might smell it and report us. It's so complicated here.

Everybody is bringing salads and breads and desserts. It's going to be a feast.

I'm so excited. I've been trying to remember the pictures Mama showed me before we left, but what if I call someone by the wrong name? I hope they like me. I don't want to disappoint Mama. Maybe I'll just stay back and watch everybody so I don't miss anything or make any mistakes.

Angelika

* * *

Marta came down the stairs to find her mother standing over Angelika as she sat at the table. Angelika was clutching a notebook to her chest. Her mother's forehead was puckered. "Give it to me. We'll be arrested if someone sees it."

"It's just stuff about our visit, Oma. And besides, they won't be able to read it. It's in French."

"*Mein Gott*! They'll think you're a spy."

"Mama, please help." Tears shimmered in Angelika's eyes. "Oma wants to throw my *journal* in the fire."

Marta moved to her mother's side and took her gently by the elbow. "Come, Mutti." She steered the old woman to her rocker beside the stove. "Now, tell me, what's wrong?" She pulled a chair up beside her. Marta caught her breath at the fear clouding her mother's faded eyes. She'd always been so indomitable. What was this regime doing to her?

"It's illegal to write about the state. They'll put us in jail."

Marta kept her tone even. "It's just a child's writing. What could they possibly think she could reveal?"

Her mother laid her hand on Marta's knee. "They act first here, then ask questions. We could be in jail for months before they even read it." Her voice rose. "And why is she writing in French, not English?"

"It's okay, Oma. I'll hide it and only write upstairs so no one will see."

Angelika returned from upstairs and, announced she'd hidden the diary under her mattress. She put her arm around her grandmother's shoulders. "Sister Mathilde started teaching us numbers, colours, clothes, and stuff in English this year, but my school is French."

"Sister Mathilde?" Angelika's Oma covered her mouth with her hand. "A nun?" Her fear turned to flashes of anger as she turned to Marta. "You raise your daughter Catholic?"

"Mutti, we live in a small town in the French part of Canada. There is one school, one church, one language." Marta went to the sink to fill three glasses of water. "What's this big concern about religion, anyway?" She handed a glass each to her mother and daughter. "You sent us kids to church, but you and Papa never came." Marta couldn't fully smooth the edge from her voice. "And now, the government doesn't allow religious services."

Marta's mother fixed her gaze on her granddaughter. "Angelika, do you know who Luther is?"

Angelika glanced from her mother to her grandmother, as if searching their faces for the right answer, before shaking her head.

"Come, sit." Her mother patted the chair that Marta had vacated. "Martin Luther changed the world, not only for Germans but for all Christians, in the 1500s. He protested against the Pope and showed us we could be saved through our faith in Jesus Christ, not by doing good deeds to buy our way into heaven. He translated the Bible into German so everyone could read it for themselves."

"My Bible is in French," Angelika said.

"Before Luther, all Bibles were in Latin, and only the priests could read them." The old woman crossed her arms over her thin chest, a satisfied smile creasing her lips.

Angelika guzzled her water.

Marta swiped at the perspiration coursing down her neck. "This is ridiculous. Thirty degrees, and you can't open a window because of the dust. They shouldn't be allowed to dig the coal so close to town."

"They do what they want, when they want." Her mother pushed herself to her feet to the cracking accompaniment of her knees. "Come. The cellar is cooler. The family won't be here for a couple of hours."

Angelika wrinkled her nose but followed her grandmother down. While the old woman lit the lanterns, Marta and Angelika pulled the wooden table to the centre of the space and arranged three chairs around it.

"See that wooden box on the shelf over there?"

Angelika's gaze followed her grandmother's finger pointing at a box about the same size as the one Angelika's new boots from Sears had come in last winter. "Bring it to the table."

The old woman opened the box and tipped it. Photos, some black and white, others sepia coloured, cascaded across the tabletop. "Now, my girl, you are going to learn who you are."

The chair legs sank into the uneven gravel floor as they sat on them.

Marta knitted her brows. "Mutti, Angelika speaks perfect German. We keep the traditions for Advent, Christmas, and Easter. She knows where we come from."

"But she doesn't know her history."

"She's Canadian." Frustration shook Marta's voice. "She doesn't need to bear the German shame and guilt." She sighed. "We haven't forgotten who we are, but we had to plant ourselves in Canada to feel we had a home."

Her mother flapped her hand. "*Ach*, Marta. She needs to know her roots to help her understand that other history I'm sure she'll learn from the victor's point of view in her Canadian school. She needs to be proud, not ashamed. We weren't all Nazis." She began moving the photos around the tabletop.

Here we go, Marta thought. She pressed her back into the chair, arms crossed, watching her daughter feathering her fingers through the piles.

"Some of these are the same photos you showed me. Who's this lady?" Angelika held up a sepia photo. "She looks like one of those French artists with that hat."

"That's a beret, and that's your Tante Klara, my eldest sister." Marta looked closer. "*Mein Gott*, Mutti, she looks just like you did when you were younger." She picked up another photo. "Here's Klara with her three children."

"Tante Klara's the one that married Rudi the communist from Czechoslovakia," Angelika recited.

"*Ja, ja.*" The old woman held her sides in laughter. Then she held up the next photo. "Who's this?"

Angelika stared at the photo of a woman with skin that hung limply from her cheeks, surrounded by her three daughters and one son. Their eyes were all sunken. No one smiled. "That's Tante Liesbeth, with her kids Hiltrut, Rolf, Ursula, and Gudrun. I think they're sad because their dad is in jail. I can't wait to meet them."

"Might be a good idea not to mention their dad," Marta said.

"Oma, you had only three boys."

"*Na, ja.*" She shook her head sadly. "Otto died in the war. Fritz had mental problems when he came back from the war and hung himself in the shed." She stared into space, blinking the tears from her eyes. Marta reached across the table and held her mother's hands.

Glancing across the piles, Angelika grabbed another photo. "Oma, don't be sad. Here's Onkel Herman. He works all over the world. I have a whole shelf above my desk at home with dolls and snow globes he's brought me from different countries."

The grandmother smiled, taking the photo. "Herman was such an impetuous boy." Her eyes took on a faraway look. "He behaved so strangely that day, fixed everything that was broken around the house, cleaned up the shed. When he gave me all his money, I knew something was coming, but going *Schwarz über die Grenze*…" She raised her eyes. "I never expected that."

"Mama, what does that mean?"

Marta took her time in answering. "Remember the wall we saw when we crossed the border to come here?"

Angelika nodded. "It stops people from leaving."

"That's right," Marta said. "In the countryside, there's a fence instead of a wall. Back in 1954, it didn't have electricity running through it yet. One night, your uncle and one of his friends cut the barbed wire and slipped into the open space between the two parts." Marta's jaw tightened. "While they were running through the water and grass toward the fence on the West side, one of the guards in the watchtower caught them in the searchlight. The guards started shooting."

Angelika gasped. "But they made it."

Marta and her mother exchanged a long look.

"Herman's friend was killed," Marta said quietly. "Herman was hit in the shoulder. West German farmers helped him through the wire on their side."

"I asked him about the scar on his shoulder when we were at the beach." Angelika's pupils were huge. "He called it his freedom scar." Her forehead creased. "Do they call it going black over the border because they go at night?"

Angelika's grandmother nodded. "Also, because they don't take identity papers, and they never tell anyone they are going. We were interrogated for days after he left." She forced a smile. "I miss him. He's the last of my boys, so you tell him he needs to get a wife and make babies." She chuckled softly, then pressed her lips to the photo.

Angelika reached for another one. "This looks like you, Mama, when you were a teenager."

Her mother leaned over Angelika's shoulder to get a better look at the sepia-coloured photo. Marta knew it well. In it, her fourteen-year-old self was holding the hands of a little boy and girl. A sweet face smiled from beneath a lacy bonnet on the baby sitting in the shade of the baby carriage's wicker hood.

"*Ja*, that's your mother, with Herman, Liesbeth, and baby Hildegard." The grandmother giggled like a teenager. "Remember, Marta, how Papa sent you out with the little ones every time we got notice that the authorities were coming to search the house?"

"Why would they search your house, Oma?"

"Because your Opa was a political dissident after the first war."

In response to Angelika's puzzled expression, Marta said, "Your Opa was a communist. He organized protests against the socialists and handed out flyers." Under her breath she added, "And his children paid the price of social isolation when it all came to light."

"One of his friends was on the police force, so Opa would get a warning when the police were coming," Marta's mother said. "It was against the law to print and distribute propaganda. We'd hide the papers under baby Hildegard in the carriage and send your mother out for a walk with the little ones whenever the police were coming." She nudged Marta, her smile showing her three teeth. "They never figured it out."

"Weren't you scared, Mama?"

Marta pursed her lips. "I was at first, but mostly I was angry being stuck with the kids."

Angelica picked up a black and white photo of a couple posing in a park. He wore a dark suit, she a white dress with a lacy veil. She held a small bouquet of flowers in one hand, her other hand was folded through the crook of the man's elbow. *Was that—?*

"What do you have there?" Her grandmother leaned over Angelika's shoulder to get a better look.

When Angelika turned the photo around, she caught a glimpse of 'Franz und Marta' written on the back. She didn't get a chance to read the date before her mother tore the photo from her hand.

"You don't need to see that." Marta shoved the photo into her pocket. "Let's pack this up, the company is coming soon." She glared at her mother before shovelling all the photos back into the box.

They'd just returned upstairs when a melodious "Hallooo" from the back porch announced the arrival of a petite woman wearing a knee-length, slim, black skirt and a white blouse. She tossed her black-and-white jacket over the back of the rocking chair and tugged her black beret at an angle over her left eye.

"Tante Klara!" Angelika ran to embrace. She was already several inches taller than the woman.

Klara laughed. "Angelika, how did you know me?"

"By your beret. Just like in the photos." She looked to the door. "Is Uncle Rudi with you?"

Klara shook her head. "He had work to do. But he sends his love."

"Is he writing propaganda? I've never met a com—"

Marta cleared her throat loudly.

"Him," Angelika finished.

Klara embraced her mother and Marta. "What have you two been telling her?" She grinned at their expressions of chagrin. The three women settled around the table with cups of fresh coffee. Marta and her mother picked up their knitting.

While the women talked, Angelika wandered to her mother's side. With her hand cupped to her mother's ear, she whispered, "Oma moves her foot when she knits just like you do."

Marta gave Angelika " the look."

"Ah, ah, ah. There is no whispering in this house."

Angelika gave her mother an apologetic glance. "Oma, you move your foot when you knit just like Mama does."

The old woman laughed. "An old habit. With thirteen children, there was always at least one in the cradle that needed rocking. Do you know how to knit?"

Angelika nodded. "Mama taught me how."

Marta sat a little taller under the look of approval from her mother.

"Good, then one day when you have babies, you will understand."

Klara pulled Angelika close. "Why don't you go outside and watch for the others?"

* * *

After checking on the ducklings swimming in the pond, Angelika settled on a bench under her favourite tree, the largest of the plums. Soon, she heard voices approaching. The figures of three women flashed in and out of view between the trunks in the orchard. Tante Ellen, the one who lived in West Germany, had to be the one in the middle, Angelika thought, with her bright flowered dress and white leather purse over her arm. The smallest one, with black hair and a sour mouth, was Tante Anna, and Tante Liesbeth, with her bright smile and sensible shoes, was the third. She didn't look as drawn as in the picture, but she still had a very thin face, unlike her sisters. A girl Angelika's age, but a bit smaller, held a younger child by the hand—Ursula and Gudrun. Rolf, Ursula's older brother, walked beside them. Four teenagers came last. Angelika recognized one of them as Hiltrut, Tante Liesbeth's oldest.

Angelika jumped up and ran through the orchard, only to pull up short behind the first row of trees. What was she doing? They didn't know her. She smoothed the flared skirt of her sky-blue sundress and patted her blond hair into place. Then, she stepped into sight. The three women stopped. Angelika approached them. Remembering her mother's explanation that Germans shook hands when they met, she extended her right hand. "Tante Anna. Tante Ellen. Tante Liesbeth. *Ich bin* Angelika."

The first two aunts shook her hand and returned her smile. Tante Liesbeth used her offered hand to pull Angelika into a huge hug. "Come here, child. We're family."

Angelika felt her three cousins join the hug. Warmth flooded her. So this was what family felt like.

As soon as the three aunts disappeared in search of her mother and Oma, Angelika turned to her teenage cousins. "Hello, Hiltrut." She stopped in the face of Hiltrut's stern expression, uncertain whether to offer her hand or try for a hug. The other three teens pushed past, saying their names as they went—Kristel, Otto, Monika. Angelika knew they were Tante Klara's children, even though they'd been at least ten years younger in the photo she'd seen.

"Well, if it isn't the wasteful little capitalist." Hiltrut's mouth pulled into a sneer. "*Ich bin Angelika.*" She tilted her head coyly and pulled at her skirt in an exaggerated imitation. "You think you're something special with your pretty clothes. We speak our dialect here, not your perfect schoolteacher *Hochdeutsch.*"

Kristel called to Hiltrut. "Come on. Leave her be."

"What's the matter, Angelika? You going to cry?"

Rolf pushed his older sister's shoulder. "That's enough, Hiltrut. Go."

Hiltrut threw Angelika another look of disgust then turned and sauntered away. The teens laughed amongst themselves as they disappeared into the backyard.

Ursula put her arm around Angelika's shoulders. "Ignore her. We're so happy you're here."

Angelika gave herself a shake and pushed her mouth into a smile. She and Ursula wandered the orchard while Rolf took four-year-old Gudrun into the house. When he rejoined them, the three sat under Angelika's plum tree.

"Is it true that everyone in the West has a television? A car?" Rolf asked.

"I don't know. I'm not from the West. I'm from Canada," Angelika said.

"We live in the East with the Russians." Ursula pulled her arms into her chest. "The West is America, Canada, West Germany, anywhere outside here." Ursula flung her extended arms past the space around her.

"Ohhh," Angelika drew out the sound to show her understanding. "Okay. Most people in Canada have a television, and families need cars to get around because the towns and cities are so far apart."

"Can they drive wherever they want?" Rolf asked.

He has eyes like a deer, Angelika thought. "Yes, and they don't have to check into the *Polizeiwache*."

Ursula said, "I heard Canadians use dog teams and live in ice houses."

Angelika burst out laughing but pulled herself together when she saw Ursula's hurt expression. "You're serious. I'm sorry. No, we live in houses. Some of the EsTimos, the people in the North, build ice houses called igloos and use dog sleds in winter."

Ursula hesitated, then asked, "Is it true you can walk into a store and pick out anything you want to buy?"

Angelica nodded.

"Like drawing pencils and paper?"

Angelika remembered Oma had told her Rolf loved drawing.

The cousins kept pelting her with items. Angelika just kept nodding.

"Like chocolate?"

"Blue jeans?"

"Even dresses?"

The suitcase! Angelica raised her arms in the air. "Okay. Follow me."

Once in the house, she whispered in her mother's ear. When her mother nodded, she led the way as the three cousins clattered up the stairs. Angelika opened the suitcase on her bed and began pulling out skirts, pants, coats, blouses, until the pink quilted bedspread had completely disappeared under the jumble of clothes. With each new item, Ursula gasped. She held the black-and-white velvet dress against her body, rubbed the faux fur collar of the green, plaid coat against her cheek.

"These used to be mine, but they don't fit anymore. They're yours, if you want them."

Ursula's eyes were round as they moved between the mound of clothing on the bed and her Canadian cousin's face.

"I mean…if you don't want them 'cause they're used…"

"Ursula." Rolf snapped his fingers in front of his sister's face. "I'm sorry. Of course she wants them. She's never seen so many beautiful things."

Angelika exhaled. "Okay! Let's try them on. Rolf, give us some privacy and get ready for an amazing show."

"O…kay," Ursula repeated the strange new word. The two girls giggled.

For the next hour, Angelika guided her cousin through her new outfits, many of which fit immediately and a few of which she'd grow into soon. They made a separate pile of the ones that were too small and would be given to Gudrun, Ursula's younger sister. Rolf played his part as audience to perfection, commenting on the fit, the style, and how each outfit complimented his sister's eyes or complexion, while Ursula twirled to make the skirts unfurl. They'd just come to the end of their fashion show game when the call came from the bottom of the stairs that the food had been put out. Rolf ran down first, called the party's attention to the staircase, and then announced his sister.

Ursula descended, pausing on each step to show off her new green-and-pink-flowered sundress and white sandals to the calls of admiration from her family. Then, Rolf announced Angelika as the generous couturier. As the applause faded, everyone made their way to the food-laden tables set up in the courtyard.

Hiltrut bumped up against Angelika in the food line. "We don't need your charity. We are proud workers of *das Volk*. We don't need finery."

Ursula leaned past Angelika and glared into her older sister's face. "I guess you won't want the soft wool sweater and silk scarf I was going to give you." Then she grabbed Angelika by the arm. "Come on. Let's sit over there. I want to get to know your mother, my Tante Marta."

During dessert, Marta steered Angelika around the yard, introducing her to the aunts and uncles she hadn't yet met—Tante Greta, Tante Regina with her husband Friedrich and their grown son Peter, and her cousin Günther, who was really Greta's illegitimate son that Oma had raised.

After the meal, Ursula and Rolf suggested their cousin might be feeling overwhelmed meeting all the relatives. They convinced their mother to allow them to take Angelika into the village. The three children set off down the dirt road toward the shops. During the walk, it was her turn to ask the questions.

CHAPTER FIVE - 1963

Too Canadian

Marta was on her way to the kitchen, balancing plates and cutlery in her arms, when she overheard Anna and Liesbeth in conversation. She stopped in the doorway and let the screen door lean against her shoulder while she eavesdropped on her sisters.

Marta picked up Liesbeth's voice. "Hey, Anna, aren't you going to help with the dishes?"

"All I do is work. Werner is too sick to do anything, and Bärbel has broken her arm again."

Marta recalled reading in one of Anna's letters that her six-year-old daughter, Bärbel, had a disease causing her bones to break easily. She was expected to outgrow it, but Marta empathized with her sister. It was hard to helplessly watch your daughter's pain.

Marta heard the scrape of a chair.

"I need to sit." Anna sighed. "You wouldn't understand what it means to do everything for a man, what with your Herbert in jail." Of all Marta's siblings, Anna was the one who'd felt her life was harder than everyone else's when they were growing up. Being wedged between Marta, the top student, and Ellen, the prettiest, Anna didn't know how to fit into the threesome, so she'd taken on the role of tattletale and complainer.

Marta jumped at the ringing sound of a metal pot slamming on an iron stove. "I wouldn't understand?" Liesbeth's voice climbed. "You have one child in a big house. Try living in a two-bedroom apartment, in a crumbling building, with no running hot water, and four kids." The slam of another pot. "The state pays for your husband's and daughter's health costs, including those six weeks he spent in the convalescent home."

"That time was so hard." Anna was in full whine. "Going to see Werner each day, then rushing to get Bärbel from kindergarten. And the costs for all her special food."

"Paid for with the money from your husband's pension. Try raising four kids without that," Liesbeth shot back.

"Maybe you shouldn't have picked a loser for a husband, but then you always had a talent of falling for the bullshitter."

"Whoa!" Ellen's voice broke in. "What's the matter with you two?"

"*Frau DDR,*" Anna taunted Liesbeth, using the initialism for East Germany, the *Deutsche Demokratische Republik.* "Working like a good little socialist in the government cafeteria. Feeding her children for free on fancy leftovers each day."

Marta allowed the screen door to fall closed behind her and strode into the kitchen. "This is your mother's birthday. Have some respect, you two."

"Look at you," Anna spat. "Showing up here with your fancy clothes. More Canadian than German. Never a care for your family left behind in this hell."

"Shh!" Liesbeth, eyes darting around the room, held her hand in front of Anna's mouth. "You never know who's listening."

"Listening to what?" Klara asked, coming into the kitchen. She paused as if taking roll call of her sisters. "Let me guess, Anna. You're jealous of Marta and Ellen and feel your life is harder than everyone else's?" Klara may have been the smallest, but as the eldest, she commanded respect, especially since she had played a key part in raising each one of her younger sisters. "You think it was easy for Marta to start fresh in a new land? I bet not all the Canadians were happy to welcome Germans."

Marta nodded.

"And what about Ellen? Surviving the rebuilding of the West, cut off from her family." Klara looked around the room. "We've all had to adapt to survive. But everything we've done and continue to do is for the sake of our children." Her expression hardened. "And today we are celebrating the woman who showed us how to be good mothers by sacrificing for us, so *reisst euch zusammen,* and join the party."

"Mutti, Mutti," Rolf and Ursula burst into the kitchen. "They have Angelika. The *Polizei* took Angelika!"

Marta's heart dropped to her feet. Liesbeth turned to calm her children. Their voices tumbled over each other. They'd gone to the edge of town to see the coal pit. They were getting ice cream on the Hauptstrasse when two police officers approached Angelika and told her to come with them. Rolf tried to stop them, but they shoved him to the ground and told him to go home. They'd run all the way back to Oma's house.

Franz, Marta thought. *I'll kill him*. She rushed through the screen door and exploded into the yard. Her family members were pressed around the perimeter. Her daughter, restrained by Franz's hand on her shoulder, stood frozen in the middle of the courtyard. *Thank God*. In the beat of a bee's wings, Marta was pulling Angelika to her. "It's okay, *Schatzi*," she murmured into her daughter's ear as she held the quaking child against her chest.

"What the hell do you think you're doing?" Marta yelled into Franz's face.

Klara stepped to Marta's side.

Franz put his hands in the air and took a step back. "You need to calm down. There was no harm to your daughter."

"No harm! Arresting an eleven-year-old? Assaulting her cousin?"

"Marta," Franz spoke through clenched teeth, his eyes moving from Marta to his fellow officer at his side. "Calm down, or I'll have to take you in."

Marta's chest heaved as she tried to slow her breathing. Her stomach twisted at the fear etched in the faces of her family. "I'm okay," she choked, eyes dropping to the gun at Franz's belt.

"Please get your passports. Alfred will go with you." Franz signalled with his head to the other officer.

Marta took Angelika's hand and marched into the house, followed by the policeman. Behind her, she heard Franz speaking to the group. "Ladies and gentlemen, this is an illegal gathering. I will need to see your papers."

By the time Marta and her daughter rejoined the group, everyone's papers had been checked and Franz was continuing his explanation. "Groups of more than ten require a permit. You all need to leave or face fines." People muttered to each other. A few began to move toward the house to gather their belongings.

"Wait." Klara's voice rang out.

Everyone stopped.

"This is a family reunion. Everyone here is related. Therefore, I believe your law concerning gatherings does not apply."

Regina and her husband nodded. Günther stepped forward to stand beside Klara.

Franz's eyes dropped in the face of Klara's glare. He cleared his throat, then held his hand out for the passports from Marta.

"You stamped these yourself," Marta said. "It's a two-week visa, and we have only been here ten days."

"*Ach*, Marta, you need to check your paperwork. While our government might award you a fourteen-day visa, it is up to the local police to determine how long it is appropriate for you to stay in the East Zone. You will note here—"he held the passport page out for her to see"—that I stamped the expiry as today's date. We are a small village, and *Ausländer* can have a significant negative impact on our limited resources." He raised his eyebrows.

"You did that on pur—" Marta felt her mother's restraining hand on her arm.

"Franz, would your mother be proud of what you are doing here?" Her mother's quiet tone commanded attention.

Franz shrank under the matriarch's glare.

"It's time to put the past behind and behave like a *Mensch*. Kindness to each other is all we have these days."

Alfred took a step forward, but Franz shook his head at him. "I will extend the visa, Marta, but if you aren't gone by noon tomorrow, I will arrest you and your mother."

"Arrest!" The old woman spat the word at him. "You think you scare me? You'll be back here in a week anyway. We'll see about arrest then."

Regina tried to take her mother's arm and pull her away.

"Let me go." She pointed at Franz with her chin. "He knows what I mean."

Franz rested his eyes on the old woman. "Happy birthday, Frau Hoffman." He turned on his heel and the two officers marched out of the yard.

Amid the loud collective exhale, Regina asked, "Mutti, what's this about being arrested next week?"

Her mother faced the crumpled expressions of her children and grandchildren. "Today is the perfect end." She drew a creased envelope from the pocket of her skirt and handed it to Regina. Then she pulled herself upright and walked across the courtyard to where her four teenaged grandchildren clustered. "*Kommt, Kinder.* Tell your Oma what's new." The family watched the young people embrace their grandmother and move with her toward the pond.

As Regina silently sTimmed the letter, the page began to shake in her hand, and the wrinkles in her forehead deepened. "They are taking the house on July seventeenth."

Marta felt her heart beat three times into the silence. Then the questions exploded.

"Who's taking it?"

"Why?"

"They can't do that. She owns it."

Regina held up her hands. Into the silence, she explained that the whole neighbourhood was being expropriated so the coal deposit under the houses could be mined. Their mother was being moved into a senior's home on July sixteenth.

Liesbeth, Regina, Anna, and Klara gathered to discuss what, if anything, could be done.

When Marta moved to join them, Ellen took her by the elbow. "They need to figure this out. We have no role. We aren't from here anymore."

"But..." Marta's brow furrowed. "This will kill her."

Ellen nodded. "I know. We all know." After a pause, she added, "Why don't you and Angelika come with me tomorrow? Dagmar would be excited to see you, and she'll have fun showing her younger cousin around. The girls are only two years apart."

"*Danke*," Marta squeezed Ellen's arm, "but I think we'll go to Kurt's parents in Wiesbaden for a few days. It's never easy with them, but they deserve to meet their granddaughter."

* * *

Marta opened the living room window to let in the fresh night breeze. Thankfully, the gentle evening rain had freshened the air while the strengthening wind had torn apart the heavy humidity. Enjoying this quiet time to herself after her mother and Angelika were both tucked into bed, she stood in front of the billowing sheer curtain, head thrown back to let the cool air dry the perspiration from her neck and chest. Klara's words echoed in her mind. Was she being a good mother to Angelika? Her daughter was smart, worked hard at school, was polite and considerate of others. Would she continue to grow up that way? Marta hoped so.

Her hand brushed against the flimsy blue airmail envelope she'd dropped on the end table beside her. Earlier in the evening, she'd searched the meagre lines for good news. How she missed Kurt. "Wawa isn't going to be our new home," she reread to herself. "The company doesn't provide houses, wages are low, and they won't hire an underground miner who doesn't speak English." She felt his discouragement in every word. *I should be there to support him.* He did end on a positive note, with news of a mining company farther along Highway 17 looking for miners. "They provide houses. The town is completely built by the mining company, including schools, churches, and even a hospital." Marta smiled. It sounded like home. The only challenge might be learning how to pronounce and spell the name. The town was called Pusamakwa.

Leaning against her father's overstuffed chair next to the window in the darkened room, Marta lit a cigarette. Her mother and Angelika had no idea she smoked, and she wanted to keep it that way. It was a temporary vice meant to help her cope with this place where the air tasted of despondency and resignation.

It was as if the bus from West to East Berlin had crossed a time barrier as well as the regime-imposed border, dividing the population into two sides of the same coin. People moved like shadows here, furtively gathering whatever they could to survive, then slinking behind the walls of their homes. No one greeted you on the street anymore. Her dreams of swapping life stories in old friends' parlours, munching sweets, and drinking coffee while Angelika played with their children in the yard, had floated away like the cigarette smoke she blew out the window. The friends she'd grown up with who were still in the village seemed to have hardly a minute to spare for her. Did they resent her? Or were they fearful of scrutiny from the regime for associating with a foreigner? Who wouldn't be afraid when you didn't know who you could trust? And those billboards. Giant gold letters screaming slogans about *das Volk*—"the people"—on red backgrounds. The Work of the People for the Good of the People, and Socialism: The Voice of the People. Well, the voice of the few in power, anyway.

Marta caught a silhouette under the last working light on the street. There was a familiarity in the comfortable pose as the man leaned against the post. By the time she realized he'd seen her, it was too late to duck out of sight, so she held her position. His cigarette glowed red, then he threw it to the ground, tipped his hat at her in mock salute, and walked into the darkness. Franz.

Keep calm, Marta. You'll be gone tomorrow.

* * *

SYLVIA BARNARD

July 10, 1963

Chère Journal,

I met more than thirty relatives at the family reunion today. At first, I felt as if I didn't fit in because all my cousins are shorter than me, even the teenagers. And I was the only blond. But then Kristel sat with Ursula and me. We talked about food—they both hate broccoli like me and can't get enough chocolate, strawberries or peaches—and school—we're all good at math and learning other languages but find history boring. Kristel and I both love learning about the world, and she said she'd like to come to Canada one day to visit if the Wall ever comes down. Pretty soon, we were laughing together, and I thought, this is what it feels like to have sisters.

Ursula and I were instant friends. She loved all the clothes. Rolf hung around with us even though he's two years older. He said he didn't want to hang around with the other teenagers because he heard enough of the state propaganda at home from Hiltrut.

I wish we could have stayed for a few more days. Ursula was going to sleep over at Oma's. We would have had so much fun.

All my aunts complimented me on my German, but they used lots of words and phrases I'd never heard before. Mama insisted we speak high German at home so I wouldn't sound like a peasant when I met other Germans.

People brought so much food, and most of it looked just like what Mama makes, but there were some dishes I'd never eaten.

All my life, I've been German and Canadian. Sister Marie-Claire even wrote German-Canadian beside my name, like she wrote Polish-Canadian beside Kalina's name on the class list. When I asked her why she put a dash, she said that we were all more than one thing in Quebec. Lots of kids were Czech, German, Italian, or Polish at home, but we were all French-Canadian at school. Here, things feel familiar, but I feel like a stranger. Could Hiltrut be right? Maybe I'm not a real German. Will I be a real Canadian in Ontario?

The smell of cigarette smoke coming from the window below me has stopped. I wonder if Papa knows Mama smokes? I don't think I'll say anything to him. I better turn off the light.

Angelika

CHAPTER SIX - 1963

Auf Wiedersehen, Germany

The words on the page swam in front of Marta's eyes, but the book was a comforting shield as she settled into the airplane seat. Angelika wrote in her diary in the seat beside her.

* * *

July 16, 1963

Chère Journal,

In the morning after the reunion, Oma pressed a soft package wrapped in flowered tissue paper into my hands as we said goodbye. On the train, I unfolded the paper to find a pair of grey woollen mittens with red thumbs. I hope I get to see Oma again someday. She's so much more fun than most old ladies. Franz watched us get on board. It's a good thing he didn't come too close. I think Mama would have punched him, and we'd really be trapped, then.

* * *

Images of the last ten days paraded through Marta's mind. *Helpless.* The emotion she'd never been able to tolerate now tested her the most. She knew what Kurt would say: *Put aside the things you can't do anything about, and put your energy into something that you can change.* The challenges for her mother and sisters in the disintegrating infrastructure of the East weighed heavily on Marta. As Ellen had pointed out, feeling guilty about the opportunities in her Western life wouldn't put bread and meat on her siblings' tables in the East. Instead, Marta and Ellen had resolved to find ways of supporting their family members around the barriers of access the German Democratic Republic kept erecting.

Marta wished she knew what her mother intended to do in the face of the coming eviction. When she'd tried to talk about it with her after everyone had left, her mother had smiled and changed the subject. Klara and Liesbeth had both opened their homes to their mother, but she wouldn't hear of it. Everyone knew that Oma wouldn't survive long living in a single room in an institution. Marta shuddered as she considered what her mother could possibly be planning and the potentially lethal outcomes.

"Are you okay, Mama?"

Marta pulled her sweater around her shoulders and forced a smile. "I'm fine, *Schatzi.* Just a little chilly."

Angelika went back to her writing.

* * *

We took a train from East Berlin directly to Wiesbaden in West Germany because we were going to my Oma and Opa Langer. At the border, the khaki-clad Grenz-Truppen carrying machine guns walked around all the train cars. Some had German shepherds, and others had mirrors on long sticks to look under each car. Another group of soldiers walked through the aisles inside. We had to step out of our compartment and wait while they lifted the seats and poked their rifles into the coats on the overhead racks. As if people could be hiding in such an obvious place. When the train started moving again, Mama put her hands on my shaking knees. She said I looked really pale. I'm glad to be out of the East. The villages in the West speeding past the windows vibrated with colourful houses, cheerful gardens, and unfiltered bright sunshine. It's like the world has turned on the coloured lights again. I feel sorry for Ursula and Rolf growing up in such a scary place. And what's going to happen to Oma?

* * *

Marta swallowed hard. She had likely seen her mother for the last time. And who knew whether or when she'd see the rest of her siblings? Then there was Franz. As if it wasn't enough to have seen him again and put up with his petty power play, the last image of her hometown was of him standing on the platform, arms crossed, monitoring their departure.

* * *

> It was a really short visit in Wiesbaden. We got to Oma and Opa's just in time for Abendbrot. That's German for supper. It means evening bread, because you eat sandwiches, called open-faced. I guess that's because there's only a slice of bread on the bottom, not on the top, so you can see the meat and cheese, like a face. Germans eat a hot meal at lunchtime because they believe that too much heavy food at night gives you nightmares. They sure have some different ideas about food here.

* * *

Then there was Kurt's family. On the first morning in Wiesbaden, while Angelika and her Opa went to get his newspaper and the buns for breakfast, Mutter Langer had trapped Marta in the kitchen, hands on hips to block the doorway. "So how long is this silliness going to go on?"

Marta kept her back to the woman while preparing the cheese and meat tray. "What silliness?"

"You've proven you can control Kurt, so now I want my son back home. Angelika said her papa is looking for a job in Canada. There are plenty of jobs here."

Marta choked. "You think going to Canada was my idea?"

"No, but you drove him to it. Kurt told us how you pressured him for an apartment. I always said you were too expensive for him, you and your fancy clothes."

"You drove him to it with your constant disapproving looks because he didn't measure up to his number-pushing twin," Marta muttered under her breath. Aloud, she said, "We've made a good life in Canada."

Mutter Langer snorted. "Angelika told me about the blackflies and the bush, living with the French, eating wild meat. How is she going to get a proper education over there? Find a good husband?"

"Angelika is thriving. Canada has many excellent universities. But thank you for your concern." Marta refrained from slamming the plates on the counter. "You're always welcome to visit and see our country for yourself."

"What about family? She won't know who she is, growing up over there."

"If this is family," Marta said, pointing at her, "then she's better off without it."

Angelika burst through the door, bringing Mutter Langer and Marta's conversation to an abrupt end. She was full of stories about the Biebricher Schloss, the castle they'd seen. After purchasing his newspaper and a crossword puzzle book for his wife, Papa Langer had taken his granddaughter through the Schloss Park to stop at the bakery.

"Mama, we walked right up to a really big square building. It was built in 1702, and it has twenty-eight windows across the front, and fourteen on each side, with a fancy wooden door in the middle. Opa says it's a castle, but I don't see how it can be." Angelika's brow furrowed. "It's only one floor high, with no turrets for the knights to defend it from invasion."

Marta laughed. "Opa's right, Angelika. The palace was built for the prince of this area, not for war, but as a country residence to enjoy the Rhine River."

Angelika hadn't looked too convinced as they all sat down to breakfast.

That afternoon, Hans picked them up in his car. Papa Langer sat in the front, while Mutter Langer and Marta slid into the back. Angelika was squeezed between her mother and grandmother, perched half on her mother's lap.

"Everyone in?" Hans called over his shoulder before steering into the traffic. Angelika looked as if she was ready to say something about the size of the car, but she closed her mouth in the face of Marta's frown and slight head shake. As they drove, Hans provided a running commentary as though he was guiding a group of tourists. He pointed out the new buildings, the restored churches, and the modern streets.

"Angelica, that's where your Papa and I lived before we moved to Canada." Marta cricked her neck to look upward. "Our room was on the top floor."

Angelika leaned across her mother. "Your room?"

"Yes, that's all we had, one room with a bed, two chairs, a round table and a dresser where our hot plate sat."

Angelica wriggled.

"Ow! Move your elbow out of my stomach."

"Sorry, Mom, it's kind of—"Angelika stopped talking and sat up. "But what about a bathroom?"

"We shared one with everyone on our floor."

"That's the way it was after the war, *liebling*," Mutter Langer interjected. "Wait until you see your Onkel Hans's apartment. So big, with modern kitchen and bathroom. That's how we live now, how you and your Mama and Papa can live when you come back."

"Mutter Langer!" Marta silenced her mother-in-law with a glare.

"Mama, are we—"

Marta put her arm around Angelika. "No, we aren't moving back here."

Mutter Langer huffed loudly, then crossed her arms over her chest. A tight silence squeezed the air out of the car.

"Here we are." Hans's voice was laced with relief as he pulled up to a multi-storied building. "Papa, Mutti, and Angelika, you go ahead. I have to park the car in the garage." He turned to the back seat. "Marta, maybe you'd like to join me?"

Marta gave a curt shrug. She watched her in-laws and daughter enter the building as they pulled away.

"So, Canada." Hans exhaled heavily. "Seems pretty wild. Living in the bush." He glanced in the rear-view mirror at her. "My brother must be in his element; hunting, fishing. I bet he's talked you into having a boat, going camping. But that's not the Marta I remember. "

Marta saw his eyebrows raise as their eyes met in the mirror.

"We had fun, you and I, didn't we?" Hans's smile made Marta's skin crawl. "You could have it all again if you stopped this stupidity, moved back."

Marta forced an even tone. "What are you suggesting? We're both happily married."

Hans pulled into the parking garage. "But what about family? You want your daughter to grow up with family to guide her, show her who she is?" He pulled into his parking spot, turned off the ignition, and shifted to face her.

"Angelika is doing just fine as a Canadian." Marta gave a hard laugh. "And, as to you and me, we had a few dates, but that's ancient history."

"You were more than happy to have me take you to the theatre and art gallery, concerts in the park, walks along the Rhine." Hans's eyes turned dark. "Then the thanks I get is being left standing while you spent the whole evening dancing with my brother that night I took you to the nightclub."

Marta pressed her back into the seat as Hans adjusted his position so his body protruded between the front seats. She adopted a placating tone. "I admit, that wasn't nice of me. But Hans, you knew we weren't meant for each other."

"My brother always got the women. They couldn't resist his good looks, his smile. And then I met you and I thought, this time I'll be the winner." Hans's voice dropped. "I would've learned to dance for you. I would have done anything you wanted."

"Hans, look at you now. A beautiful wife, a daughter, a great office job and apparently a lovely apartment."

Hans met her eyes. He deflated like a child's balloon. "I'm sorry. It's Kristel. She's always after me about how you and Kurt are so far away and caring for Mutti and Papa falls on my shoulders." He pushed himself around, got out of the car, and opened her door.

When Hans didn't move out of the way, Marta got out and stood toe to toe with him. "There is no life here for Kurt and I. Perhaps you've forgotten but I have my own family who deserve my help more than those two," she tilted her head in the direction of the building, "ever will." She took a step toward him, forcing him to back away. "Now let's get this over with." Marta marched out of the parking garage, Hans hurrying in her wake.

* * *

When Onkel Hans picked us up the next day, his car was so small that I had to sit half on Mama's lap. When we got there, Onkel Hans sent Opa, Oma, and me upstairs while Mama went with him to park the car. I don't know what happened but when Mama and Onkel Hans came in, Mama's mouth was drawn in that line that she uses when me or Papa have done something really wrong.

Onkel Hans's living room was like being in the furniture showroom we went to when we picked out our furniture for Ontario. My legs kept sticking to the plastic cover on their sofa. Tante Kristel sounded like the saleslady trying to sell us on how rich they are because they own their tiny one-bedroom apartment and two cars. I wanted to ask Mama why Jutta, who's four, still sleeps on a pullout bed in her parents' closet if they're so rich, but I remembered Mama's rule about asking questions only when we are alone.

Looking at my Papa's family is like seeing them in two different mirrors in a fun house. Onkel Hans and Oma are in the mirror that makes you look short and fat. Opa and Papa are in the tall and skinny mirror. It's hard to believe Onkel Hans and Papa are twins. I'm glad I look like Papa. I wouldn't want Onkel Hans's chubby cheeks and saggy belly. I hope their daughter Jutta takes after her mother.

I can't wait to see Papa and our new house. Maybe I'll meet some kids and learn English before school starts. I hope they'll be friendly.

Angelika

* * *

Marta shifted in the narrow plane seat and took a sip of water. The drone of the aircraft's motors smothered the memory of Kristel's incessant chronicling of their supposed wealth and success over coffee and cake. Marta had been too relieved to be insulted when Kristel suddenly rose and announced that the visit was over because she needed to pick up Jutta from kindergarten. *Looks like Hans found himself a replacement for his mother*, Marta thought. He had always been a mama's boy. She let out a snort.

"What's so funny, Mama?"

Marta smoothed the strip of yellow paper she was using as a bookmark. She missed Kurt. It hadn't been easy for him to find a new job. She trusted that the place he'd found would be just as perfect for their family as Beaupré-sur-lac had been, but why did it have to be so far from everything? It had been hard enough learning French, and now she'd have to learn English, make new friends, find her way in a new town. *You're beginning to sound like Angelika.*

"That's Papa's telegram!" Angelika leaned against Marta's arm and read aloud. "'Job, house in Pus-a-ma…whatever… Fly Toronto. Train to White River.' How'm I ever going to live in a place that I can't pronounce!"

Resting her hand on her daughter's knee, Marta said, "I don't know how to say it, either, but we'll learn together."

"How long will we be on the train?"

"I don't know," Marta said, "but we'll see Papa and our new house at the end of it."

Angelika gave her mother a narrow-eyed look. "Fine." She dropped her eyes to her lap.

"Still nervous?"

Angelika fidgeted with her fingers, then nodded slowly.

Marta put her arm around her daughter and pulled her close. "It's okay to be scared, you know. This is a big change. I'm nervous, too."

"Why did you and Papa move to Canada? Were you nervous then?"

Marta gave a short laugh. "I was more than nervous—I was terrified." She stared off into the distance for a moment. Then, reaching into the carry-on bag at her feet, she pulled out knitting needles and wool. "You're making good progress," she said. "But you made the wrong stitch here."

"Mom, stop!" Angelika stared in horror as her mother pulled the stitches from the needle and began unravelling five rows of knitting. "It doesn't show that much."

"If you don't correct it, all you'll ever see is the mistake. Knitting isn't just knit and purl. A knitter has to know how to unravel, too. Now watch." Marta worked the knitting needle back through the stitches and redid the five rows correctly before handing the piece back to her daughter. Then she picked up her own knitting.

"What was it like when you first moved to Beaupré-sur-lac?" When Angelika saw her mother's hesitation, she added, "Please. We have a long flight. And you and Papa never talk about it."

Marta's needles began to click. "Well, it was your father's idea…"

CHAPTER SEVEN - 1951

Time to Go

Kurt stowed his fireproof work gloves, hard hat, steel-toed boots, and overalls in his locker, then grabbed the soap and pumice stone and joined his fellow workers to take advantage of their employer's free ten-minute hot shower. They scrubbed quickly. Six years since the end of the war, and people were still barely surviving. Talk about escaping Germany for America in search of a better life swirled around the men's heads while the inky water carried black soot and iron filings across the concrete floor to swirl around the drain.

Kurt's friend, Felix, talked of his plan to move his wife and four children to Waukesha, Wisconsin. He painted a picture of rolling hills with blue rivers sparkling through green fields. He had work lined up in a foundry and planned to buy a farm. "They need men like us who know iron," he said, "and we can live off what we grow on the farm." His visa was due to arrive any day.

Another man spoke of opportunities in Canada, a land of open spaces, rocks, lakes, and forests that reached to the horizon in all directions.

Kurt grimaced as his hand sTimmed lather over the puckered scar on his abdomen. Screams as his friends dropped around him. A searing pain as the Russian bullet tore through his side. Choking on the pungent smell of gunpowder and blood. Kurt tilted his face into the shower spray to subdue the memories. Mere months after his conscription at sixteen into Hitler's disintegrating army, Kurt and his comrades had been mowed down in a skirmish with the advancing Russian forces. Remembering the stories of brutality, he'd feigned death rather than be taken prisoner by the Russians. After hours of slowly sinking into the mud, he'd moaned when a British soldier stepped on his hand. The soldier called to his comrades. Sucking sounds as hands lifted him from his bed of sludge. Kurt had ridden out the last year of the war as a motorcycle courier carrying messages between the Americans and the British on the Baltic Coast. His comrades who'd been captured by the Russians were never heard from again.

"What about you, Kurt?" Felix's voice broke through Kurt's thoughts. "Have you and Marta decided where you're going?"

"We're still discussing it." Kurt's eyes clouded. Marta firmly refused to discuss it each time he suggested emigrating. How long, he wondered, could they continue with him working twelve-hour night shifts at Wiesbaden Rheinhütte Pumpen Company while she worked twelve-hour days as a chambermaid? They'd never have a family with only one night a week together. Perhaps that was a blessing in their current living conditions.

On his way home, Kurt's temple bounced against the window as the bus wound between the potholes along Rheingaustrasse. His gaze followed the green grass of the Biebricher Schloss Park streaming by. The few remaining trees in the park pushed uncertain leaves up to the sun from scorched limbs. He caught a tiny glimmer of red and yellow from the shards of stained glass embedded in the castle's doorframe. Gazing through the bombed-out window openings was like looking through vacant eyes into a decimated soul. He looked away.

On the other side of the street, lines of women in kerchiefs, waiting for their turn to purchase a handful of rubbery green beans or a kilo of maggoty meat, choked the sidewalks. Children played king of the castle on rubble piles in the alleyways. Kurt shuddered. Images of a place to start a family, of a house instead of a single ten-by-twelve foot room. A toilet, sink, and bathtub just for them instead of sharing with three other couples, air fragrant with green forests, fresh rain, and life. That's what he wanted for his wife and the children they were yet to have. It was time to go. Tomorrow, on their only day off together, he'd take her to the park. They could sit on the bench by the Rhine, and he would ask her again.

* * *

Marta leaned out over the windowsill of their sixth-floor room overlooking the courtyard of 27 Mainzer Strasse. She pulled her woollen sweater tightly around her thin frame against the early morning September chill. At this hour, all the buildings were in black silhouette against the sun's rays, camouflaging the charred, roofless ruins still marking the skyline five years after the 1947 Marshall Plan had begun. When the Displaced Person's Relocation Committee had assigned them this room, Marta had been relieved they were on the top floor. While it was a long walk up, it was the quietest spot for Kurt to sleep during the day.

She sang the first verse of "You Are My Sunshine" to herself, continuing to hum the melody because she hadn't learned all the English words yet. She heard the song on the radio throughout the day when she cleaned the hotel rooms of the American officers in charge of the occupation and reconstruction of her city. It was a struggle for two to exist on the German government's weekly rations. Fortunately, her American employers encouraged her to take home leftovers from their cafeteria. Chambermaid wasn't her dream job, but in these times, she felt lucky to be employed. When things settled down, she intended to pursue her dream of becoming a teacher.

The cuckoo called eight times. Six floors below, Kurt stepped through the arch and into the courtyard. Marta caught her breath at the weary motion of his fingers brushing back his blond hair. He'd feel better after breakfast and a good day's sleep. Hugging her sweater closer, she opened the door to their room. Her husband's upward progress was marked by the creak and groan of the ancient wooden stairs.

"Good morning, *Liebling*." Marta wrapped her arms around Kurt's neck as he stepped onto the landing.

Kurt kissed her deeply. Stepping back, he gave a loud sniff. "Is that real coffee?"

Marta grinned. "American coffee, with none of that government ration chicory. Sit." She pushed him gently toward one of the two chairs at the round café table. "We have four American eggs. I boiled them just the way you like."

"I hope I don't have to speak American to eat them." He chuckled.

A satisfied smile lightened Marta's sharp features as her hand grazed over the napkin covering the fresh golden rolls nestled in the basket. "And fresh *Brötchen*."

Kurt wrinkled his brow. "Oh, no. And here I was looking forward to that tough, black ration loaf."

Marta punched his arm playfully, set two chicken-shaped china egg cups holding the boiled eggs in front of him, and took her place at the table. They were soon eating with gusto.

"That was delicious. Thank you." Kurt sat back from the table.

"See, we can have a good life here." Marta pushed the plate of peeled, sectioned oranges toward him. "Maybe tonight we could go dancing. Get together with Ingrid and Alfred. I heard the Kochbrunnen Trinkhalle has reopened." *And afterward, I'll sleep in Kurt's arms*, she thought. Saturday, the one night a week free from the memory of the whistling of Allied bombs over Hamburg before their explosions had shaken every bone in her body. In Kurt's arms, she wouldn't wake screaming at the nightmares of melting streets and the roar of the Elbe river as it burned. Her head would stay free of the stink of human waste and body odour from days crowded in the darkness of the bomb shelter.

*   *   *

Kurt stretched his arm across the back of the park bench to drape it over Marta's shoulder. They both stared out at the sparkling waters of the Rhine. "How's the ice cream?"

Marta's face lit with the smile that had pulled him in when they'd met three years ago, the smile he hadn't seen for a very long time. "Delicious. And chocolatey, just like in the old times."

A father and son walked by, tossing a ball between them. Marta sighed. "People are coming out on Sundays just like before. Things will soon be normal again."

A couple pushing a tall wicker carriage strolled past, a chubby cherub face framed in a lacy bonnet barely visible under the canopy. Kurt watched the smile slide down Marta's cheeks. "Our time will come," he whispered.

Marta took a lick of her ice cream.

"You know it won't be like the last one. I won't leave you to cope alone, no matter what."

She nodded. "I know. You're nothing like Franz." She sighed again. "But we agreed, no baby until we can get our own apartment."

"Or…"

"Please, not that again." Marta moved out of his embrace to face him. "We'll have the money for a rent deposit soon. The Someday Jar is almost full."

Kurt's heart lurched. He longed to remove the deep purple circles from around her eyes. "You can't go on like this. Walking back and forth to work after twelve hours on your feet just to throw a few *Pfennige* into that jar. You're exhausted." He shifted to stretch his back.

"I'll take the bus when you stop working all those extra hours." Marta gave his shoulder a gentle shove.

They sat back, finishing their ice cream and squinting out over the glistening river.

Her hand found his. "I love it here. The water's so calming."

"Me too," said Kurt. "There are beautiful rivers in America and Canada. And Australia has lots of oceanfront." He paused, then plunged on. "And we could have a house with a garden. No rubble. No rations, or burned-out buildings. Just clean, bright countryside and plenty of fresh food."

Marta put space between them on the bench.

"I know you don't want to hear it, but please, just listen one more time." Kurt cast Marta a pleading look. "Then, if you say no, I promise, I won't bring it up again." He held his breath. She hesitated for a long time. When she nodded, he exhaled loudly, then launched into all he'd learned as he'd researched each of the three countries—the costs, the processes to obtain a visa, and the employment opportunities for a blacksmith.

"It sounds perfect, but what about our families?" Marta turned to him with a frown. "Liesbeth is having her baby next month, and she can't even get diapers. And what about my mother, all alone in the house?" She grasped his hands in hers. "My brothers and sisters need me."

Kurt struggled to swallow his frustration. "But West Germans aren't even allowed across into the East right now, and if you did get through, you know what would happen.

Remember our last visit?" Kurt and Marta had carried two suitcases filled with coffee, soap, detergent, chocolate, towels, diapers, and baby clothes. After the East German border guards had finished their inspection, they were allowed to pass through the gate with a pound of coffee and a few articles of clothing.

"They had no right to steal our things. Those things were for my family." Marta's shoulders tightened with anger.

"I know, but yelling at them like you did almost got you arrested."

Marta glared at him. "I'd like to see them try."

Kurt shook his head. "Anyway, it's all pointless now. Who knows how long they'll keep the border closed." Kurt wasn't sure he wouldn't be tempted to lift a few items from travellers, call it a border tax, if he were one of the guards. After all, their families lived under the same shortages. His voice became cajoling. "You'll be able to write. Letters are still going through, and maybe soon, parcels will be allowed. They might even be more lenient with foreign mail. You aren't likely to be planning an escape for a relative from across the ocean in America."

And as for his family, he thought, leaving would finally release him from seeing the disappointment in his father's eyes because he chose to work with his hands instead of in an office like his twin brother. It would render mute his mother's nagging about what she saw as his doomed marriage to a divorced woman nine years his senior.

"Australia's too far." Marta wrinkled her nose as if she'd picked up a bad smell.

Kurt quelled his excitement. "And America or Canada?" His hands clenched in his pockets.

"I need to think." Marta's eyes clouded.

Kurt knew he'd pushed as far as he could. "How long? I can't keep living in this limbo."

"This week?"

Kurt nodded.

* * *

Marta jolted awake, bathed in a cold sweat. Someone was pounding against the wall from the room next door. Her throat felt raw. She must have cried out in her sleep again. Pulling the blanket around her like a shawl, she moved to the window. Fingers of yellow dawn creeping through the black city banished her nightmare's shadows to the corners of the room, but not from the depths of her mind. Cold hands groping pockets for theft-worthy possessions while assaulting her body in the inky darkness. Choking coughs of inhaled dust as the bombs thumped and the earth shook. Marta had been born in one world war and scurried into bomb shelters in a second. What kind of mother would she be to subject her daughter to the constant fear of violation or starvation when a third war came? To subject her son to the dangers of battle? Maybe Kurt was right. Maybe this was the time to leave, to start fresh in a new world whose shores were less likely to be visited by war.

That day at work, Marta asked Captain Dave, one of the American officers on her floor who spoke German, how long it took for immigrants to get a visa for the United States.

"Two years," he said. "Are you and Kurt thinking about emigrating?"

"Kurt thinks it would be a better place for us to raise a family." Her fingers pleated and un-pleated her apron. "And who knows when the next war may come. Besides, things are difficult with his parents because…well…"

Captain Dave smiled. "I can't imagine anyone objecting to you as their daughter-in-law. Let me know if you decide to apply. I can speed things up for you."

Marta felt her eyes widen. "Oh, thank you, but we wouldn't want to put you to any trouble."

"No trouble at all. And I know my wife will be happy to meet you."

Marta smiled weakly and continued her rounds.

The following morning, she waited for Kurt to come home before leaving for work. If she took the bus just this once, she'd still make it on time. And the cat would have to wait until she walked home before getting a meal. It wasn't uncommon these days to see gaunt figures barely recognizable as cats prowling through the rubble in search of food. Marta's heart went out to these desperate animals that had lived as pets until the bombs had destroyed their homes and, in some cases, their owners. In the struggle to feed families and recover from loss, people had little time or resources to care for these homeless pets.

Several weeks ago Marta had encountered a grey cat meowing plaintively from a tiny cave-like space under a mound of bricks and stone. Marta recognized the sound. They'd had cats at home to keep the mice down. A closer look confirmed her suspicion. The poor animal was giving birth to a litter of kittens and she appeared to be barely out of kitten-hood herself. Marta left half her sandwich at the mouth of the cave. On the way home that day, she brought two chipped bowls from the hotel kitchen, a jar of milk, and a handful of leftover meat and vegetables from the officers' supper plates. And so their understanding began. Marta would provide for the cat and her kittens and respect the cat's independence and privacy, never attempting to see the little ones. And the cat would not follow Marta in hopes of finding a permanent home.

Kurt's face contorted with fear when he walked through the door and found Marta at home. "What's wrong? Are you sick? Hurt?" He covered the room in two strides and pulled her to him, running his hands over her body.

"I'm fine." She pushed back and took a shaky breath. "I'll go to America."

Kurt swept her off her feet and twirled her around the room, laughing at the top of his voice.

"Shh, you'll disturb the neighbours," Marta said, but she couldn't help laughing along with him.

Suddenly, he stopped and set her feet on the floor. "Or Canada?"

"Yes, or Canada." *America, Canada, what's the difference?* she thought. Either way, visas would be years away, and maybe things would be better here by then.

A week later, Kurt came home waving two tickets to Quebec and freshly-inked Canadian visas in their passports.

The blood dropped to Marta's feet. "How can that be? I thought it took two years to get a visa?"

"To America. But the Canadian office said there's a boat leaving in two weeks. Isn't that great?"

"We don't have enough money for the fares." Marta pushed her words through stiff lips.

Kurt grinned. "We had enough in the Someday Jar for yours."

"But that money's for the deposit on an apartment."

"An apartment we won't need anymore." Kurt's eyes shone. "And the Canadian government gave me a loan. They need my skills. All I had to do was sign a contract."

"What kind of contract?" Marta grimaced at the sharpness in her voice.

"When we arrive in Quebec, we have three days for me to find a job."

"Three days!"

"It'll be fine. Employers hire immigrants right off the boat."

Marta covered her face with her hands. "It's too fast. I need to go see my mother, my family."

Kurt pulled down her arms. "We don't know if or when the border will open." He gently wiped the tears from her cheeks. "I promise you can come back for a visit when things open up."

She had no argument left. Kurt had done what she'd agreed to. It was time to think of their future children. She was a good wife, and a good wife followed her husband. But the warmth of his lithe, six-foot frame as he gathered her against him didn't fully thaw the icy fear she'd felt rising from her toes.

They departed two weeks later.

CHAPTER EIGHT - 1951

Welcome to the New World

Marta grasped the round iron rail in front of her. Her knees locked and unlocked, absorbing the ship's rhythm as she pressed her back into Kurt's body, safe in the circle of his arms. Seagulls wheeled over the white crests of the waves, their screeches lost on the wind. A V-formation of brown birds with black heads and white chests announced their arrival in a cacophony of honking as they emerged over the towering cliffs of the approaching shore. Over the past twelve days, Marta had come to think of this corner by the front rail as their spot. It was the only place where she could find relief from the constant nausea as their ship, the *Homeland*, pitched and rolled its way from Bremen to Quebec. One hundred and ninety-nine hopeful, terrified immigrants were carried away from everyone and everything they knew. Perhaps *Angst* would have been a more fitting name for their ship.

Kurt's chin resting on the top of her head pulled Marta back to her new reality. "Only a few more hours," he murmured. "You'll feel better as soon as we get you on solid ground."

She turned her head to meet his eyes. "And once we have something to eat other than fish soup, stale bread, and rancid butter. What I wouldn't give for a bath!" The fresh water reservoir serving the three wash basins for the passengers had run dry three days out.

"And a real cup of coffee." Kurt leaned over and brushed his lips over hers. "The trip was rougher than I expected." Marta's body crumpled against him. "Something wrong?"

"Just thinking about the Schmidts. The tiny body of their baby,"Marta sniffed, "wrapped up tight and sliding down the board into the black water." She shuddered.

"And grandfather Romanski's body, too. What a hard way for their families to start their new lives."

"There were days when I wasn't sure I was going to make it until you found this spot and got me out into the air." Marta pressed herself into Kurt's embrace.

He breathed into her ear. "Look out there, Marta. A whole country is waiting for us."

She forced a smile to meet the anticipation dancing in his blue eyes.

Soon the deck was crowded with passengers pressing for their first view of the city of Quebec. Marta leaned over the rail to get a better view of the rows of six-storey, rough-stone buildings crowding the shore, their red, grey, and blue metal roofs gleaming in the sunlight. No blackened skeletons of bombed-out buildings. No piles of charred beams and broken bricks. "I didn't know Canada had such old buildings. And cobblestone streets."

Kurt grinned. "See the *Schloss*?" He tilted his chin up at the green-roofed turrets crowning red brick walls of windows.

"That's the Château Frontenac." The couple turned toward the thin girl of about thirteen squeezed against the rail next to them. "It's not a castle. It's a hotel, and they built it to make it look old." Her high-pitched tone was tinged with self-importance. "It was built by the Canadian Pacific Railway in the 1890s."

"How do you know that?" Marta asked.

The girl's slim fingers disappeared into the pocket of her oversized coat. "My papa told me right here." She held up a crinkled page marred with fingerprints. "And he knows, because he works for the CPR. We're coming to live with him."

"Anna Maria Leibner, get over here right now!"

"That's my mother. I have to go. *Auf Wiedersehen*." The slender girl slipped away through the crowd. Kurt and Marta shared a smile.

Soon, the crew of the *Homeland* nestled the ship into its berth. Marta clung to Kurt's hand as he threaded a path down the gangway and through the chaos on the dock. She choked back bile at the stench of unwashed humanity pressing into her until her cheeks reddened with the realization that she, too, must smell.

Waiting on the dock, they scanned the crowd. Marta saw Kurt's dreams reflected in the multitude of faces. She heard inflections of her fears voiced in the different languages swirling on the breeze.

Suddenly, the crowd began to separate into groups.

"*Deutsche, hier Bitte. Deutsche.*"

Kurt pulled her toward the man waving a black, red, and gold banner reflecting their homeland's flag. The German translator shepherded his group of about forty people to the medical screening station. Marta hesitated to let go of Kurt's hand as the lines split, men to the left, women and children to the right.

Kurt gave her shoulder a squeeze. "I'll meet you on the other side." He pointed ahead to where the lines reconnected. Then he disappeared into the crowd.

A nurse dressed in white cap and navy cape greeted her in broken German while guiding her by the elbow into one of the canvas-sided booths. "You're looking very pale," she said. In response to Marta's questioning expression, she added, "You feel *schlecht?*"

Marta forced herself to stand straighter. "*Ja, seekrank… das Boot.*" She swayed back and forth to simulate the rocking of the ship.

The nurse smiled sympathetically as she took Marta's temperature, checked her throat, listened to her heart and lungs, measured her height and weight, and did a quick examination of her limbs and abdomen.

"*Alles gut,*" the nurse said and stamped Marta's paperwork.

Relieved, Marta rejoined Kurt. He was looking around with eyes as wide as a child with a penny in his pocket in a candy store.

The translator beckoned them forward. "Now you will be interviewed by an immigration officer to confirm the information on your application."

They took their seats in front of the immigration officer's desk. Kurt responded easily to the officer's German/English mix as they worked their way through the questions about where he was born, where he'd grown up, and his schooling, including his qualifications as a blacksmith.

He confirmed his birthdate, "May 18, 1927."

"*Ja*…Yes," said Kurt.

"Did you fight in the war?"

Kurt nodded. His hand pressed involuntarily to his side, reminding Marta of the crenelated skin where the Russian bullet had penetrated.

"Why didn't you go home after the war?"

Kurt's brow folded into a frown. Marta held her breath. *Don't mention anything about the house and farm that was handed over to Poland after the war*, she urged in her mind. *This man won't care that it was in your family for hundreds of years, or that your mother had to flee ahead of the Russians with only what she could carry on her back.*

"The Displaced Persons Relocation Committee found work for me in Wiesbaden. My mother had been relocated there and had an apartment for our family." The translator repeated Kurt's German response in English. The officer's expression remained neutral.

Marta quietly released her breath.

"You must pay back the full amount of your fare to the Canadian government within five years, or you will be sent back."

Kurt nodded.

"You have three days to find a job, or you will be sent back. You must remain employed until the loan is repaid, or you will be sent back." The man repeated the required statements in a monotone while the translator whispered them in German for them.

"*Ich verstehe*. I understand."

"You may not live in Quebec, Montreal, Toronto, or Vancouver until your loan is paid."

"*Ja*, no city."

Marta remembered thinking how strange that condition seemed, until Kurt shared what the agent in Germany had told him. Immigration was Canada's solution to its labour needs for the development of its natural resources. And those resources were found around the small towns, especially across the North.

Stamp. Stamp. Stamp. The officer handed Kurt his paperwork. "Welcome to Canada."

Marta took a deep breath and squared her shoulders. The warmth of Kurt's hand on her leg reassured her. Her interview began with the same easy questions.

The officer confirmed her birthdate, "October 23, 1917." Marta nodded.

"Divorced?" The officer raised his eyebrows.

Her gaze dropped to her hands clenched in her lap. Would she never escape the stigma? What was the point in telling this man about the late nights of drinking and gambling, the other women? The marriage had only lasted two years. Her mother had been right: you couldn't trust a musician. Feeling Kurt's hand squeeze her knee, Marta raised her head and nodded.

"Children?"

Her heart lurched before she shook her head. Her baby son had come too soon. For three days, she'd sat alone beside the incubator, watching his struggle for each breath. In the end, her son had never fully taken hold of life. She was the only one by the graveside when they laid him in the ground. "No."

"What did you do during the war?"

She swallowed hard. "I worked in Hamburg as a shop clerk." It wouldn't serve any purpose to tell him about the days and nights spent in bomb shelters while the Allies flattened the city. That was another time, and this man wouldn't care. Maybe he'd think the Germans deserved it.

The officer made a few notes, then stamped her passport and her visa. "Welcome to Canada. *Bienvenue.*"

Kurt and Marta rose and extended their hands. When the officer's hand remained flat on his table, they awkwardly moved away. Perhaps Canadians didn't shake hands as they did at home.

A guard clad in military olive lifted the barrier. Kurt swept Marta into his arms and carried her through the gap like a groom carrying his bride over the threshold. She flung her arms around his neck, and they both dissolved into jubilant laughter. Suddenly self-conscious of their emotional exhibition, Kurt set Marta back on her feet. She patted down her hair and smoothed her coat before catching the eyes of those passing. Some looked away with derisive expressions, but others smiled. The corners of the guard's mouth twitched upward when he pointed them toward a rank of long, low buildings at the end of the wharf. The translator called his farewell before turning to help the next German family.

Marta's smile drooped. Surrounded by a milling crowd of foreigners, she suddenly felt completely alone. Her hand tightened its grip on Kurt's.

"Everything will be fine." Kurt squeezed her hand back.

They joined the steady stream of their shipmates moving in eerie silence past the guards stationed along the wharf's edge. Marta waited to the side while Kurt waded through the sea of baggage. She'd never seen such an assortment of suitcases, bags, trunks, even slatted wooden crates and barrels. Kurt found their two suitcases containing their clothing. Marta checked the cardboard labels flapping in the breeze. When he deposited the wooden steamer trunk at her feet, she breathed a sigh of relief at its undamaged condition. Its cargo—a forty-eight-piece place setting of dark green depression glass given to them by her American employer on their wedding day and the six sets of hand-painted Bavarian porcelain cups, saucers, and cake plates they'd purchased on their honeymoon to the Alps—was wrapped in embroidered tablecloths and nestled in straw. They were the only pieces she had from her homeland to adorn her new life. Losing them would pierce a hole in her soul.

Another guard pointed to the line forming in front of a warehouse. Marta took in his dark hair and olive skin. Was he an immigrant once?

At the entry, a female guard directed women and children to the left, while a male guard pointed the men to the right. Marta froze in the designated doorway. Endless rows of cots. Rough timbered walls. Naked lightbulbs swinging on lines strung from rafter to rafter. Her heart pulsed in her ears. She couldn't breathe.

"Go." She felt Kurt's push on her back. "I'll meet you in the dining hall."

A woman muttered something in a language Marta didn't understand as she pushed her through the door. The tide of anxious women dragged her into the space. Staggering to the next vacant cot, she choked back her tears and unwrapped her scarf. Continuous murmuring, punctuated by baby cries, washed over her. Children shouted excitedly as they chased each other up and down the aisles.

"It's overwhelming at first, but you'll get used to it," a soft voice said in German.

Marta turned to the woman burping her baby on the next cot while feeding spoonfuls of mushy green into the mouth of the dark-eyed toddler corralled firmly between her knees. She couldn't be more than twenty. And two babies. Marta gave herself a mental shake. Time to stop feeling sorry for herself. This was a new start.

Two hours later, she followed her new friend, Monika, to the dining hall for dinner. Marta carried the baby while Monika kept a firm hold on little Frederik's hand.

Monika stepped to the side, out of the way of the entrance. "This is where Richard and I meet. It's easier than trying to find each other at the tables."

Marta gently rocked back and forth to soothe the sleeping baby as she took in the spectacle of several hundred people seated on benches at rows of tables. Others picked up plates of food from the counters along one side of the room. Her mouth watered at the aroma wafting through the hall. The sight of passing plates heaped with meat and potatoes garnished with rounds of carrot all swimming in a rich brown gravy brought a rumble from her stomach. Real food at last.

Suddenly, Kurt materialized at her elbow. "Here you are!" He glanced from the baby to her face with a raise of his eyebrows.

"This is Monika, my bed neighbour. She and her husband, Richard, have been here two days. She showed me where everything is."

Monika nodded a greeting. "We leave tomorrow on the train to Capreol. It's in Ontario." Her brow creased as she pushed her tongue around the foreign words.

"Papa!" Frederik escaped his mother's grip and ran to jump into his father's arms.

While the women collected the food, the men found seats and settled the two children. Over dinner, Kurt and Marta learned that Richard had decided on a job with the railway.

Lingering in the dining hall was discouraged because of the number of people waiting, so after finishing their meal, the couples separated. Although immigrants were prohibited from going into the city by six-foot-high fencing and gates controlled by guards, they were free to walk along the wharfs and explore the few shops tucked into the face of the cliff.

"You seem brighter," Kurt said as they strolled among groups of their shipmates who had also decided to brave the stiffening breeze and stretch their legs. "Seasickness gone?"

"I feel better." Marta stopped and faced Kurt. "I'm sorry I've been so difficult."

Kurt made a dismissive gesture with his hand.

"No, I have. I promise I'll be better."

Kurt pulled her into his arms and kissed her deeply. They continued their stroll until the cold and damp forced them back to their respective cots. When everyone had settled for the night, Marta grabbed the towel provided and slipped between the cots to the shower room. The warm water pounded over her head and massaged her shoulders, but it didn't entirely wash away her fear at what was to become of them.

In the morning, they joined the hundreds of other newcomers in the employment hall. Kurt was offered a job with CPR right away. The pay was generous and included an apartment, but it meant he would be away from home from four to seven days at a time. Marta told him she'd return to Germany before agreeing to that.

The next day, the lumber companies wanted him, but Kurt would have to start as a feller, which meant four months away in the bush each year. Not a chance, said Marta.

At supper that night, Kurt was deflated until they heard several men talking about the mining companies—good pay, a house, a real town with stores, doctors, schools, and churches. At noon on their third and final day, as specified in their contract with the Canadian government, Kurt signed on with a gold mine and the next morning, they boarded the crowded company train to the town of Beaupré-sur-lac in Northwestern Quebec.

They sat crammed shoulder to shoulder with their fellow travellers on hard wooden benches. *Nothing but rocky outcroppings, lakes, and trees. Where were the towns, the cities, the people?* Marta thought. *It's so wild here. How did people survive?* What if their house was one of those log cabins without heat or plumbing that she'd seen in pictures? Would they have to hunt for their food? Marta shivered.

Kurt gripped her hand. "It's so beautiful. So much room to spread out, places to go fishing, hunting…" His voice drifted under her hard stare. He pulled her into him. "Sleep, *Schatzi*. Everything will be all right. You'll see."

Fourteen hours later, the crisp fresh air on her face revived Marta as she stepped onto the rough wooden platform in front of the Beaupré-sur-lac Railway Station. A man, dressed in a suit, flanked by four smiling women, greeted their group of sixty-five nervous immigrants, referred to as *fros*, foreigners, by the locals. As the man explained in French how everyone would be sorted into temporary housing, each of the four women translated his words into English, German, Polish, and Czech. Single men boarded the first school bus and were driven to the bunkhouse. Families with children were directed to the next bus. They were to be settled into motel units during the probationary work period, after which they'd be eligible for a house. Three months of motel bills, living in one room without a kitchen? Marta cringed at the thought—and the expense.

A matronly woman, dressed in a full-length mink coat, approached them, firing questions in rapid French.

Marta put out her hands, palms up, and tried to look pleasant as she responded, "*Ich verstehe nicht.*"

"*Les enfants?*" The woman held out her hand, waist high, then posed her arms as if cradling a baby.

Kurt shook his head.

"*Seulement vous deux?*" The woman held up two fingers.

The German-speaking translator came over to help. "This is Madam Pelletier, the wife of the mine superintendent." The translator introduced herself as Elisabeth Erb. She and her husband had arrived off the train three years ago. "She's offering free room and board in her home for a couple, in exchange for childcare and light housekeeping duties." Deciding this could be a significant financial saving for them, Kurt and Marta accepted the offer.

CHAPTER NINE - 1951

Making a Home

Marta stirred the *rouladen* as they simmered in the pot on the single hotplate, then dipped a spoon into the velvety brown gravy and slurped. She restrained her impulse to duck her head. *Ladies don't slurp.* She heard her mother's voice in her head, words that were usually accompanied by a flick of the dishtowel that seemed to always be in her mother's hand.

All afternoon, Marta had dashed between her daily household chores for the Pelletier family upstairs and Kurt's and her room in the basement to check on the beef-and-moose-meat rolls. She brushed angrily at the tears trickling down her cheeks, then dropped into one of the two mismatched wooden chairs at the rickety café-style table. Her shoulders sagged as her eyes sTimmed their tiny room divided by a dull curtain which hid the double bed and toilet. A lumpy, legless sofa sagged against the stone cellar wall in the space that passed as a living room. Had it only been a month? She felt as if they'd been stuck in this hole for much longer. This was far from what she'd envisioned for their new life. She wasn't sure how long she could continue to hide her desperation to return home from Kurt.

The aroma of fresh baking wafting down the stairs reminded Marta that her last task, the Pelletier family bread, was ready to be removed from the oven upstairs. As she came to her feet, a wave of nausea pushed her back into the chair. Her hand drifted to her abdomen. There was no doubt. With a steadying breath, she stood and smoothed her hands down the apron that protected her best dress. What better day than their third anniversary to tell Kurt. Upstairs, the five Pelletier children had all been fed, their homework completed, and the meal for their parents prepared and set waiting in the warming oven. There couldn't possibly be another thing she needed to do for her employer/landlord this evening. She climbed the stairs one last time to remove the loaves.

"Ah, there you are."

Marta jumped at Madam Pelletier's voice behind her.

"Jean-Paul has vomited all over himself." The woman held the baby out at arm's length, his front covered with green and yellow mush. "I need you to bathe him."

"But…" Marta felt helpless without the words to explain about their anniversary dinner.

Madam Pelletier thrust the smelly baby at her. "Kurt's not home yet. You have time." She pointed at her wristwatch.

Marta didn't understand all the words, but she grasped the general gist of her employer's expectations. With a sigh, she slid the last loaf onto the counter and took the child. Nine-month-old Jean-Paul grabbed Marta's hair and pulled himself into her embrace. The wet goo transferred from his chest to hers through her dress. She groaned.

* * *

Kurt's shift partner, Gordon, nudged his elbow into Kurt's side as they strode home along the frozen ground at the edge of the recently paved mine road. "Smells like snow. You ever seen snow, Kurt?" Their silver metal lunch pails bumped against their legs as they walked.

"*Schnee? In Oktober?*"

"*Ja, ja, Schnee,*" said Peter from Kurt's other side. Peter and Elisabeth Erb, the woman who'd translated for them upon their arrival, had become good friends, helping Kurt and Marta navigate their new world. "What did the housing foreman want with you today?" Peter continued in German.

"He said we are getting a house next Wednesday."

"Impossible. You have to prove yourself for three months." Peter then spoke English to Gordon. "Have you ever heard of anyone getting a house before three months?"

Gordon shook his head. "Kurt, you must have misunderstood."

"No, no," Kurt said, then went on in German for Peter to translate. "He said *Haus*. Then showed me next Wednesday on the calendar." Kurt was worried about Marta. Despite her efforts to hide it, he knew that she continued to be sick each morning. She hardly ate anything, and her eyes either glistened with tears or were red and swollen from crying. Kurt would be the first to admit that the accommodations were less than ideal, and the light housekeeping and childcare duties had been grossly underestimated, but each day, he reminded Marta that it was only temporary. And each night, he held her in his arms while he lay awake wondering whether he'd made a terrible mistake.

The men moved from the shoulder to the sidewalk as the mine road became *la rue Main*. A dozen two-storey cube-like buildings, each sporting a facade extending above the roofline, reminded Kurt of the towns he'd seen in the pictures of the Wild West. According to Peter, all the boom towns in the North looked like this.

The whole community was plopped onto a flat clearing in the dense forest of spruce and fir. There was nothing like the Schloss Park here. Only treeless streets crowded with identical one-and-a-half-storey company houses for the workers. Peter and Gordon peeled off on *Avenue Centrale Nord*. Kurt continued up the residential part of *la rue Main* to "snob hill." He always felt eyes peering at him from behind the lacy curtains of the two-storey clapboard houses, each unique in style, that housed the managers and their families. He was grateful that the Pelletiers had taken them in, but he still felt like a chicken among swans in this neighbourhood.

Kurt smelled the burning as soon as he came through the back door. Without taking off his outdoor clothing, he rushed down the stairs to their room and pulled the smoking pot from the hot plate. Steam hissed as he dropped the pot into the metal basin they used for washing.

Marta ran in behind him. "Oh, no!" she wailed. "The *rouladen*! I couldn't leave Jean-Paul in the bath alone. It was going to be perfect, and now it's ruined. It's all shit." She dropped to a chair, hands over her eyes. "Our life is shit."

Kurt unplugged the hotplate, then came to kneel beside her chair.

"Don't!" She pushed him away. "You made me come here. I hate Canada! This isn't a dream. It's a nightmare!"

Kurt moved to sit across the table from her.

"All I do is cook, clean, and run after children. What kind of mother leaves her children for someone else to raise while she plays cards and has tea parties with the other managers' wives? She practically lives at the church, organizing bazaars and gambling nights called *bingo*." Pulling a white handkerchief adorned with delicate embroidered yellow flowers from her sleeve, she wiped her eyes and blew her nose.

Kurt reached across the table, his eyes imploring her to take his hand. Slowly, she rested her fingers in his open palm.

"Don't worry about the *rouladen*. We can eat the leftover sausages."

"But it's our anniversary."

Kurt closed his hand over her fingers. "I have a surprise." He looked like a balloon about to burst. "We're getting a house!"

Marta's eyes widened. "Kurt, that can't be. They said you have to work three months." Her expression softened as she squeezed his hand with both of hers. "Could it be you misunderstood?"

"Why does everyone think I'm stupid?" Kurt exhaled loudly, then softened his tone. "The housing manager was very clear. House is *Haus*, and he drew a picture, then pointed to next Wednesday on the calendar."

Marta rushed to him, and he pulled her onto his lap. Their kiss was interrupted by a loud crack. Kurt fell backward, taking Marta with him. The seat of the chair skittered away while the back remained pinned between Kurt and the concrete floor.

"Are you okay?" Kurt ran his hands over Marta's body.

"Yes," she choked out between giggles. The giggles turned to laughter as Kurt joined in.

They were still chuckling as they struggled to their feet and settled on the sofa.

"Did he say why we're getting it early?"

Kurt's eyes clouded. "Most of the men that arrived with us have left. Some couldn't bear being underground. Others found the work too hard."

"But shouldn't a family living in a motel get the house before us?"

"I guess." Kurt frowned. "But I don't know how to ask. I think we need to trust the company knows what it's doing and be thankful."

The following afternoon, Marta ran into Elisabeth in l'Épicerie Cartier Grocery Store.

"Congratulations! Peter says you're getting a house next Wednesday. You must be so happy," Elisabeth said.

Marta beamed. "I can't wait to get out of that horrible basement. But—" A nervous pang shot through her chest.

Elisabeth rested her hand on Marta's forearm. "But what?"

"I didn't want to say anything to disappoint Kurt, but we have no furniture and no money to buy it. Because we live free at the Pelletiers, I've been putting all our money into paying back Kurt's loan." She turned worried eyes to her friend. "I suppose we can sleep on the floor with blankets, but how am I going to cook? We have nothing."

"*Ach*, don't worry. The company has an arrangement with the furniture store. Tomorrow, I'll go with you to the warehouse to order what you need."

"The company gives furniture?"

"It costs fifteen dollars a month for a couch, side chair, coffee table, two lamps, kitchen table with four chairs, fridge, stove, a double bed with two side tables, and a dresser. After two years, it's yours. And when you need a crib…"

Marta nodded.

Elisabeth raised her eyebrows.

"Don't say anything to Peter. I want to surprise Kurt once we're in the house."

Elisabeth hugged her. "A crib and small chest costs a dollar extra each month."

Stepping back, Marta wrapped her arms around her middle. "I want to make blankets and clothes for the baby, but no-one sells wool in town."

"No problem. You can order from the Sifton Products catalogue and it will come in the mail."

Marta's eyes widened.

"Don't worry," said Elisabeth. "I'll help you.

Marta smiled her thanks.

"Now back to the furniture. They will deliver it on the day you move in. The company takes the money out of Kurt's pay each month. All you need is the sixteen dollars for the down payment." She gave Marta another quick hug. "And the kitchen things will come. You'll see."

Marta's eyes dropped to her hands. "How will I tell Mme. Pelletier we're leaving early? She's going to be very upset."

Elisabeth squeezed Marta's shoulder. "It'll be fine. She knew you wouldn't be staying for long. Now, let's practice what you need to say to her."

Immediately after Kurt left for work on Wednesday morning, Marta rushed upstairs, fed the children their breakfast, and was cleaning up when Mme. Pelletier came into the kitchen, carrying a wooden crate. The ping of metal against metal marked each of her employer's steps. Pot handles protruded through the slats of the box as she set it on the table with one final *clang*. Mme. Pelletier then beckoned Marta to follow her down the hall. She stopped in front of the linen closet and proceeded to heap towels, sheets, pillowcases, and two blankets into Marta's arms. The employer followed Marta back to the kitchen, carrying another crate, this one providing a symphony of glass clinking as accompaniment. "For you and Kurt. To help you get started," said Mme. Pelletier, pointing first to the two boxes and pile of linens, then at Marta.

"*Pour moi? Merci, Madame. Merci beaucoup!*"

Mme. Pelletier unleashed a flood of French, smiling and gesticulating as she spoke. Marta understood *bon travail… les enfants…bonne chance…*when suddenly her employer swept her into a tight hug. Marta struggled to make sense of this uncharacteristic behaviour when a howl from Jean-Paul waking from his morning nap pulled the two women apart. But as Marta turned to fetch the baby, her employer stopped her with a hand on Marta's arm.

"*Non, non. Tu as fini. Va à ta maison.*" Then she turned and called, "*J'arrive mon bébé*," as she headed toward the children's bedrooms.

Marta carried the generous gifts down to their rooms where she left them on the trunk for Kurt to collect later. Then she grabbed their two suitcases and headed to their house. She and Kurt had walked past it every day since they'd received the address, dreaming of how they'd make it their own. Setting her two cases down on the small concrete porch, she pulled the key from her pocket. Her palm was sweaty as she slid the key into the lock and turned. The smell of fresh paint and paste wax filled her head as she stepped over the threshold. She gasped, taking in the white walls and gleaming hardwood floors. A whole house. All to themselves.

Removing her shoes but keeping on her coat against the chill in the house, Marta twirled, arms spread, in the empty living room. Laughing, she danced through the doorway on the right and found the kitchen. A place to put their table under the front window. Cabinets and an L-shaped countertop across the back and down the side. A second window above the sink overlooked the backyard. She could already smell the aromas of the roasts she'd make. She imagined her little daughter or son—boys needed to learn to cook, too—standing on a stool beside the counter while they made cookies together. Back through the doorway, she ran up the stairs to the second floor. A bedroom under the eaves on each side with a bathroom between them. A sink and toilet and a full-sized bathtub. She turned on the tap. Hot water. She hugged herself.

A knock on the front door interrupted her exploration.

"Hello, anyone home?"

Marta came down the stairs just as a man was backing in through the door with her two suitcases. "I found these on the step." He set them on the floor, then extended his hand. "Madam Langer? *Je suis* Jean-Guy Robichaud."

Her hand disappeared into his huge callused one.

"*Nous avons votre meubles.*"

Marta drew down her forehead. "*Meubles?*" she repeated.

A bright voice came from behind the man. "Yes, furniture, *meubles*," a petite woman said in English as she stepped into view on the porch. "Hi, neighbour." She put her hand to her chest. "Edna." Then she gestured toward the house on the kitchen side.

Marta's eyes moved from the man to the dark-brown head nodding and smiling at her. "Marta." She imitated the woman's action. "Naa-brr." She paused. "*Nachbar?*" She caught sight of the moving truck in her driveway. A couch and dining table caught the sunlight penetrating the open door at the back of the vehicle. She read the sign on the side. "*Meubles?*" Her eyes lit up. "*Möbel!* Fer-ni-shur." Kurt was going to be so surprised.

Jean-Guy grinned. "So can we bring it in?" He gestured at the truck and mimed carrying something.

"*Ja…Oui!*"

Edna came to her side, and Marta took in her neighbour's matronly figure. She looked about Marta's age.

Jean-Guy and a second man carried in the couch. "Brr. It's cold in here," the second man said. "I'll go down and light the furnace?"

Marta looked to Edna, who nodded. The man opened the door behind the staircase and disappeared into the cellar.

"Hopefully, there's some wood for the furnace?" Jean-Guy said in English for the benefit of Edna.

"Should be enough to get it started. My husband can get them set up later," Edna replied.

Marta smiled and nodded even though she had no idea what the two were saying.

* * *

Kurt rushed ahead of his friends on their way home after work. He was in a full run by the time he peeled off *la rue Main* and into the workers' residential town site. A right at the second block put him on *Rue Laval*. Five driveways down on the left stood their white house. He was vaguely aware of smoke rising from the chimney before he raced up the walkway and burst through the door.

"Marta, I'm home!" He'd been waiting so long to say that. He froze in the doorway.

Marta rushed into his arms. Tears were streaming down her face as she laughed at his slack-jawed expression. "Come! You need to see this!" She took him by the hand, led him into the kitchen, and pushed him into a chair at the table under the front window. Opening cupboards and drawers, she said, "Look, dishes for two and utensils." She held up each piece of mismatched cutlery in turn, saying their name in French and English, "*Couteau*, knife, *fourchette*, fork, *cuillère*, spoon." Then reverting to German, she explained, "Edna, our neighbour, taught me the words. All day, the neighbours have been bringing these things for us.

And there are two crates waiting for you to pick up at the Pelletiers. Madame has given us linens, pots, and glasses."

Kurt's blond eyebrows climbed his forehead.

Marta nodded. "She said I did a great job, and she hugged me!" she said with a girlish giggle.

"Look." She opened the fridge to reveal several casseroles. "Welcome gifts from the neighbours. And in here." She opened the stove. "Supper." The aroma of tuna wafted through the room.

"But where did the furniture come from?" Kurt gaped as Marta explained how Elisabeth had helped her with the arrangements. "You mean this is all ours?"

"Yes, as long as we pay fifteen dollars a month for the next two years. Come! See the bedroom." She pulled Kurt by the hand as she bounced up the stairs. After checking out their bedroom and marvelling at the bathroom, she stopped him in front of the closed second bedroom door. "We'll have to pay another dollar each month for this." She flung the door wide.

Kurt stared at the crib and tiny dresser. His eyes darted from Marta back to the crib. "You mean…"

Marta's eyes sparkled as she placed his hand on her abdomen. Without a word, he swept her up into his arms and carried her back into their bedroom.

CHAPTER TEN - 1963

Ontario

Kurt stood on the wooden railway platform. Above his head, a sign creaked on its rusty metal hooks in the light summer breeze. "White River," he read under his breath. He couldn't wait to hold Marta in his arms, feel the softness of her hair against his cheek, breathe in her lavender scent. He smiled at the thought of how Angelika would regale him with the details of their trip. They'd be excited to see their new house, but how would Marta feel about the surprise he had waiting for them?

Was the train on time? He could have asked at the station ticket office, but he still felt shy using his few English words. So he stood, rocking from foot to foot in time with the swaying sign, looking down the track.

The distant whistle of the train ignited a fire in Kurt's heart. "From Toronto?" he asked as the stationmaster emerged from his office.

"Yes." The man flipped open his pocket watch. "And right on time."

"Right on time," Kurt murmured.

Angelika jumped onto the platform and into her father's arms before the train had even stopped. Kurt pulled Marta into the embrace as she joined them. This was home.

Once their car was filled with gas, they ate lunch at the restaurant attached to the Husky Station. Kurt ordered hamburgers and French fries for all of them in English. He even ordered chocolate milk for Angelika.

"*Shocolat* milk," Angelika said, grinning.

"Let's hit the road," Kurt said, feeling proud to show off the English he'd learned in just a few weeks.

"Hit the road," Angelika wrapped her tongue around the words.

After finding only one station on the radio, a CBC talk show, Angelika gave up playing with the knobs.

"You must be tired," said Kurt. "First, eight hours on the plane, and then—how long was the train trip?"

"Seventeen hours," said Marta with a grimace. "We must be halfway across Canada."

Kurt shook his head. "Still in Ontario. Was it boring?"

"No, Papa. Mama told me all about how you two came to Canada." Angelika laughed.

"What's so funny?"

"She told me about the time you went next door to borrow an onion from Edna. You didn't know the word, so you pretended to peel something round and she offered you a potato and an apple. You must have looked really funny pretending to cry."

Kurt nodded. "And I felt silly, but I got the onion." He grinned at Marta. "Did Mama tell you about the horse shit?"

"Kurt, language!" Marta gave him a warning glare.

"Mama said horse shit? Tell me, Papa, tell me."

"Never mind, young lady." Marta knew by Kurt's expression that the story was going to come out, despite her admonishment.

"The neighbours wondered why your mama's vegetables seemed to grow so much faster and bigger than theirs." He chuckled. "She told them it was because of the *merde de cheval*."

Angelika gasped and looked from her father to her mother.

Kurt pulled on his cigarette and blew the smoke out the window. "All the ladies covered their hands with their mouths and their eyes went wide as she explained that she shovelled up the milkman's horse droppings from the road each day."

Angelika screeched in laughter.

"Come on, it's not that funny," said Marta, trying to keep a straight face.

Angelika struggled to pull a serious expression, but each time she caught her father's eye, they both erupted in laughter again, until tears streamed down their faces. Eventually even Marta couldn't hold back her mirth.

Once they'd quieted down, Angelika exhaled loudly. "I wish we could have stayed in Beaupré-sur-lac."

"Angelika," Marta's voice carried a note of reproach. "Your Papa has done his best—"

Kurt caught his wife's eye over their daughter's head. "Angelika, I know this is hard. But I think you're going to like our new home. Just give it a chance, okay?"

Angelika nodded, then yawned. Soon her head was bouncing against Kurt's shoulder as she dozed between her parents in the front seat of their blue Impala.

"How was the visit?" Kurt asked. "It's so good to have you back." He reached his arm across Angelika to touch Marta's knee.

Marta smiled at him over her daughter's head. "I missed you, too." She took a deep breath. "I'm happy Angelika got to meet her family."

Kurt's heart paused at the sadness in his wife's voice.

"The East is worse than what Anna described in her letters."

"So no regrets that we left?"

Marta turned clear eyes to him. "You were right. There was no point in staying. The war blew up all the memories."

Kurt felt Angelika slump more deeply into sleep against his shoulder as Marta told him about their trip.

An hour into the ride, Angelika sat up. "Are we there yet?"

"Just another hour," Kurt said as he turned off the highway and onto a gravel road with construction signs. He caught Marta's frown. "They're paving this part of our highway, so it will be a little slow here."

Soon, dust swirled through the interior of the car, forcing them to close the windows. Angelika started coughing.

"Why don't you go into the back?" Marta suggested as she brushed dust from her daughter's hair and shoulders.

Angelika clambered over the back of the bench seat. "What's our house like?"

"It's green on the outside and has three bedrooms. Your room is pink."

Angelika groaned. "I'm sick of pink. Can we paint it blue?"

"Sorry." Kurt winced. "The company just painted it fresh for us. They paint bedrooms blue for boys and pink for girls." Kurt tried to distract Angelika's disappointment. "But we have a backyard big enough for you to play and still have lots of space for Mama's vegetable garden."

"But will there be horse shit?"

"Angelika!" Marta said.

Kurt shook his head, his mouth turned down at the corners. "Sadly, no. There is no milkman." He coughed to cover his snort of laughter.

Marta sighed. "How does the furniture fit?"

Kurt hesitated. "We have a very large kitchen, so our table and chairs fit perfectly. And so many cupboards. I brought all our things from Beaupré-sur-lac in a U-Haul last weekend…" His voice petered out at the expression on Marta's face.

"But what about the new furniture?"

Kurt worked to keep his expression neutral. He'd contacted the store as soon as he knew their address so the new living and bedroom furniture they'd purchased in Montreal before Marta and Angelika had left on their trip could be delivered, but—

"Papa, look! There's a moose in that pond!"

"Good eye!" Kurt exhaled, thankful for the distraction. He wouldn't have to answer Marta's question yet. He slowed the car. Water droplets dribbling from the sides of the moose's mouth sparkled in the sunlight as it chewed pensively on a waterlily. "Ah, here, we are at the end of the construction."

"But it's still gravel," Marta said as she stared ahead.

"Yes, but it's not so dusty as the new gravel." Kurt opened the window.

Marta swiped the perspiration from her forehead, scowling at the brown stains on her hankie. "Where have you taken us?"

Kurt reached across the seat to take her hand. "I know it's a bad road, but wait 'til you see the town. You'll love it. And look around. Doesn't this feel just like Beaupré-sur-lac—trees, rock cuts, rivers, lakes?"

Marta made a small *humph* sound and sat back while Angelika quizzed her father about the town's amenities.

A half hour later, they followed the road around a long curve circling a three-storey high granite outcropping. Marta caught her breath as the town suddenly unfolded below them. Angelika stopped her questions.

The valley, surrounded by hills bristling with evergreens, opened before them, and so did Pusamakwa. Skirting along the top of the valley, Kurt pointed out the recreation centre, arena, curling club, hospital, and library, all built by the mining company as enticements for workers and their families to live in the middle of nowhere.

Continuing the tour, Kurt drove through the downtown—a Chinese food restaurant, a drug store, a post office, a bank, a diner, a convenience store, and the Hudson's Bay where you could buy everything from beans to bras, apples to zippers. Beyond the central parking lot stood the motel with another restaurant and bar.

"Where's our house, Papa?"

Kurt pointed through the windshield to the opposite side of the valley. "There." As they drove down into the valley, he pointed out the three churches clustered on a rise between the two town sites. Three schools rested around a large running track below the churches. "The small one is the Catholic school. The big one is the high school for everyone, and over there, that's your school."

"But I go to the Catholic school." Angelika looked from her mother to her father.

"Not anymore," said Marta. "You went to Catholic school because that's all there was, but we're Lutheran, so we will go to the United Church, and you will go to the public school."

"But why? I have to learn English, and now I have to learn a new religion, too?"

"Don't whine." Marta turned to fix a firm gaze on her daughter. "Just be thankful that you can go to church and have a choice of schools, not like your cousins."

"Look, Angelika." Kurt was pointing straight ahead. "That hill up there is the ski club."

When Angelika was three, her father had strapped skis to her boots. Within a year, she'd traded in her driveway snowbanks for the challenge of the downhill ski centre near their home.

"Wow! It's bigger and steeper than my old one. I hope they have a racing program. It looks perfect to help me get ready for the Olympics."

Marta made a small *tsk*ing sound.

"And here is our street." The street curved away from them, flanked by a repeating pattern of two styles of houses, bungalows and one-and-a-half storey homes neatly arranged on flat lots. Kurt slowed so his passengers could read the sign.

Angelika read aloud. "Wen-o-nah Dr. There's our house!"

Kurt pulled into the driveway. Angelika was out of the car as soon as it stopped.

"Welcome home." Kurt looked into Marta's eyes.

The corners of Marta's mouth quivered into a smile as Kurt took her hand. Their attention on each other was torn away at Angelika's shout. "Papa! There's a tent in our backyard!"

"Surprise," said Kurt, his voice shaking. "The furniture won't be here for three more days." His eyes pleaded with Marta. "So I bought camping equipment."

Marta stared open mouthed.

"We can use the bathroom and the kitchen in our house and sleep out here. I bought cots and sleeping bags, a cooler and camp stove." Kurt gave a queasy chuckle. "Fun, *neh*?"

Marta raised her eyebrows.

"Everyone goes camping here, so this will be a chance for us to practice before we go to White Lake Provincial Park."

Marta's expression relaxed. She burst out laughing. "It's always an adventure with you. Now, come on. Show me our house."

As they all settled into the tent that night, Kurt lay back on his cot, one hand holding his wife's on the cot next to him. He'd hoped for a more romantic reunion, but this would have to do for the next few days. Marta seemed happy with the house and the town. She'd agreed to a puppy, so tomorrow, they'd go to his new friend, Bill Barnett, and let Angelika pick one out. He sighed as he drifted into sleep.

Marta rested her hand on Kurt's thigh. When she felt him relax into sleep, she turned tentatively onto her hip, trying not to tip off her cot. She loved how hard he tried to make things perfect for them. This place was so far from everywhere, but it had everything they needed. On Sunday, they'd go to the United Church, and in a couple of weeks, they'd register Angelika at the public school. The girl who lived next door seemed friendly. Marta hoped the people would be kind, especially while they learned English. *I'll have to check tomorrow if they have the meat for rouladen in the grocery store*, Marta thought. *I can make them on the kitchen counter and cook them on the camp stove.* She drifted off with designs for the vegetable garden floating through her mind.

* * *

July 18, 1963

Chère Journal,

We're sleeping in a tent in our backyard for a few days because our furniture hasn't arrived yet. I thought Mama was going to be angry that we are camping but she just laughed and hugged Papa. She seems very happy to be here. Papa said we are going to go camping once we're settled, just like a lot of people do here. I'm going to ask him to get me an air mattress. The cot feels too tippy.

I like my new town. It's more modern than Beaupré-sur-lac, but it feels kind of temporary, like living in a town that popped up in the centre of a book and will disappear if someone turns the page.

Judy, the girl next door, waved to me within minutes of our arrival. When I waved back, Judy came to our shared property line and introduced herself. When she started asking me questions, I shrugged my shoulders and my eyes filled with tears. "No English," was all I could say.

"That's okay," she said. Then she made some hand signs while she talked. I think she said she will teach me. I smiled and nodded a lot.

Maybe Pusamakwa isn't going to be so bad, after all.

Angelika

CHAPTER ELEVEN - 1963

A Place to Stand

"Fast, Angelika. The bus comes soon."

"It's *hurry*, Mama, not *fast*," Angelika corrected with a sigh. They'd been in Pusamakwa for almost three months, but Angelika was still spending most conversations with her parents correcting their English. It was hard to be responsible for teaching her parents a language she was still learning herself. Why couldn't they just speak German at home like they used to?

Trudging behind her mother, she skittered through sleet-covered ruts on the gravel street. How she envied the smiling children pictured in her school reader kicking through mounds of coloured leaves on sidewalks with paved streets.

The twelve other kids waiting at the bus stop turned their backs when Angelika and her mother walked up. Mrs. Watson, the manager's wife, beckoned to them. A well-meaning woman, she was teaching Angelika's mother "Canadian ways." But why was she here? Her kids were grown.

Mrs. Watson's smile didn't reach her eyes as she put her hand on the shoulder of a boy standing next to her. "This is

Arthur Nanibush. He's come to live with us." She shielded her red-lipsticked mouth behind her hand as she whispered, "He's a rez kid. We're saving him."

Arthur's deep brown eyes went flat.

Her mother's crinkled forehead announced she had no idea what Mrs. Watson was talking about. Her mother smiled fleetingly, then turned to Angelika. "Don't be late after school. Today we the Sifton Products order fill out."

Angelika grimaced, hoping no one had heard her mother's mixed-up word order. "It's called Mary Maxim now, Mama." Since the age of seven, she'd been completing catalogue orders for her parents—Sifton Products/Mary Maxim, Eaton's, Sears—in French when they lived in Beaupré-sur-lac, now in English. By ten, she was writing cheques whenever money orders or cash were not accepted as payment.

"Okay," Angelika murmured.

Her mother bade her goodbye and walked toward the downtown to her job as baker in the bunkhouse cafeteria. Mr. Watson had offered her mother the job after sampling the German breads and cakes she made for the church dinners.

Angelika knew there'd be questions tonight about what a *rez* was. Admitting she had no idea what the word meant would not be an acceptable response, so maybe she could find out from Arthur and hope he wouldn't think her rude.

Arthur's hair glinted raven blue in the early morning sun. The scent of pine and wood smoke, underscored by Ivory soap, floated in the air around him. She recognized his jeans puddling over his scuff-free sneakers from the Sears catalogue. Angelika's fingers itched to touch the flannelly newness of his blue-and-black plaid jacket.

When the school bus arrived, everyone charged the doors.

"Hi," Angelika said. "I'm Angie. You can sit with me if you want." Her teacher couldn't master pronouncing Angelika's name, so she had suggested the short form, Angie—a name familiar to the other kids and easy for everyone to say. Angie appreciated the change because the kids didn't laugh anymore, but her parents were less receptive.

Arthur shrugged but followed her on. Angie led him to her usual bench, halfway down the aisle, then positioned her father's worn leather satchel across her lap.

"Nazi."

"Kraut."

"Frog."

The bag couldn't silence the names, but it did block most of the spit. Heat crept up her neck to her face. She gritted her teeth at the pity in Arthur's eyes.

"It's okay. In another couple of weeks, we'll be walking to school like everyone else," she said.

"Why aren't we now? It's not far."

Angie wrinkled her brow. "Something about a bear in this part of town near the bush... a kid chased by it." She shrugged.

Arthur snorted. "Kid probably bothered it. Bears don't hurt people unless they feel threatened."

"Anyway, once the bear sleeps for winter, we walk."

Ronnie Bartlett stopped beside Angie and Arthur's seat. "Hey, we don't want no rez kids on our bus," he yelled, pointing at Arthur.

George, the wiry bus driver, turned around and locked eyes with the fifteen-year-old. "Shut up, and sit down."

Ronnie hung his head under the driver's glare and walked to his seat. On her first day on the bus, a girl had told her George's war story, but she'd needed her dictionary that night to decode the true horror of it. George had chopped off his own leg as it hung from a demolished knee joint, then pulled his injured buddy back to the trench while bullets whizzed over their heads. You didn't mess with George.

After Ronnie passed them, Arthur said. "Come on." He pressed his hand against her shoulder.

She stood in the aisle and followed him to the front of the bus.

"Excuse me, sir," Arthur said. "May we sit up here behind you?"

"Sure, kid."

Arthur pushed her into the seat. "From now on, we get off first, and we get on last."

She frowned at him.

"Good thinking, kid," said George. "No traffic passing you."

Everyone settled down for the five-minute ride to the school.

Angie's mind burned with questions. Why was Arthur living with the Watsons? Where were his mother and father? Why was he friendly to her?

"What grade are you in?" she asked.

"Seven, but who knows where they'll put me this time."

"I'm in six. Maybe you'll be in my class. It's a six/seven." She smiled at the thought of having someone to talk to. "What do you mean, *this time?*"

Arthur shrugged. "They think 'cause I'm Ojibwe, I must be stupid. Every place I go, they put me back a grade."

She frowned. "Every place?"

Arthur puffed out his cheeks. "The Watsons are my third placement this year."

Angie opened her mouth with the next question.

"I don't want to talk about it, okay?"

She clamped her mouth shut.

His expression softened. "You talk funny. Where are you from?"

"My parents are from Germany, but I was born in Beaupré-sur-lac. It's in Quebec."

His gaze measured her.

She slumped against the window. "I miss *mes amis*—"she winced"—er…my friends. Papa says Ontario is better for work. Mama says there's a better future for me in English Canada. I hate it here."

Arthur murmured sympathetically.

"Everything was fine in Beaupré-sur-lac. I was German at home and French at school. But here, I had to learn English. The kids call me names because of the wars, and they laugh at my mixed-up accent. My parents tell me to act Canadian, but what is that?" She brushed at her tears. Why was she telling him all this?

"Don't ask me." Arthur shrugged. "They call me an Indian."

"What did Mrs. Watson mean when she said you're a *rez* kid?"

Arthur gave her a long look. "You really don't know?"

Angie shook her head.

"*Rez* is short for *reservation*. It's the land the government let us keep when they took over the country." He exhaled deeply. "It's complicated."

The bus stopped, and Arthur pulled Angie from the bus before anyone else could get up the aisle.

Angie was in heaven when Arthur ended up in Mr. MacNamara's grade six/seven class. At recesses, they hid down the hill, behind the swings and monkey bars. Angelika told him all about her trip to Germany and finally feeling what it was like to have family. And Arthur's eyes glittered as he talked about his six younger brothers and sisters. "It was really crowded in my Nokomis's two-bedroom house, but she always had time for each of us, and she made good food. Me and my little brother spent summers on the land with my uncle and cousins. We caught and dried fish for winter food."

"Why didn't you live with your mother and father?"

"My mom was very sick, and my dad was away a lot, trapping and logging to make money."

Angie stayed quiet, watching the faraway look in Arthur's eyes.

"Last year, a social worker and two police officers walked in and took all us kids. I haven't seen my family since. At first, I'd run away, but they always caught me before I could get back home."

"I'm sorry. I miss my Oma, too."

When Arthur gave her a puzzled look, Angie added, "I think *Oma* is German for *Nokomis*. My Oma is dead." She blinked hard.

Arthur gave her hand a squeeze. "I'm sorry. Was she sick?"

Angie shook her head. "No. The government made her leave her house because they wanted to dig out the coal under it. They took the whole town." Angie brightened. "But my Oma didn't make it easy for them. She boarded up the downstairs windows, locked all the doors, and sat in her rocking chair in the window upstairs. When the machine with the wrecking ball came, she shot at the workers from her perch."

"Oh my God!" Arthur's eyes were wide.

"Boy, were they surprised! They didn't know she was there. It took them three days to get her out because she just kept shooting when someone came near. Finally, she couldn't stay awake anymore, and that's when they broke in and took her."

"Did they put her in jail?"

"No, they put her in a home for old people, but it might as well have been a jail. That's what my Tante Liesbeth said in her letter to my mother. Oma's mind went crazy. She kept trying to get home to her children. It was like she forgot most of her life. Then, she stopped eating, until one morning she just didn't wake up. I think she just gave up living."

It was Arthur's turn to stay quiet.

"My Oma was a very strong woman, and she had a hard life, but she always had time to laugh. She knitted me grey mitts with red thumbs. I loved her stories."

Arthur turned to face Angie. "The last thing Nokomis said is that she won't rest until she finds me. I will be strong until she does."

"Oma told me to be proud of who I am and to stand up for what is right. I'm going to be strong, like her."

Angie and Arthur squeezed hands, as if sealing a pact.

On the weekend, Arthur showed Angie how to build a shelter using evergreen boughs in a scoured-granite clearing behind the last houses of the new town site. When it was finished, he lit a tiny bundle of cedar fronds, then blew them down to embers.

"We need to smudge the shelter."

"Smudge?"

"It's a cleansing ceremony. First, fill your heart with an intention for this place."

Angie stared at her feet. An intention? *A place for being yourself,* she thought.

"Ready?"

She nodded.

"Now, follow me."

Imitating Arthur, using both hands, Angie brought the sweet smoke to her heart, over her head, and down the front and back of her body.

"Next, we need to smudge our place."

She kneeled beside him on the dirt in the middle of their upside-down bowl. They rotated on their knees as Arthur waved the smoke toward the perimeter walls using an eagle feather. Angie snuck a sidelong glance at him, admiring his pride in who he was and wishing she could be like that.

When he was satisfied, he extinguished the stick of cedar in the dirt. Then he set it aside. "For next time."

She dropped a tiny cedar stem into her pocket.

* * *

Arthur and Angie met at their shelter every weekend. She knew he snuck out there sometimes at night. He said it was the one place he felt at home.

One Saturday afternoon, as she slipped between the trees for their usual meeting, arms grabbed her from behind and flung her to the ground. A rough hand covered her mouth.

"Don't make a sound, Kraut, or we'll cut your tongue out." Ronnie Bartlett's lips were drawn into a snarl above her face. "Tie her hands."

A second boy bound Angie's wrists behind her back. Ronnie cracked the back of her head against a tree trunk. Black spots filled her vision. The tang of blood coated her tongue. And then the deep throb of pain hit. They left her slumped against the tree and headed toward the shelter.

By the time her head cleared, smoke was snaking under the branches, burning her nostrils.

"Help!" Angie screamed. She struggled to her feet and ran back to the houses, hands still behind her back, evergreen branches grabbing at her hair. "Fire!" she yelled.

Men ran toward her. Someone untied her wrists.

"They've got Arthur." Angie pointed back at the bush. "They're burning our shelter."

Suddenly, her father was at her side. "You stay here." He pushed Angie to her mother, who was running down the road toward them.

Angie ran into her mother's arms, sobbing against her shoulder. "They're burning Arthur." Her mind roared with images of flames licking through the boughs, the dream catchers they'd made burning like torches. Her mind stopped before she conjured the image of Arthur in the fire.

When everyone emerged from the woods, Ronnie was whimpering, his hand covering his ear. The other boy walked doubled over, holding his stomach. Angie's heart raced as Arthur appeared at Mr. Watson's side. She ran to him. His arm was bent at a funny angle, and he cradled it to his chest.

"I'm okay," he murmured, then motioned toward her mother with his chin.

The men gathered around the boys.

Her mother pulled her away. "Come, *Schatzi*. Let's go home."

On Monday, Arthur wasn't at the bus stop.

"The Watsons gave your rez kid back to the authorities," Ronnie taunted. "He's going to live at the Church School now. I told Mr. Watson we caught him dragging you through the bush with your wrists tied and that he beat us up when we rescued you."

"Liar!" Angie kicked him in the shin.

Ronnie hopped on one leg. "You Nazi bi—" He lost his breath under George's grip on his neck from behind.

"George, Ronnie's lying. They attacked me—" Angie pointed at the two boys "—and burned our shelter."

"Leave it to me, kid," George said.

That afternoon, Ronnie and his friend got the switch from Mr. Watson, but it was too late for Arthur.

* * *

October 20, 1963

Chère Journal,

Judy, the girl next door, lives with her older sister and her sister's husband and new baby because it wasn't safe for her to live with her mother in Manitoba. Something about her stepfather that I don't understand. She was really nice and taught me some English words before school started in the fall. But now school has started I don't see her very often because she goes to the Catholic School. I wish I could go there with her, but Mama was firm. We aren't Catholic so I have to go to the public school.

When Arthur came, he became my friend at school and we hung around together on weekends. Arthur's Ojibwe and lived on the rez with his grandparents until a white lady and a policeman took him and his brothers and sisters away. They said their grandparents' house was too small for them and that they needed to live in proper families. All the kids were split up. Arthur lived with two other places before he came to live with the Watsons. When Ronnie and his friend started a fire and burned the shelter Arthur and I built, they blamed Arthur and sent him away. Judy wasn't allowed to play with us because her sister didn't want her near a rez kid. That seemed weird since Judy's family is Native.

I miss Arthur. No matter how mean everyone was, he looked them directly in the eye. You could see his strength shine from his eyes.

I don't like Ontario. Everyone is mean to people who are different. They're mostly all English or their families have been in Canada a long time. The French kids stay to themselves. They won't let me join them because I'm not "pur laine."

I've pinned the small sprig of cedar that I took when we smudged our shelter to my picture of Oma on my bedside table. In my window, I hung a dream catcher that I found in the wreck of the fire. It has one red bead still clinging to the charred leather lace. I feel so lonely at school now that Arthur is gone but maybe Judy can be my friend again. I've started looking people right in the eye when they call me names. Now no one talks to me at all, but at least the name-calling has stopped. Mama says it will get better. I just nod.

Angie

CHAPTER TWELVE - 1964

Pen pals

Kurt returned from his day shift on the third Friday in August to find the camping equipment arranged in the garage.

"I think this stuff should fit in the trunk, Papa." Angie swept her arm like a game show host to encompass the tent, poles, a Coleman stove, and two cardboard boxes—one with dishes and cooking pots and a second with dried and canned foods.

"What's this for?" Kurt lifted an empty box from the pile.

"I needed something to take the place of the cooler so I could figure out the puzzle."

Kurt laughed, tousling his daughter's hair. Then he went into the house to get the packed cooler from Marta.

Father and daughter moved the equipment from the garage into the trunk. When Marta brought out the sleeping bags and the suitcases with the clothing each had packed the night before, Angie's expression sagged. "I forgot about those."

Kurt managed to adjust the trunk contents to absorb the three small suitcases. As he stood staring at the rest, Marta opened the door to the backseat. "Angelika, bring me that stuff." Within minutes, Marta had stowed the sleeping bags and pillows on the floor and seat behind the driver, then covered the pile with a blanket. Standing back, she said, "Angelika, you can sit behind me, and Robbie can sit on top of the pile. You know how he likes to look out the window." The cocker spaniel bounded into the car and flopped onto his elevated perch as if on cue.

Kurt grinned. "Let's get going."

Two hours down the highway, they pulled into Neys Provincial Park. Lake Superior glistened through the trees surrounding their campsite. "Let's set up camp, then we can explore the beach before it gets dark." Kurt's plan to leave after shift instead of waiting until the following day was working. He already felt like he was on vacation.

While Angie helped Kurt erect their twelve-by-twelve-foot orange canvas tent, Marta set up the stove on the picnic table to make an evening cup of coffee. The sound of the waves lured the family to the beach. Kurt and Marta sat on the sand, backs against a log as they sipped their coffee in the red and yellow glow of the sunset. Robbie barked at Angie's heels as she ran in and out of the crashing waves. Kurt wiggled his toes in the warm sand, his arm around his wife. They both laughed at Angie's squeals when the icy water sprayed up her legs. Kurt had dreamed of this when he bought the camping equipment a year ago.

When the lake swallowed the red ball of the sun, Kurt announced it was time to return to camp.

"Can we make a fire, Papa?"

"Not tonight, *Schatzi*. It's almost time for bed." Kurt's hand steadied Marta as they moved into the gloom under the trees. "Whoa. It's darker than I thought." He gave an embarrassed chuckle. "Guess I should have brought the flashlight."

"I can't even see my hand in front of my face." Marta grabbed Kurt's upper arm in a vice-like grip. "Where's our campsite?"

"I'm sure we'll see the car," said Kurt.

"Or we can feel the numbers carved in the little posts," said Angie. "What's our number?"

No one remembered. The family stood in the middle of the gravel roadway, paralyzed under a black sky pricked with a sea of twinkling stars. "Where's Robbie?" Marta's voice broke their trance. A single bark floated back to them.

"Robbie! Come, boy," Angie called.

"Shh, Angelika. Other people will—Oh!" Marta's words were cut off by the dog bumping against her shins.

Suddenly, two flashlights emerged from the bush beside them. "You lost?" Came a man's voice.

"Sorry if we disturbed you," said Kurt. "We forgot our flashlight."

A young girl laughed. "We've done that. Come on. We'll guide you."

"But we don't remember our campsite number," Marta said.

"No problem," said the man. "You're just down here. We saw you arrive. Besides, I think your dog knows where he's going." The man shone his light to catch Robbie's rear end swaying along the road ahead.

Once at their camp, Kurt pulled their flashlight out of the trunk, and their rescuers returned to their site. Kurt carried the cots and sleeping bags from the car to Marta in the tent. Angie shone the light along his path, then held it while her mother set up the sleeping accommodations.

"We'll buy a camping lantern tomorrow," Kurt said.

The family settled into their beds, sleeping in underwear and shirts instead of trying to find pajamas in the suitcases.

"And an air mattress, Papa?" Angie asked. "These cots are—"

Crash!

"Robbie!" Marta yelled.

Kurt's flashlight caught Marta sitting on the tent floor, her cot tilted against her back. "You okay? What happened?"

Robbie pressed himself into the corner of the tent.

Marta explained she'd been sitting at the foot of the cot to remove her shoes because the dog had been lying in the middle. When he jumped off, the cot tipped, spilling her onto the floor. Once Kurt had ascertained that Marta was unhurt, he set up her cot and returned to bed. Angie pulled Robbie beside her on the floor.

Kurt drifted on the shushing of the waves in the distance. When he'd set up the tent in the backyard last summer, he'd pictured their family camping every summer weekend beside their fellow Pusamakwans. With gardens to dig in preparation for next spring planting, a garage to build before the snow came in October, and storage shelves to be erected in the basement, camping never came up for the remainder of their first summer in Ontario. Once the snow had cleared in the late spring, it seemed every weekend was consumed with planting vegetables and constructing wire fences to protect the gardens from invading wildlife. It had occurred to Kurt that Marta might be devising these chores to avoid camping. Still, she'd enthusiastically greeted his suggestion of a week's vacation on Lake Superior when he'd offered a day trip for shopping at the European Delicatessen in Fort William and the wool shop in Port Arthur.

The tent's zippered door whined, jolting Kurt upright.

"Papa, Robbie's gone!"

Kurt disentangled himself from the sleeping bag, grabbed the flashlight, and hopped out the door, pulling on his shoes as he went. Angie and Marta heard his urgent whispers for Robbie to come. Moments later, he pushed through the zippered opening, dragging the dog by his collar. "He must have heard an animal." Shining the light around the tent, he found the dog's leash.

"Give it to me, and I'll tie him to my cot," said Marta. She knelt on the floor to loop the dog's leash around the aluminum leg.

"Maybe that's not a good idea," said Kurt.

"Just shine the light over here," Marta said. "He's not strong enough to pull me."

Everyone settled again.

Kurt sank into the rhythm of guttural bullfrog croaks from the swamp behind them. "*Who, who,*" called an owl over the top of their tent. Marta snored softly beside him. High-pitched raccoon chattering followed the plop of several branches hitting their canvas roof. Robbie charged through the zippered door. The leash twanged. Marta's cot jerked forward, then tilted, dumping her onto the floor.

Kurt grabbed into the dark and pushed the cot's leg upward. The slack leash disappeared through the door, Kurt in close pursuit. A few moments later, he returned to the tent without the dog.

"Where's Robbie?" Angie asked.

"In the car. Now let's get some sleep." He slipped into his sleeping bag.

* * *

After breakfast, the family drove ten minutes into Marathon to pick up the missing equipment and supplies. Once she'd blown up her air mattress, Angie decided to to explore the nature trail near their campsite.

"Hi."

Angie lurched to the side of the trail and pressed her back against a large silver birch. Where had this girl come from?

"I'm Gail Higginson."

Angie stared at Gail's extended hand, then looked up to meet her hazel gaze. They stood eye to eye. "Where'd you come from?"

Gail's laugh tinkled. "I've been wanting to meet you."

Angie recognized the laugh. "You're the girl with the flashlight last night."

"My mother says I'm not allowed to march into people's campsites without an invitation, so when I saw you leave, I snuck through the bush to meet you head-on. It would be creepy if I just followed you." Gail blew a dark brown curl off her forehead.

Angie didn't move.

"Damn. I scared you, didn't I?" Her hand flew to her mouth. "Oops, I'm not supposed to swear. Mom says it's not ladylike, but who says I want to be a lady? I'm going to be an explorer when I grow up, and explorers swear and drink beer and do whatever they want. I've been practicing walking silently through the woods. You didn't even hear me go past you, did you?"

Angie shook her head uncertainly, feeling breathless at the girl's outburst. She turned to walk away.

"Please, wait." Gail took a deep breath. "Let me try again." She slowed her speech. "I'm Gail Higginson, and I'd like to be friends."

This time, when Gail offered her hand, Angie took it. The two girls smiled as their eyes met again over their clasped hands. "I'm Angie Langer."

"I'm from Winnipeg. Where are you from?"

Angie remembered seeing Winnipeg on the map of Canada, and it was a long way from here. "Pusamakwa."

Gail looked confused.

"It's a small town," Angie added.

"No, I mean, before that."

Oh no, here it comes, thought Angie. She's going to make fun of my accent. She took a step back.

"Don't go!" Gail's hand brushed Angie's forearm. "I didn't mean to offend you. You sound so exotic. Wish I could talk like that."

"Ex-oh-i..." Angie stumbled over the word.

"Exotic. It means different, foreign, as if you come from somewhere romantic and far away."

Angie tilted her head as she sized up Gail. "I come from Quebec, but my parents are German."

"So you speak French and German?"

Angie nodded. Gail's open interest was a new feeling for her.

"See, I was right; you're exotic. Not like me. My great-grandparents settled in Winnipeg from England almost a hundred years ago. All we speak is English. But I'm learning French in school. Hey, maybe you can help me."

Angie took a step toward Gail. "I'll help you with French if you teach me more English words like exotic."

"Deal." Gail extended her hand. "Now, come on. I found a trail to take us over the rocks to the next beach."

* * *

August 20, 1964

Chère Journal,

I met a girl named Gail Higginson. Her family is camping three sites away from us. She's from Winnipeg, and she has a brother two years older than her who teases her and a pesky (a new word she taught me) seven-year-old sister she has to babysit after school until her mother comes home from work. Gail's in Girl Guides like me.

Gail didn't laugh at my accent. She said I sound exotic (another new word, it means foreign but in a good way). She thinks I'm interesting! We've walked all the trails through the park and even visited the shacks where the Canadian army kept German prisoners they'd captured during the war. My papa says he wishes he would have been brought here when he was arrested because, after the war, Canada let the German prisoners stay if they wanted to.

Gail's family invited us to their campsite last night. We roasted marshmallows over the fire and put them between crackers with chocolate. They called them S'mores. So gooey! Mama says she'll get the ingredients so we can make them again.

Tonight, Gail and her family had dinner with us. Mama made rouladen in a big pot on the fire, and Mrs. Higginson brought potatoes and carrots cooked in foil in the fire. I was so scared they'd laugh at the meat, but they loved it! Mrs. Higginson asked Mama for the recipe.

We are going home tomorrow, and Gail's family has to drive back to Winnipeg, but Gail gave me her address, and I gave her mine. She said I could keep her Anne of Green Gables book until I finish reading it and then send it back to her. She said we'll be pen pals. That means we write letters to each other and maybe next year our families can camp in the same place.

I wish there were kids at school that were nice, like Gail. She said I might find someone if I join a team or a club so the kids can see me as more like them. She suggested basketball because that's what she plays and I'm tall like her. I might try that if I can fit it into my skiing. Even if I don't, I still have Judy to hang around with after school when her sister lets her.

Angie

CHAPTER THIRTEEN - 1965

Too German

February 1, 1965

Chère Journal,

Judy and I have to take her two-year-old nephew wherever we go. Her sister just had a baby and expects Judy to help out. I don't mind. It feels like having a sister and a little brother when we're together. My birthday is coming soon and I think Mama wants me to have a party so she can have a daughter that's like everybody else's.

Angie

* * *

Angie feigned excitement when her mother suggested a sleepover with five girls to celebrate her thirteenth birthday.

"So I'll make a nice big pot of *rouladen*..." Marta's voice slowed as Angie's eyes grew wider. "What's wrong?"

"You can't make *rouladen*." Angie's voice dripped desperate derision. "Canadians don't eat *rouladen*."

"But it's your favourite, and we always have it when we have something to celebrate." Marta put up her hands in surrender as the tears gathered in Angie's eyes. "Okay, what do Canadian girls eat at sleepovers?"

Angie hugged her mother. "Hamburgers and fries. Thanks."

They planned the meal together. Angie picked out the snacks for later in the night—chips, popcorn, Coke, orange pop, pretzels, and chocolate bars. She begged her mother to make a chocolate cake out of a box, like the other kids' mothers made, instead of her usual buttercream torte. Her mother pasted a quick smile on her face at her daughter's request, but not before Angie saw the hurt in her eyes. "You know I love your cakes, Mama, but—

Her mother nodded. "—it's not what the other kids have. I know."

The following week, Angie saw two Betty Crocker boxes peeking out of the grocery bags. Maybe there was no reason for the trepidation that had started to settle into the pit of her stomach as the day grew nearer. Feeling she'd solved the food issues, Angie elicited her father's help in figuring out how to accommodate the invitees in their unfinished basement. Only the party would tell her whether she'd invited the right girls.

Angie sat at the head of the table in her kitchen, watching the five girls she'd invited as they ate her birthday dinner. She couldn't comfortably call them friends, except Judy.

"Mrs. Langer, do you have mustard?" Sharon's red-gold curls bounced against her shoulders as she picked up each of the bottles in the centre of the table. Sharon was the only one of the group who flirted on the edges of being a cool girl. Her mother had helped Angie's mother become involved in the church, and Angie and Sharon were in the same Sunday school class. Sharon wasn't her kind of person, but she'd invited her to keep her mother happy.

Angie's mother passed the jar of Dijon.

Sharon opened it. "It's brown." Her nose wrinkled as she sniffed the khaki-brown paste. Replacing the lid, she asked, "Do you have yellow mustard?"

Five pairs of eyes swivelled to Angie's mother's face. Her mouth quivered into a smile. "No." She shook her head. "Try this one. It makes the meat taste better."

The girls shared a look of disbelief.

"No, that's okay." Sharon whispered something behind her hand to Debbie, one of Angie's ski teammates. Angie couldn't hear them from her spot at the other end of the table, but she felt her face flood red when they both giggled.

"Mrs. Langer, I think the relish is bad. It's yellow," said Sally, her hazel eyes narrowed. Sally sang next to her in the church junior choir. Thanks to her, Angie managed to stay in tune.

Angie groaned inwardly.

"No, sweetie. The relish has mustard in it."

Sally frowned. "But I don't like mustard. I only like relish."

"I'm sorry. Maybe try pickles instead." Angie's mother gave her head a slight shake, muttering in German about spoiled children, before turning back to the stove to flip the burgers. Fortunately, only her daughter understood her.

The fries were perfect, fresh cut and boiled in oil. "Can someone pass me the ketchup, please?" asked Debbie, waving her arm from the opposite end of the table.

Angie held her breath. Did they even have ketchup? They hardly ever used it.

"Wait, I'll get it," said Judy. "I have to go to the bathroom, anyway."

For Judy to get out, Katy, a girl from Angie's patrol in her Girl Guide company, had to get out of her seat. Katy puffed out her cheeks as she squeezed her chubby body between the table and the wall. Angie's father had put the leaf into their kitchen table so all the girls could fit around it, but it didn't leave much space to move. "Mrs. Langer, I don't see the ketchup on the table," Judy said on her way out of the kitchen.

"It's in the fridge. Don't you use vinegar and salt on French fries?"

Debbie and Katy screwed up their faces.

Angie wanted to shout, *That's the way they eat them in Quebec,* but she kept her mouth clamped shut.

Most of the girls left half their hamburger on their plate. "Didn't you like it?" Angie's mother's brow furrowed as she cleared the table.

"It was delicious, just a little big." Katy's blue eyes moved from Angie to her mother.

"Yeah. And the buns were really crusty." Sally's mouth turned up in a half smile.

Angie's mother sighed as her brow cleared. "Yummy, yes? I couldn't give you those horrible flat buns, so tasteless, and they feel like Kleenex in your mouth."

Debbie and Sharon silently mimicked her while the others giggled. Angie gripped the edge of her chair to stop herself from running away.

"Now, girls, just wait a few minutes, and we will have dessert."

Oh, no. Here we go again with musical chairs so she can get the ice cream from the freezer, Angie thought. Instead, her mother disappeared into the living room. The conversation around the table turned to comments about Ralph, the new boy who'd moved into town after Christmas.

"He must be blind without those Coke bottle glasses." Sharon held circles made by her thumbs and index fingers in front of her eyes and blinked rapidly. Everyone laughed.

"And his hair. Bet he has a sore neck with all that flicking it into place." Sally threw her head back and to the left.

More laughter.

Ralph looked like a movie star to Angie when he brushed his straight brown hair out of his face with his hand. "I think it's cute the way he looks like a baby horse with his long arms and legs." Why did she say that? Everyone stared at her.

Sharon said, "Ooh! Angie likes Ralph!"

"Ralph and Angie under a tree," Katy began the rhyme.

"K-I-S-S-I-N-G," they all chorused.

The front door opened and closed. Angie's mother came into the kitchen carrying the ice cream. She'd stored it in the snow on the porch. "Who is this Ralph, Angie?"

"Ralph's her boyfriend, Mrs. Langer." Sally smiled saucily.

Angie was dizzy from how hard she shook her head.

Her mother's eyes hadn't left her. "Boyfriend?"

"No, Mama. He's just a new boy at school." Angie felt her stomach drop.

"We'll talk tomorrow, my girl." She turned to the kitchen counter.

Everyone went silent. A few girls mouthed, "Sorry." Angie shrugged her shoulders, trying to show she wasn't scared of her mother's reaction.

When her mother turned around, she was holding a tall, round chocolate cake. Cherries perched on the puffs of whipped cream decorating the top. Thirteen candles burned between the puffs.

"It's beautiful," Debbie whispered.

"One, two, three, Happy—" Her mother counted everyone in as they joined her singing.

"Make a wish," the girls chanted at the end of the song.

Angie wished she could be more Canadian so she'd have real friends who didn't make fun of how her family did things.

Her mother cut the cake into generous slices and added two scoops of ice cream to each piece.

"Wow! It's four layers!"

"There's cherries and whipped cream on every layer!"

"The cake is really chocolatey, but this icing..." Debbie screwed her upper lip. "It tastes like...butter?"

Angie's mother nodded. "Good, *neh*? It's buttercream."

"Butter icing?" the girls whispered around the table. They picked out the cherries and whipped cream, ate the cake and ice cream, but most of the buttercream icing remained on the plates.

Angie glared as her mother cleared the plates while muttering more comments in German about the children of peasants. Why couldn't she just be like other mothers?

With the meal behind them, Angie led the girls downstairs to continue the party. She and her father had worked all afternoon to transform the big concrete space into a party room.

"Keep your slippers on," her mother called from the back of the line. "The floor is a little cold."

Walls of blankets and sheets had been strung down the middle of the basement like a tent, separating the party space from the furnace with its glowing orange mouth, the laundry, and the crowded storage shelves. The Christmas lights that her father had hung on the front of the house in December twinkled from the beams overhead. Six beds—three camping cots, a roll-away cot, and two air mattresses resting on a plywood platform supported with bricks above the concrete floor—were ready for pillows and sleeping bags. Snacks, stacked on a side table, waited to be dumped into bowls. A cooler filled with ice and drinks sat under the table. On the opposite side, Angie's record player was poised to be called into action, and her father's transistor radio kept it company in case the WLS Chicago signal wafted its way across Lake Superior tonight. Warm air floated from two air vents above that her father had redirected downward so the girls would stay cozy overnight.

"This is magical," said Judy.

"Thanks. My papa helped me."

"Okay, let's party!" Sharon yelled.

Once the girls had picked their beds and laid out their sleeping bags, Debbie put on a record. Katy and Sally broke open the snacks, and Judy fiddled with the radio.

Everyone sang along to "I'm a Believer," "The Letter," and "All You Need Is Love." Angie moved her mouth, pretending she knew the words to songs she'd only ever heard once or twice. She didn't have older siblings who played the hits at home like the other girls. Angie and her father listened to German top hit albums she'd brought back from her trip with her mother. Her father taught her the waltz, cha-cha, and foxtrot to Dean Martin, Perry Como, and Doris Day. While those ballroom steps and her ballet movements gave her rhythm, she felt uncoordinated waving her arms and wiggling her hips like everybody else.

Conversations centred around questions like who was the cutest Beatle—Paul; which new Elvis movie was better, *Double Trouble* or *Clambake*—*Clambake*, of course; and whether the Monkees, the Beatles, or the Dave Clark Five was the best group. Angie said the Beatles because they were the only group she'd seen on *The Ed Sullivan Show*.

Sally pulled out her sister's copies of *Seventeen* and *'Teen* from her bag, and the girls started planning their summer wardrobes from the photos.

"Angie, you'd look amazing in this." Sally pointed to a bright-red miniskirt, striped red, orange, and yellow turtleneck sweater, and black knee-high boots.

"Yeah, Angie. With your long legs," Debbie said.

Angie felt heat rise to her face. Did they really think she could look good?

Sharon huffed. "Your mother'd never let you wear that. And besides, you need breasts for that sweater."

Angie crossed her arms over her flat chest.

Sharon patted Angie's thigh. "Don't worry. They'll come. German women always have big tits." She turned to the group. "So, ladies, pointy or rounded bra cups?" Sharon pushed her chest forward. "Personally, I prefer rounded ones, more comfy and natural looking." She posed sideways.

While Sally, Katy, and Debbie joined Sharon's bra-cup discussion, Judy touched Angie's arm. "Don't pay attention. You know Sharon's mean."

"I'm saving for purple velvet bell-bottoms, just like these," said Katy, holding up a page from *'Teen*.

Judy broke the awkward pause. "They're great, Katy."

Sharon started laughing. "Come on, Katy. Even if you could fit that fat butt into those pants, you'd look like a hippo waddling around."

Debbie and Sally gasped. Tears sprang to Katy's eyes. Angie put her arm around Katy's shoulders.

"Hey, that's mean." Judy glared at Sharon.

"It's only mean if it isn't true." Sharon sneered.

Katy threw herself face down on her bed, her shoulders shaking with silent sobs.

"You should take it back," Angie said to Sharon.

Sharon looked at the wide-eyed expressions around her. "What? You all agree with this Kraut? What does she know about apologizing? Her people started the war. Her father probably killed your relatives that died saving us from her Nazi family." Her green-eyed glare fixed on Angie. "My dad says you and your family should go back to Krautland and take your smelly cheese and weird meats with you." Sharon turned to the others. "They eat ground-up pig's heads and tongues in Jell-O. It's not normal. You don't belong here." As she spoke, the spittle from Sharon's mouth flew like venom into Angie's face.

Debbie stepped between them. "You need to stop," she said to Sharon in a low voice.

"You're with her? Unbelievable." Sharon took a deep breath. "I'm leaving." She started to pull her jeans and coat on over her pyjamas.

The others stood around, not sure what to do.

"Come on, Sharon, you don't need to go." Sally put her hand on Sharon's shoulder.

Debbie sighed. "Yeah, stay. It's really late, anyway."

"Katy, are you okay if Sharon stays?" Judy asked from where she sat at the end of Katy's bed.

Katy sat up. She sniffed and swiped at her wet cheeks. Angie handed her a tissue.

"I'm okay if she stays if you are, Angie." Katy fixed her eyes on Angie's.

Everybody stared at her. Angie was wishing she hadn't given in and invited Sharon. If she said she had to go, she'd lose the others. "Sure, she can stay," Angie murmured.

She took a ragged breath to settle the tightness in her chest. "Anybody want a chocolate bar?"

* * *

Monday at school, kids whispered behind their hands and pointed at Angie as they hung up their coats. Sharon was talking to a group of the cool girls. As Angie walked by, she heard her say, "The hamburgers were like huge meatballs of beef guts. Her mama—who calls their mom, *mama*?—gave us brown mustard so it would disguise the taste."

Angie couldn't believe it.

Debbie and Katy stood just outside the group, but they didn't say anything. They looked away when Angie's eyes met theirs.

"Come on, Sharon. You're kidding, right?" Polly, the leader of the cool girls, pushed her shoulder into Sharon's.

"It's true. And the cake was made of ground-up pig's head in jelly." She did a fake gag. "You should have seen it jiggling in the middle of the table." She tossed her curls. "They made us sleep in the basement on cots. I felt like I was in one of those camps where they put the Jewish people in the war." She shuddered.

"That's not true!" Angie launched at Sharon, grabbing her hair as she pulled her down. The girls tangled into the coats, slipping on the wet floor around the snow boots. "The cake was chocolate with whipped cream and cherries. We slept in a tent my papa made for us downstairs."

Angie felt a heavy hand on the back of her neck yanking her to her feet. Mr. MacNamara loomed over the two girls. His six-foot-four football linebacker frame blocked the light from the classroom's bank of windows.

Sharon stayed on the floor, crying. "I don't know what happened, Mr. MacNamara. I was talking with my friends when, all of sudden, she—"—Sharon pointed at Angie"—attacked me." Crocodile tears slid down her cheeks.

"She was telling lies about me and my family." Angie looked around at her classmates. "You heard her. Tell him." But her desperate glances were met with downcast eyes. Sharon threw her a sideways grin.

Angie was sent to the office for fighting.

* * *

February 12, 1965

Chère Journal,

I'm NEVER having a birthday party again and I'm NEVER speaking to Sharon Douglas AGAIN. I'm not going to tell you what happened. I don't want to ever be reminded of the horrible things Sharon said and did. When I got into a fight with Sharon because she told lies to everybody at school, none of them stood up for me. Then I was the one who got sent to the office. I was so scared that Mr. Savoie was going to call my mother, but he was really nice. He reminded me that young ladies resolve their disagreements with words, not fists, but he also seemed to understand that maybe it wasn't all my fault. I guess that's why he's a principal. He said that since it was my first time in trouble, he wasn't going to suspend me and he wasn't going to call my mother. Instead, he gave me a week of detention as long as I promised to never fight again.

I had to serve my detention in the kindergarten class every recess and lunch hour, hanging up artwork, cleaning up paint and glue, pulling up zippers, and tying boots. The kindergarten teacher was so grateful for my help that after the detention was over, she invited me to return any time. It was the best punishment! I love the little kids.

Gail has stopped writing to me. I guess she feels that thirteen is too old to have a pen pal, but my life feels full. Katy and Sally are nice to me when we see each other in church. Judy and I hang out after school. I still have skiing, and Miss Virtanen— Mrs. Savoie—works at the library now. She was the Kindergarten teacher until one day she was gone and a new teacher took over her class. A few weeks later, she married Mr. Savoie and started working at the Library in the Rec Centre. Mom says she heard that pregnant ladies aren't allowed to teach. That seems kind of weird since teachers who are moms probably know lots more about children. Anyway Mrs. Savoie and I have become friends over our love of books. She has great suggestions for me like Tale of Two Cities, David Copperfield, Nancy Drew Mysteries, and all the Anne books. When she is busy with someone else, I play with her baby. Besides skiing, I love reading.

Angie

CHAPTER FOURTEEN - 1965

Friends

June 30, 1965

Dear Diary,

I'm writing you in English now. French and German will always be part of who I am, but I live in an English world, and I think in English now. My parents have settled into our new town. They make it look so easy. Dad has his work friends, and even though Mom doesn't let him go for beers at the hotel on Fridays with them, they invite him to go fishing and hunting on weekends. (Like the other kids, I've started calling my parents Mom and Dad.) When Dad was building our garage, six men showed up on a Saturday, weighted down with stuffed tool belts to help out. Mom started volunteering to make snacks for Sunday school. She's helped organize the annual church picnic and donated to the

Christmas bazaar. Now, she has friends who call her for coffee in the afternoons. Mom and Dad play cards most Friday nights with three other couples. Only one of them is German. They even joined the curling club. It's easy for them. They can avoid the people who hate Germans and make fun of the French. But I can't. Those people's kids are in my class, and they use their parents' words against me.

I joined the basketball team as Gail suggested. I'm the starting centre. Miss Boyko, our coach, says I'm a natural. She keeps putting me on the court more than Mary, who used to be the centre, so now all the girls hate me. They don't even cheer when I score a basket. I go to all the activities Mom has signed me up for, but the only place I feel myself is on the ski hill. I don't participate in my teammates' conversations after a hard training day, but I like listening to them tease and encourage each other, and I pretend I'm one of them. Debbie sometimes says hi and once said, "Good run." The others don't notice me but don't pick on me.

Angie

* * *

"Angelika, telephone!" Angie came out of her bedroom, still wearing her pyjamas, and gave her mother a quizzical look as she took the receiver. Her mother shrugged.

"Hello?"

"Hi, Angie? This is Katy."

Angie remained silent, uncertain how to respond. Her mother stood beside her.

"We were wondering what you're doing today?" Katy continued. "Angie, you there?"

"Um, yeah, sorry. We?"

"Yeah, me and Sally. We're going to the second railway crossing today on our bikes. You have a bike, right?"

"Yeah," Angie said carefully.

"Good. We're meeting at my place at 10. Bring a lunch."

Angie's mother was nodding vigorously.

"Okay. Where's your house?"

"34 Essa Place. Just off Mona before the stop sign out of town. See ya."

The line went dead.

"I'll make you a nice salami sandwich and pack extra cookies to share." Her mother bustled off to the kitchen. "You go get dressed."

Angie wandered into her bedroom and stared at herself in the mirror above her dresser. Katy called *me*. Katy and Sally actually want *me* to join them on a picnic bike ride. And Mom said I can go. The sounds of food preparation from the kitchen brought Angie out of her trance.

"Mom, maybe a ham sandwich on white bread?"

"But in the heat, the sala—"

"Mom, please." Angie drew out the word.

Her mother hesitated.

Angie held her breath.

"Ham on white bread it is. And the cookies?"

Angie grinned at her reflection. "Of course, the cookies. Everybody loves your baking."

Ten minutes and four clothing changes later, Angie returned to the kitchen wearing her orange shorts and matching green, orange, and yellow striped top. Her lunch box waited for her on the table. "I put apple juice in your thermos; it's cooler than milk, *neh*?" Mother and daughter shared a smile. "Now, do you want me to walk there with you? Make sure you find the house?"

That was the last thing she wanted. Angie forced a neutral expression. "That's okay, Mom. I'll find it."

"Okay, have fun. And be home by four-thirty." Her mother stood at the door as Angie walked her bike out of the garage, dropped her lunch pail in the basket, and rode up the driveway. Angie was surprised her mother was allowing her to go. The railway crossed the fifty-six-mile road from Pusamakwa to Highway 17 seven times. The second crossing was popular for kids to bike to as it was six miles out of town, far enough from prying parent eyes, yet an easy enough distance to cover on a bike. And it was a short hike in the bush to Bare Head Lake along a wide track. Angie was positive her mother had no idea where she and her friends were going.

Angie pumped her pedals to get up to coasting speed. She was a confident rider, having ridden her bike through both town sites many times last summer, always on her own. There were two styles of houses for the workers in the town sites: bungalows, like hers, and one-and-a-half-storey homes. Up the hill along Mona Drive and the crescents off it, the houses were larger and more varied in style. That's where the "big bosses"—what her father called them—lived with their families. Everyone rented from the company. As she'd ridden, she'd wondered about the families who lived in these identical houses. She imagined the families with the messy yards were messy in how they lived: loud, boisterous, parents playing with their children, a place full of activity without care for appearances. Like the Dusomes with their six daughters whom she babysat. Did the houses with carefully cared for lawns and gardens regiment their children, ensuring they were well-groomed and controlled? Her home had immaculate gardens front and back. Nothing was ever left lying in their yard.

Angie used her arm to signal a right turn onto Neebig, a quick left onto Adjala, and another right onto Mona. The entrance to Essa Drive was just ahead. A glance at her watch told her she was a few minutes early, so she decided she'd take the long way around the circle to Katy's house, maybe catch sight of the yard. As the house came into view, Angie suddenly felt her stomach knot. What if this was a setup? What if they were luring her to the second crossing, where other kids would be waiting to hurt her, maybe tie her to the track? *Don't be stupid.* Her mother always said she had a too-active imagination.

Katy was in the driveway waving to her. It was too late to turn back. A game with wire wickets and posts was set up in the side yard, and a basketball net was suspended above the garage door. The grass was cut, but there weren't any fancy gardens. Angie stood on her pedals and coasted into the driveway. Katy and Sally were good girls. They never picked on her, and they went to church with her. Everything would be fine.

Katy and Sally grabbed their bikes as Angie arrived.

"Everybody ready?" Katy looked at Sally and Angie. "Okay. Let's go." Katy led the way with Sally behind her. Angie tucked in at the back of the threesome. The girls covered the six miles easily, often riding three abreast to chat, then pulling into a line to allow the occasional car to pass. At the tracks Katy popped off her bike and walked it along a narrow path through the trees. Angie and Sally followed and dropped their bikes beside Katy's at the foot of a lichen-covered granite rock cut. Scrambling up the side, the girls dropped onto the moss and began their lunch overlooking the railway track.

"Are you guys going to choir practice tonight?" Angie asked.

"I have to go early," Katy mumbled around a mouthful of cookie. "It's my turn to do the solo on Sunday."

"I don't see why we even have to do choir in the summer." Sally's voice was almost a whine.

Katy nodded. "I know, hardly anyone comes. They're all on vacation."

"And Mrs. Bray is so mean." Sally mimicked the choir leader's voice. "Sally, stop slouching. Your voice has to come from *here*." Sally pressed her fingers into her diaphragm.

"Watch me!" Katy snapped her fingers and pointed to imaginary children in the back row.

"I want to hear one 's'. You aren't snakes." Angie giggled as she closed her fingers to her thumbs like Mrs. Bray did when they sang the end of a line. She watched her new friends as they imitated more of their choir master's gestures. Angie felt her shoulders relax. It felt good to be included in a conversation.

The girls then mulled over the possibilities of who the new grade eight teacher would be now that Mr. McNamara was moving back south. They all complained that their mothers prohibited them from wearing mini-skirts or bell-bottoms.

As Katy awkwardly cleared her throat, Angie looked up and stopped packing the wax paper from her sandwich into her lunch box.

"You look like a scared deer," Katy said.

Angie forced her eyes out of their wide-eyed expression. "Sorry, I, um…"

"We want to apologize." Sally took over the conversation.

"Yeah," said Katy. "We should have told the truth that day in the classroom when you got into trouble, when—"

"What she's trying to say is we feel bad for not standing up for you after your birthday party. We wanted to tell you sooner, but—"

Angie felt her mouth hang open as her gaze moved back and forth between the two girls.

Katy looked Angie in the eye. "We're not mean girls, but we didn't know what to do. Then we were scared to stand up to Sharon because of what she and her friends would do to us."

Sally inhaled audibly, "We're sorry that we didn't say sorry sooner, but we hope you'd like to hang out with us, you know—"

Katy gave an uncomfortable laugh. "We want you to be our friend. We think you're nice."

"And interesting," Sally added.

Angie kept staring as the silence grew. She couldn't believe it. They wanted to be friends. They thought she was *interesting*. Suddenly, the looming summer vacation didn't feel so empty.

"Angie, are you going to say something?" Sally pulled on a brown curl at her neck.

"Yes! Oh yes!" Angie hugged her new friends.

Katy and Sally broke into grins.

"Okay, Let's go up the trail to Bare Head Lake." Katy led the way down the rocks to where their bikes stood propped against a pine. As the girls prepared to ride, Angie asked, "You really think I'm interesting?"

"Naw."

Angie felt her shoulders slump.

Sally pushed her on the arm. "Kidding! You're different and not afraid of it."

"Hurry up, you two!" Katy called. "Enough of the chit-chat. We've got swimming to do."

Fifteen minutes later, Angie and Sally stood on the cliff bank, watching Katy swing over the lake and plunge into the tea-coloured water. Bare Head Lake was a popular picnic and fishing place for families in Pusamakwa. Somebody's dad from town had strung a three-inch thick rope from the overhanging branch of an enormous pine. Angie held her breath until Katy's head popped to the surface. "Come on, the water's great."

Angie and Sally exchanged glances, arms wrapped around their chests, skinny legs jutting from their underwear. The girls had all stripped off their shorts but kept on their t-shirts since none of them wore a bra yet.

"You go," Angie said to Sally. "I've never done this before." She saw a moment of nervous fear flit through Sally's hazel eyes before her friend grabbed the rope, gave it a testing jerk, and then ran and leaped into the air. She splashed in well beyond Katy.

"Your turn, Angie," Katy called.

Angie grabbed the rope and prepared for her running start when Katy's scream froze her in place. Sally surfaced, flailing her arms and sputtering. When she sank again, Katy dove. For an agonizing second, the surface of the lake remained unbroken. Then both heads popped up. Sally struggled against Katy's efforts to assist her. Angie ran with all her might and felt herself fly through the air. The cold water pushed the breath from her lungs. Then, with several hard kicks, her head and shoulders burst into the sunshine. She put all her energy into her newly mastered front crawl to where Katy trod water and wrestled to keep Sally's head up.

"Get on her other side." Katy panted. "Sally, we need you to lie on your back. We'll pull you to shore under your arms."

Sally was crying between coughs. "I can't. I'm sinking."

"Sally," Katy's voice was firm but not screaming. "Trust us."

Angie floated on her stomach beside Sally and slipped her arm under one of Sally's shoulders. "See, I got you." She felt Sally relax a little. With a few strong kicks, Katy and Angie brought Sally into shallow water and helped her stand up. The three girls strode against the water, arms linked. They dropped on the narrow, shallow sandbar in front of the cliff. The rope creaked in the breeze above them while they caught their breath.

* * *

September 7, 1965

Dear Diary,

I had the best summer ever. Katy and Sally were my friends all summer. We had sleepovers in our tent in my backyard or in the rec room in the basement at Katy's house. That game with the wire wickets I saw in her yard is called croquet. You hit a wooden ball with a hammer, called a mallet, through the gates. If you hit another person's ball, you can put your foot on your ball and hit it so the other ball goes flying. Once, when I did that to Katy's ball, it went to the neighbour's yard. When Sally laughed, Katy threw her mallet at her, then started screaming I was a cheater. Katy's mom made her apologize to us, then sent us home, and Katy was grounded for three days.

Sometimes, we played board games like Monopoly and Clue in Katy's rec room. She is taking care of her missionary aunt's collection of records while she's away, working in Africa. We learned all the words to My Fair Lady, Camelot, Sound of Music, and Mary Poppins. I'd never heard of those plays, but when I'm grown, I'm going to Toronto to see them.

We rode our bikes all over town. One time, we rode past Sharon's house when she was in the driveway. When she asked if she could join us, Katy said no, and we rode off. I felt kind of bad for Sharon, but Katy said we couldn't trust her, and besides, she deserved to get some of her own medicine. When I'm with Katy and Sally, I feel like a Canadian.

We start Grade Eight today—the last year of public school. I'm nervous, but I feel I can face anything with friends at my side. Yesterday my mom came home from shopping and gave me a bra! Katy and Sally started wearing one during the summer, but I still don't have enough to fill one. Mom said since I started my period last month, the rest would come soon, and since my friends were both wearing one, she didn't want me to feel left out. My bra is the smallest size, and the cups don't need anything in them to stick out, but it's a bra! I think my mom is as happy as I am that I have friends. Now, her daughter's not the weird one that's alone.

Gotta go, or I'll be late.

Angie

CHAPTER FIFTEEN - 1966

Facing Uncomfortable Truths

September 5, 1966

Dear Diary,

I hate my life. I started Grade 9 with no friends. Katy moved to North Bay in August because her dad got a better job, and they wanted to be closer to her mother's family cottage in Muskoka. Sally moved last week to Picton, somewhere near Lake Ontario. Her grandfather died in June, and Sally's dad quit his job and moved them to the farm. Sally says it's actually an apple orchard. Farm, orchard, who cares? She's gone.

Yesterday, Judy came over to say bye. Her mom has left Judy's step-dad, and moved to Winnipeg, so it's safe for her to live with her mom again. Judy's sister drove her to Thunder Bay to catch the plane.

> Mom said I'd be able to make friends with the kids coming from the Catholic School, but they all stick together. Polly and her friends called me "browner" in the halls. I felt branded from the start. They all stood around and laughed when I couldn't open the lock on my locker. Turns out, they glued it shut. Now, I'm the smart girl who doesn't even know how to work a combination lock.
>
> I wanted to cry, but I remembered what Arthur taught me, so now I walk through the halls with my head up, glaring at anyone who looks at me, and I pretend I don't care. With four hours of running and strength training for skiing every day and ensuring I keep my marks up, I don't have time for friends anyway.
>
> Angie

* * *

Angie sat at the kitchen table. The ticking of the cuckoo clock hypnotized the silence in the house. Open reference books littered the tabletop. The scratch of Angie's pencil scraped her insides as she recorded each atrocity in her notebook.

The back door opened. Angie froze over her work as she heard her mother stomp the snow off her boots. A quick blast of cold air curled around Angie's feet as her mother entered the kitchen. When her mother closed the door behind her, echoing shivers continued to ripple up and down Angie's spine.

"You're home early." Her mother's expression morphed from interest to concern at the sight of the vertical anger line between Angie's eyes. "What's wrong? Are you sick? Did you get into trouble at school?"

"Why didn't you tell me?" Rage strangled Angie's voice.

Her mother wrinkled her brow. "Tell you what? What are you talking about?"

"What you did. What Dad did. What the Germans did." Angie stood. Her chair toppled over backward and banged on the tile floor. "You let me be proud of being a German. Did you never consider that I needed to hear from you what we did in the war before I learned it at school, read it in a book, or heard it from the other kids?"

Her mother dropped the bags of groceries on the table and caught her breath as she took in the photos and maps displayed in the open books scattered across her kitchen table. "Angelika, You can't believe everything you read in those books."

"Are you telling me the Germans didn't starve, torture, and kill six million Jews during the war?"

Her mother dropped into a chair at the table. "Sit."

Angie remained standing, taut as a violin string.

Her mother pulled a book toward her. Angie saw her flinch at the photo of skeletal bodies surrounded by liberating Allied soldiers under the sign *Arbeit Macht Frei*. Her mother's expression hardened as her eyes roved over the pages of gas chambers, ovens, and piles of bones in mass graves. Then, with a vicious abruptness Angie had never witnessed, her mother slammed the books shut. "Lies!"

Angie felt the air leave the room. The cuckoo called three times. Angie picked up her chair and perched on its edge. "Mom, these can't all be lying." She swept her hand to encompass the books. "You were there. You must have seen it."

Her mother's face seemed chiselled in stone.

"Jews forced to wear yellow stars. *Kristallnacht*. People marched through the streets, loaded onto cattle cars."

Her mother didn't move.

"Mom, say something."

The clock kept ticking.

"Of course, we saw those things happening," she began with a shaky breath. "They weren't all Jews, but your precious books," she gestured to the material, "don't tell you that. *They* don't mention the German children torn from their families because they were different—blind, deaf, lame, slow, imperfect. Their parents were told they would receive specialized care in institutions. Still, whenever the mother tried to visit her child, it was mysteriously at a medical appointment, on a trip, or receiving medical tests." Her mother's lip curled with bitterness. "And your books certainly don't tell you what the Nazis did to those who dared to question, inquire, or stand up against them." Her mother paused.

Angie waited, hands gripping each other in her lap.

"Angie, those books were written by the winners, and the winners don't know what it was like for the ordinary Germans. We weren't all Nazis."

Her Oma's face flashed through Angie's mind. *She needs to know we weren't all Nazis.* Angie hadn't understood what Oma meant at the time, but she did now.

"But all those scenes where thousands of people are screaming *Sieg Heil* and giving the salute to Hitler. You telling me they didn't have a choice?" Angie spat the words like bullets from a machine gun. She felt her nails pressing into her palms.

Her mother kept her tone even. "I was rounded up once on my way to work and marched at gunpoint to one of those rallies in Hamburg. Out-of-uniform soldiers were stationed throughout the crowd."

Angie saw her mother's throat contract as if trying to swallow the memory. "If you didn't scream and salute, one of those soldiers stabbed you from behind, the first time in the upper arm, the second time in the back."

Angie gasped.

"When people start falling to the ground around you, you do whatever you must to stay alive." Her mother's face softened. "There was no television. The Nazi machine operated the only radio station. When Hitler told you that the enemy was lying about Nazis killing Jews to turn you against your government, you didn't know what to believe. I remember once he asked us, if he was gassing Jews, wouldn't we know about it?"

Her mother's face crumpled. "If only they'd listened to him and stayed in their own neighbourhoods. They had their own ice cream shops; they didn't need to come into ours." She rushed out of the room. Angie heard the bedroom door close. The cuckoo called four times. Angie tapped on her mother's door a few moments after their scene in the kitchen. Her query concerning her mother's state was greeted with a grunt and a rough "go away," so Angie returned to the kitchen and piled the closed books on the table's edge. She opened her math text. The numbers kept twisting into tortured skeletons.

* * *

When Kurt arrived home from work an hour later, he found Angie sitting at the table, staring blankly into space. No scent of meal preparation greeted him, no sign of Marta.

"Angie, where's your mother?"

No response.

He shook his daughter's shoulder. "What's wrong?" Then, kneeling in front of her, "Angelika, has something happened to Mom?" His heart was racing.

Angie pointed toward her parents' bedroom.

Without waiting for further explanation, Kurt rushed down the hallway and burst into the room. Marta lay on her side of the bed, staring at the ceiling. "Marta, what is it?" He touched her forehead. "Are you sick?"

"She knows." Marta turned tortured eyes to his. "We should have prepared her."

"Knows what? Prepared her for what?"

"The lies. Just like Mutti said, Angie has read the lies written by the victors, and now she thinks we are evil." Marta began to sob. Kurt pulled her to his chest and held her.

When he sensed that she'd cried herself out, he pushed her back against a pile of pillows and looked into her eyes. "Better?"

Marta nodded.

"Now, start from the beginning and tell me what Angie knows and what lies she has read."

Marta related the scene she'd encountered when she'd arrived home earlier that afternoon: the photos, Angie's anger, and her accusations about her parents' role in the Holocaust. "She doesn't understand. No one understands. If Hitler had killed all those people, we would have known. And we didn't know." She leaned toward Kurt. "Sure, there were camps, but they told us they were work camps, not death camps the way those books claim." Her words began to slur, and her hand shook as she reached for the glass of water beside the bed.

Kurt noticed the pill bottle on the bedside table. "Marta, how many pills have you taken?"

"Just a couple, for my head."

Marta had complained of piercing headaches a few weeks ago, and the doctor prescribed something "a little stronger than just aspirin."

"A couple? You sure?" Usually, when she took two pills, they cleared her head but never caused her to slur or shake.

"Yeah." She gave him a wobbly stare. "But the thoughts wouldn't stop, so maybe a couple more…" Her head slumped against the pillows. "She's mad because I didn't tell her. But it's my job to protect her. I'm a good mother, aren't I?"

Kurt smoothed the tears from her cheeks. "You're a wonderful mother." He checked the number of pills against the total prescribed and decided it was safe just to let her sleep, checking her regularly. No need to compound her distress by calling the doctor unless she worsened. He pocketed the pill bottle, kissed her forehead, and quietly closed the door behind him.

"Is she okay?" Angie turned anxious eyes to her father as he entered the kitchen.

He nodded. "She's sleeping. We'll need to keep checking on her. I don't think she'll be up until tomorrow morning." Her father ran his hands backward through his hair, then looked around the kitchen. "So, supper."

"Mom took out hamburger." Angie pointed at the brown paper-wrapped lump on the counter. "I think she was going to make a casserole."

"Let's just make some hamburgers. It'll be faster."

"Sure." Angie rose. "I'll get some buns from the freezer and make a salad."

Father and daughter worked side-by-side. Her father formed and fried the burgers while Angie defrosted and toasted the buns. She made separate salads for each of them instead of in one bowl the way her mother did, topping the lettuce with onions in her father's, tomatoes in hers, and green pepper in both. They ate their meal in silence. Angie forced down half her hamburger before the images of emaciated prisoners completely closed her throat.

"It's okay, *Schatzi*," Her father's warm, callused hand on her arm steadied her.

A HYPHENATED LIFE

With the kitchen cleaned up, her father sat back at the table instead of settling in his chair in the living room. "So, these are the books?" He gestured at the pile still sitting on one side of the table.

Angie nodded. "We started learning about World War I in History. After class, some kids called me a loser, saying the Germans lost the war."

"We did."

"I knew that. But then Colin Hale said the Germans were worse in World War II. That we killed six million Jews, he said his dad had told him all about it. He called it the Holocaust."

Her father's mouth hardened.

Angie's eyes filled with tears. "Then they chanted *murderer, murderer, murderer*, as I walked away. They followed me and kept chanting."

"Didn't the teachers say anything? Stop them?"

"They kept whispering it, but no teachers were around anyway. I ducked into the bathroom and waited until the next class started. Then I went to the library and found these books." She took a deep breath. "Dad, is it true? Mom says the books are lying. That the winners of the war wrote them to make the Germans look bad. But—"

"It's all true." Her father spoke so quietly she could hardly hear him. He dropped his gaze. "We didn't tell you because we thought you were too young." It was as if he was talking to himself. "It was in the past. We never thought it would come up in your studies." He gave a rough laugh. "Now, I see how wrong that was." Her father looked directly at her. His eyes were suddenly

173

old, and the sharp edges of his high cheekbones pressed against his leathered skin. "Angelika, I'm sorry. What do you want to know?"

Angie realized she wanted to know her mother— the ghosts that lived in her mind, all she kept hidden. "I'm not sure Mom believes the Holocaust happened. But how could she not know? She was there when it happened."

Her father exhaled heavily. "It's complicated, Angie."

At her expression of frustration, he held up his hand.

"I'm going to give you the best answer I can. Your mother worked in Hamburg, away from family, during the war. You know she lived through the bombing and burning of the city."

Angie nodded. "I saw a picture. There was nothing left of Hamburg."

"People in the countryside knew their neighbours better, saw more of how the government—" he *tsk*ed, "the Nazis, treated the citizens."

"But soldiers ordering Jews out of their homes, putting them on trains, the beatings—" Angie's voice rose in frustration.

"Absolutely. Your mother explained about the soldiers in the crowds, about the messages on the radio from Hitler. Like many others, she chose to believe what they heard and read. It was easier to believe Hitler's reasoning than to face the fact that as a German, you might be letting the Nazis carry out these atrocities."

"But you believe it all happened, don't you?"

Kurt nodded. "We lived in a small town. We all grew our food and helped each other. When the war came, I was too young at first to be a soldier. I hated going to *Die Hitler Jugend*, but we had no choice. If you didn't go, you'd be taken away from your parents, and they'd be arrested." A grin began to spread across his face. "But when our Jewish neighbours were no longer allowed to shop in the stores or grow their food, my mother and many other women assembled food packages and other household items. My mother would leave the box or bag in an old wagon Hans and I played with as a child. When I came home from a *Hitler Jugend* meeting, I'd pull the wagon out of the shed, go through the back allies to my mother's close friend, Frau Rosenblatt, and leave the package in their shed. If anyone confronted me, I would explain that I was doing a delivery for the *Hitler Jugend*. I was still wearing my uniform so no one would question further."

Angie giggled. "My dad, the dissenter. Weren't you scared?"

"At first, then I started to see the funny side."

"That's like the story Oma told me about Mom taking the baby for a walk with Opa's communist pamphlets hidden under the mattress in the carriage." Angie pressed her lips together. "Did you see the camps?"

Her father rubbed his palms against his thighs. "No. But when I was in the prisoner-of-war camp, other soldiers told stories of the fences, the stench, the smoke." He leaned his forehead on his hands, then met her eyes. "Look, Angie, in Germany after the war and even today, there are things that no one talks about. Things so shameful we buried them in a secret cemetery, but our hearts can't let them go for fear if we do, we risk repeating them." He took a shuddering breath. "And some Germans have never been able to allow themselves to see how the Nazis' propaganda manipulated them."

"And that's how Mom feels?"

"I believe in her heart that your mother understands the holocaust happened, but if she can deny the truth, she can fence off the guilt in her mind."

Her father's reasoning made sense to Angie. Her mother insisted that what went on in their home remain private, reminding Angie to keep her opinions and thoughts to herself. External appearances, what people thought, counted more than the reality underneath. Angie could see how this approach probably helped her mother cope with the teasing when she was a child because her father was a communist, the horrors of the war, the move to Canada, and life in Pusamakwa. She was a master at fitting in. Today, Angie had disrupted the depth of what she'd told herself about the war.

"Angie, you okay?"

Angie raised her head. "Yeah, I think I get it. I won't bring the war up again."

"I think that's a good idea."

Her father made to stand up.

"Dad, who is Franz?"

Her father's eyes narrowed. She could almost see the wheels in his brain turning as if he wasn't sure he understood who she was referring to. Or maybe he was trying to decide if he should tell her? He took a deep breath. "That's a question only your mother should answer."

He stood. "I'm going to check on your mother and watch TV."

"I've got homework to finish." Angie pulled her math book to her. "Thanks, Dad."

He ran his hand over her head as he passed her.

CHAPTER SIXTEEN - 1967

The Good Girl

October 30, 1967

Dear Diary,

Coach says he knew I was destined for greatness the first time he saw me charge through the practice course last year. He says I could be on the junior team this year and I'm even better than Christine Murray. I feel sorry for Christine. She lives across from me. In the summer when the windows are open, I hear her dad screaming and glass breaking. Sometimes I hitch a ride to the ski hill when her brother drives her. I've seen bruises on her brother's face and he always reminds Christine not to go in the house until he comes home. I've never seen her mom. Christine says she has a lot of bad headaches and has to take pills that make her sleepy. I've tried to be friendly with Christine but she seems to only have time for Jeannie, her training partner.

The other girls talk about the anti-war demonstrations on TV. They giggle as they chant "Make love, not war" in the halls. My mom swung her dishcloth across my face when I repeated the chant at home. She told me to remember that good girls wait until marriage. When I asked wait for what, she told me not to be fresh and go do my homework. I knew exactly what she meant thanks to Seventeen and Tiger Beat. I keep my magazines hidden under my mattress. Mom would have a bird if she ever found them.

Angie

* * *

Trudging home after school one day under a sky as dark as her mood, Angie panicked at the acrid smell of smoke coming from her house. She found her mother poking a rake into a smoldering pile in their backyard fire pit. Angie gaped at the bluish yellow flames consuming David Cassidy's face. "Mom, stop!"

"No more of this nonsense." Soot streaked her mother's brow. "We didn't leave our homeland and family so you could read trash. You're in high school. It's time to prepare for university."

"That's still four years away."

"You need top marks to get a scholarship. We can't send you to university on a miner's pay." Her mother pointed to the house. "Go. Do your homework."

That night over supper, her mother announced, "There will be no more ski racing."

"Skiing is my life!" Flying free, the cold wind fighting to steal her breath, her skis chattering over the ice. How would she survive without it?

"It takes time from your studies."

Angie turned pleading eyes to her father.

"Marta, the girl needs something outside of school." His tone was level as he glared at his wife. Turning his faded-denim eyes to his daughter, his tone softened. "Angie, you can ski as long as you keep up your marks."

Angie hugged her father. "Thanks, Dad." Old Spice tickled her nose. She knew from watching her parents' relationship what standing up to his wife for his daughter was going to cost him.

Her mother didn't speak to either of them for three days.

* * *

In addition to on-hill practices on weekends, the coach held dry-land training during the week in the chalet. When her dad worked evening shifts, Angie hitched a ride to the hill with Christine. One Tuesday night, the coach asked Angie to stay and work on her schuss, offering to drive her home afterward. Crouched over her skis, knees over her toes, Angie's thighs began to shake after barely twenty seconds.

"We need to strengthen those if you're going to schuss to the finish." The coach reached for her legs.

She jumped backward.

"Hey, it's okay. I only want to massage out the knots." He smiled. "You can trust me."

From then on, the coach always drove her home after practice. Once everyone had left, Angie and the coach would sit on the worn couches, sharing his thermos of rum-laced tea and counting the stars through the chalet's wall of windows. The cedar beams absorbed their frustrations.

"My wife spends all her time with our sons. It's like I don't exist."

"No dances. No boyfriends," Angie said, mimicking her mother's accented English. "I live in a jail."

Sometimes, she'd sit on his lap in his basement office, sharing the headphones as they listened to his HAM radio. He'd wrap her long blond hair over his balding head or tickle her waist. She'd giggle.

Angie felt safe under the weight of his arm draped across her shoulder as they walked out to the parking lot.

One evening , he opened the passenger door for her. As she slipped past him, he put his hand on her arm. "I know I told everyone to call me coach, but when we're together, you can call me Ian." He gave her a little peck on the cheek.

Angie caught her breath. "I don't know . . ."

"It would make me really happy." His tone cajoled.

"Okay, coa—Ian." Angie giggled as she slid onto the seat.

* * *

December 19, 1967

Dear Diary,

We're taking a Christmas break from training so I won't see Ian alone again until January. I feel so flat inside, like all the light is gone from my life. I just want to curl up in a ball until the New Year.

I could tell Ian was sad too. Instead of giving me a kiss on the cheek like he always does before we get in the car, he pulled me into a big hug, then he kissed me on the mouth. He tried to put his tongue in my mouth! It felt slimy so I jerked away. His eyes looked angry at first but then his mouth drooped and he said he was really sorry. When he got in the car he asked me to forgive him, that he couldn't help it because he likes me so much. He thinks I'm beautiful and much smarter than my age so he got carried away. He looked so contrite that I couldn't help but laugh. Soon he was laughing with me. Then he asked if he could kiss me again. He said it was okay because he would never hurt me and it was a way we could show how we felt about each other. The second time, he was slow and gentle. At first, it felt strange and scary, but then I started to really like it.

I know I should feel bad because it probably is wrong to kiss him like that, but all my friends have boyfriends and they kiss. And he is right, when he kisses me I do feel like he likes me. He wouldn't do anything to harm me.

It's going to be hard seeing Ian at the hill every day during the holidays without being with him. But he'll be with his sons and I'll be teaching ski school. I'll just put on the mask I wear whenever we're together with the team. Maybe I won't even go every day, but then everyone will wonder what's going on because no one is as crazy about skiing every minute as I am.

Joyeux Noël, Frohe Weihnachten, Diary.

Angie

CHAPTER SEVENTEEN - 1968

Innocence Lost

Angie shared a hotel room with her female team-mates during the season's final race in Thunder Bay. While in the bathroom, she overheard them talking about the coach.

"It was really weird," said Jeannie. "Coach leaned in like he wanted to kiss me."

"He tried that with me," said Debbie. "Told him my dad'd break his balls if he ever came near me again."

The girls laughed.

Angie gripped the heart pendant the coach had given her for Christmas, where it nestled between her breasts, safely hidden from prying eyes.

After dinner, the coach asked each team member to come to his room for an individual race review. Angie was last. Soft music played on the radio when she arrived. He was lighting candles on the dresser.

She pressed her back to the closed door. "The girls say you tried to kiss them."

"Who said that?" His eyes narrowed.

"Is it true?" She searched his face.

He shook her by the shoulders, thumbs digging into her flesh. "I said, who…told… you… that?" His face was purple.

Her head whipped forward and back. "Ow! You're hurting me." She pulled at his hands.

His arms dropped to his sides. "I'm sorry, baby." His finger ran over her cheek, eyes soft. "Of course, it's not true. They're just jealous. You didn't say anything, did you?"

"No. They didn't know I heard."

"You know you can't tell anyone about us, not even your best friend."

"I don't have a best friend," Angie whispered.

He put his arm around her. "You don't need one—you've got me. And nothing to your mother, eh?"

Angie shook her head. "She doesn't want me to ski, so I don't talk about it at home."

The coach steered her into the room. "That's okay. We have to keep our secret until we can be together. Understand?"

She nodded. "When I'm sixteen."

He pulled her into his arms and kissed her, moving her backward until her legs hit the bed. Her knees crumpled, and she dropped to the mattress.

"I've wanted you for so long," he murmured. He kissed her breasts through her shirt, then lifted it to kiss her skin. She tried to pull her shirt back into place. Then he was pulling off her pants, opening his fly. Her body stiffened; he kissed her softly.

"You're so beautiful," he whispered. "Touch me." He pressed her hand against his penis.

She whimpered.

"It's okay. I'll be gentle."

"No, stop." She pushed at his shoulders. "Please, no." The springs pressed into her back until it felt as if the mattress was swallowing her. She wished it would. His rummy breath caught in her throat.

"This is what people do when they love each other." He captured her arms over her head with one hand.

"But I never—"

"You knew this was going to happen. You know you want it."

A searing pain. Maybe if she stopped resisting, it would be over soon. Her mother's voice echoed in her head. *Good girls do what they're told.* Angie squeezed her eyes shut and imagined the wind in her face. The regular rhythm of the bed became the shushing sound of snow beneath her skis.

When it was over, she huddled into the corner of the bed, knees pulled to her chest. Crying.

"It'll be better next time." He planted soft kisses on her neck. "I'll leave my wife. We'll make a family."

On the radio, the Everly Brothers sang that all she had to do was dream.

The next night, Angie again tried to resist him.

"You say you love me. You lying?" His eyes clouded. "I'm not some pimply adolescent. Don't you want a real man?"

A fist gripped her heart. "I'm sorry." Angie's mind took to her skis. When it was over, she stumbled to the bathroom, running the water in the sink to cover the sounds of her sobs as she gingerly wiped herself clean. She jumped at the knock on the door.

"You okay?" His voice sounded genuinely concerned. "Come on out," he said in a singsong tone. "I have a surprise to tell you."

Angie took a few moments to compose herself before opening the door. The coach was reclining on the bed. "Join me." He patted the vacant space beside him. She turned her eyes from his limp penis resting in his underwear. "I have to get back, or the others will wonder where I am."

"Just sit for a minute."

She balanced on the edge of the desk chair, feeling it roll backward until it hit the wall behind her.

"At the coaches' meeting today, we selected the racers for the national junior team."

He rubbed his hand backward over his scalp. That usually meant he had bad news. The list would be announced tomorrow after the final race, so why was he telling her now?

"The junior team members are selected based on race points and potential. You've attracted a lot of attention in the past year." He paused. Then, his face broke into a huge grin. "You made the team!"

* * *

March 20, 1968

Dear Diary,

My head is spinning, and my heart keeps racing. I feel like I'm going to pass out. I'm on the Junior Ski Team! I'm going to race in Europe next month.

But I can't stop the images from the last two nights. Ian made me do it when we were in his hotel room. I said I didn't want to, but he wouldn't stop. It really hurt, and I cried afterward. He said it will feel better as we do it more. My life's like a Giant Slalom course. I'm flying down the mountain, clearing the gate where my mother nags me about school. Then I slow for the gate where Ian is on top of me, telling me he's a man with needs. On the straightaways the voice in my head is saying that what we are doing is wrong. I know I have to do it if I want him to keep loving and coaching me. He has a family, even if his wife doesn't love him anymore. I really want to stay on the team.

When the other girls giggle about kissing their boyfriends or letting them feel them up, I want to tell them, "Don't go too far. It's not as exciting as you think!" Instead, I smile, stay quiet, or pretend to read my book. Sometimes I wish I didn't know what I know, but I must be doing a good acting job because last night, when they were talking in the room, Jeannie looked over at me and said, "Look at her. Poor thing. She has no idea what we're talking about." Christine laughed. "Yeah, she probably still plays with Barbie dolls."

> The season is ending soon and I won't be seeing Ian for a few months. Maybe when we get back together, he'll be over me and I won't have to do it anymore.
>
> Inside, I don't feel like myself. I hope I can hide it from my mother.
>
> Angie

* * *

The shy April sun warmed Angie's shoulders as she bounced on her skis from one patch of snow to the next. The potentially disastrous outcome of hitting a patch of mud and stone at this pace buzzed through her body on this last run of the season. At the bottom of the hill, she joined her teammates and the ski club members as they put the ski hill to bed for its summer hibernation. Two mechanics worked in the tow house cleaning and oiling the transport truck engine and transmission that powered the rope tow. Four guys a few years older than Angie were wrestling the four-inch diameter rope onto the hooks sticking out from the tow posts about six feet off the ground.

"Guys, I told you, start from the top of the hill and work your way down," The coach shouted. He walked away, shaking his head. "Kids. They never listen."

Angie was counting, stacking, and straightening the bibs, gate posts, drills, and various tools when the door to the racing shack blew closed, plunging her into deep twilight. Suddenly, strong arms encircled her from behind.

Ian's warm breath tickled her neck, sending gentle electric shocks through her frame.

"I miss you."

They'd only been able to see each other surrounded by other people at the hill for the last few weeks. Angie had begun to wonder how he'd react the next time they would be alone together. She nodded her head against his chest. "Me too. But with the season over…" She turned to face him. "I mean…I didn't hear from you, and I thought maybe—" Her eyes swam. "I hate endings."

Ian dropped his arms as if she was a hot piece of coal. He backed up until he was leaning against the closed door. "Endings?" His lips were tight.

"What's wrong?"

"Are you saying you want to end *us*?" The muscles along his jawline tensed.

"No, but how are we going to see each other? We don't have the practices and training, and my mom won't let me out without a reason."

His jaw relaxed. "You scared me." He pulled her against his chest. "Leave it to me."

Voices were building outside as everyone gathered at the celebration bonfire. Ian headed to the door. "Wait five minutes before you come out." Then he was gone.

Angie kept moving things around until the voices passing the shack stopped. She peered through the crack in the door. A few stragglers were still joining the group, but most were standing around the fire. She joined Christine and Jeannie.

"Hey, where were you?" Christine asked.

Angie felt the heat rise up her neck. "I...um...was straightening the race shack." She pointed behind her. When she turned back, Christine and Jeannie were deep in conversation with Adam and Danny, two of their team-mates. Angie stood alone, hands thrust into her pockets, watching the crowd. Her fingers began to play with a roll of paper. *That wasn't in my pocket earlier.* Ian caught her eye across the fire. She nodded toward her pocket, then tilted her head at him. He gave his head a slight shake, then turned to one of the club's senior members to continue his conversation. Angie left the paper where it was.

* * *

Kicking off her boots, Angie hung her jacket on the hook by the back door, called a brief greeting to her parents, and descended the stairs to the rec room. Last summer, she'd worked with her father, banging in nails, painting walls, and rolling out carpet. Within a month of working most evenings, they'd created a living space with a bar and a lockable door in one half of the basement. Her mother hadn't been a fan, but a promise to purchase new living room furniture and move the old stuff downstairs convinced her not to argue against the project. To sweeten the deal, her father removed the wall between the living room and the narrow third bedroom Angie used as a study space on the main floor. Her mother would have the open living room/dining space she'd talked about for several years, and Angie moved her desk and books to the rec room. Her parents even agreed to install a phone extension in the downstairs room when Angie offered to pay the monthly cost. Her mother could still listen in on her conversations, but Angie felt she'd gained a new level of privacy.

Settling on the couch, with her knees folded under her, Angie unrolled the mysterious paper she'd found in her pocket.

> *Union Office Wed. 4:30. Call union number from pay phone if you can't make it.*
>
> *O my Luve's like a red, red rose That's newly sprung in June.*

Angie clutched the note to her chest and smiled.

"Angelika, Supper!"

Jolted from her daydream, Angie called, "*Ich komme,*" She tilted the couch forward so the top of the back rested against the coffee table, reached through a slit in the liner fabric to the secret pocket she'd attached with string to the wooden frame and removed her diary. Carefully flattening the tiny paper, she slid it into an envelope with the collection of other notes.

"Angelika!"

Angie replaced the diary and dropped the couch back in place. Casting a glance to ensure everything looked undisturbed, she raced up the stairs to join her parents for supper.

* * *

Angie jerked the knob of the scarred wooden door on the back of the long two-storey brick building housing the pharmacy, smoke shop, diner, jewelry store, and pool hall.

Ian had pointed out the window on the second storey where the union office was. As a union steward, he had a key to the office. Three doors confronted Angie at the top of the narrow staircase without signs or numbers to identify what lay behind each. She knew apartments were above the stores on both sides, so she knocked hesitantly on the centre one. Ian opened the door and pulled her through. "I'm so glad you made it." He hugged her, then led her to the cafe-style table with four unmatched chairs in the front corner. "Sit. So, how did you get away? And how long have we got?"

"I have this friend, Tim. He uses me as a cover when he wants to meet his friend. So I asked him to be my cover today. We're saying we're working on a joint project and have to use equipment at school to do it."

"But he doesn't know what you're doing?" He raised his eyebrows.

Angie shook her head. "We never ask for explanations."

"That's good. That's really good." Ian sat back. "So, you could use Tim this summer?"

"As far as my parents are concerned, Tim and I go to a movie almost every Friday night. We walk up to the theatre together, then I go in and he disappears. When the movie ends, he's always waiting for me outside, and he walks me home."

"And you have no idea what he does?"

Angie felt her smile wane. "I know he meets someone, someone he can't be seen with."

"Ah, an illicit love affair. Maybe with a girl from the wrong family?" Ian grinned. "So he's not likely to say anything to blow your cover."

"Maybe not a girl," Angie said softly. "And no, we're safe with Tim."

"I see." Ian looked genuinely sympathetic. Then his expression brightened. "So we'll meet every Friday night. We can stay here or go for a drive." Ian dropped to his knees in front of her. "I'll bring snacks and wine. I know a few private places in the bush. You make me so happy. We'll have a great summer." He pulled her to her feet and steered her to the couch that slumped against the side wall. In moments, he had her shirt and panties off and was slipping himself inside her. Angie stared at the brown water stains on the ceiling until the sound of skis on snow transported her.

CHAPTER EIGHTEEN - 1969

The Final Schuss

Two days after her sixteenth birthday in February, the team was competing on the World Cup ski circuit in Val d'Isère, France. Angie woke early on race morning. She was going into the final run with the best time, just like her hero Nancy Greene did in the Olympics. Today was the right day to share her news with the coach.

Angie tiptoed through the foyer of the hostel while the security guard snored on the front desk. She sprinted the two blocks past the shuttered stores huddled under the lightly falling snow. The kitchen door at the back of the half-timbered inn stood open, so she mounted the back stairs to the second floor. Angie waited until a woman dressed in a black, gauzy nightgown disappeared down the hallway. She tapped on the door to room twelve.

The coach opened the door. "Did you forget—what the hell?" His smile flipped into a scowl.

What was that black lace thing he was slipping into the pocket of his dressing gown?

"What are you doing here?" He yanked her into the room and shut the door.

Angie flung her arms around his neck. "I love you so much."

He pushed her away. "You aren't allowed to be here."

"But I couldn't wait to tell you. Our dream's coming true." Her eyes fixed on his. "I'm going to have our baby."

He stepped out of her reach, scrubbing his hand backward over his bald head. "I always use a condom."

Angie struggled to keep smiling. "Remember, in Austria, when you couldn't find one? You said it would be okay…" She reached for him.

"Get away, you little tramp. After all I've done for you. It's not mine."

Her eyes widened. "There's no one else." She clung to his waist.

"Get out. Now!"

She stumbled under the hard push on her back. The boards of the hallway floor bruised her knees as the door's lock clicked behind her. She hung her head. *Why did he say that? He knows he's the only one, forever. Did I do something to make him angry? No, I've always done everything he wanted.* She mustered the strength to stand. *He must have just been surprised. Yes, that was it. I should have prepared him better instead of just blurting out the news.*

Angie ran down the stairs and onto the sidewalk, choking back sobs. The awakening street smelled like her mother's kitchen on baking day. Her ears rang with imagined "I told you so" proclamations once her mother learned the truth. *What'll I do if he doesn't want me and the baby?* Angie breathed deeply. *He's stressed*, she told herself. *He'll be happy tomorrow.* Now it was time to focus on the race.

Back at the hostel, racers were beginning to stir. Angie grabbed her gear and struck out to the gondola. An army of workers crawled like ants over the mountain below her, filling ruts and icing the fresh snow on the course for the coming race. All she saw was the memory of the coach's scowling face.

At the top of the course, she closed her eyes and hurriedly went through her visualization, swaying as she imagined driving her knees through each gate. When she was called to the start, the coach was nowhere in sight, so the assistant stepped forward. The counter beeped down from ten. The bar clicked open. And Angie charged like a rodeo bronco out of the stall. The fresh snow gripped her skis, but she held the line, knees in a perfect schuss with hands low as she took the rise just above Gate Six. Ice. *It hadn't been there yesterday.* She skidded sideways, hit the orange snow fence hard, and took to the air.

* * *

Angie opened her eyes to a mound of white bandages swaddling her right knee. Frost etched against the blackness outside the window. She struggled to keep the coach's face in focus as he leaned over her.

"Where am I?" Her mouth felt like cotton.

"You're in the hospital," he said.

Angie shivered under his icy glare.

"You cut too close out of Gate Six. Told you you'd lose an edge on that line."

She winced as she moved her toes.

"They had to operate to reattach the tendon in your knee, and your ligaments are strained."

When she tried to sit up, ripping pain cascaded through her middle. Angie hugged her abdomen.

"You lost it. I assured the doctor I'd inform your parents." The coach sneered. "Of course, that's not going to happen." He leaned his face inches from hers. "You tell anyone, and I'll make sure you're just another delusional little girl who had a crush on her coach." He turned and stalked out.

Angie closed her eyes, surrendering to the dark hole in her heart, wishing she could forget to breathe.

* * *

Back home, everyone in town looked at her but no one met her eye. Her name was on everyone's lips but no one spoke to her. They shook their heads when they walked past her, gazing at some point just beyond her head. One of her teammates, in a letter home, had complained about the special attention the coach gave Angie. Suppositions bounced from bridge club to Bible study, from curling club to coffee shop. Kids at school bombarded her with questions.

Angie's mother only spoke to her about it once. "How could you let this happen? Our family is disgraced."

"But he told me he loved me. He wrote me poems, gave me presents." Angie started sobbing. "He promised we'd be together."

"Every man says those things when he wants sex. How could you be so stupid?" Her mother stepped toward her. "Do you have any idea how hard I've worked to gain people's respect here? Now, I'll never be able to hold my head up again."

"I was barely fifteen when it started. He was thirty-two. I believed him."

"You're lucky you didn't get pregnant." Her mother grabbed Angie's arm. "You will never talk about this to anyone. You won't admit anything happened." She shook her daughter. "Understand?"

Angie nodded. She realized she'd been a fool, but nobody understood. It was almost as if he'd hypnotized her with his attention. She never told her mother about the baby.

That evening, while her mother was out at her weekly bridge night, Angie's father put his arms around her and let her cry into his shoulder. "I'll kill him if I ever see him again."

She had no words to erase the pain from her father's eyes.

Later that night, Angie heard her mother walk past her bedroom door.

* * *

Marta moved through the dark living room, using the crushed velvet back of Kurt's recliner under her hand as a guidepost as she made her way to the kitchen in the dark. She thought of making herself a cup of coffee but opted instead for whiskey, straight. Staring out the kitchen window at the snowy backyard, ghostly under the half-moon, Marta took a big swig from her glass. She held her hand over her mouth to muffle her coughs as the amber liquid cut a path down her throat. The tears she'd been holding back flowed freely. Angelika must have been so afraid. Why hadn't she said anything? Why hadn't she noticed that something was going on? Marta took another swig. Had she done something wrong as a mother? No, she'd done everything right. She brought her up to be a good girl. But Angelika had become so stubborn as a teenager. She thought she knew everything better. And her father always gave in to her.

The creak of the living room floor signalled that she soon would no longer be alone. She swiped at her tears. Strong arms pulled her from the window and enveloped her. Her shoulders shook as she leaned into Kurt's embrace.

"We should call the police." Kurt's murmur didn't disguise the fierceness in his voice.

Marta pushed back to look into her husband's eyes. "I don't think so."

"But he has to pay for what he's done!"

"Shh, keep your voice down," Marta whispered. "The police will investigate. He will deny it, maybe even blame Angelika."

"Oh, please. A fifteen-year-old girl seducing a man over thirty? Who would ever believe that?"

Marta's voice hissed with anger. "It's all your fault. You had to be the hero, let her keep racing. And now she's ruined. What boy will ever marry her?"

Kurt backed up, arms across his middle as if she'd punched him in the stomach.

Marta took a final swallow of her drink. "This time, you'll listen to me. There will be no police report. We ignore the rumours, talk only about our concern for Angelika's injuries."

"So say nothing and hope things will die down?"

Marta nodded. "It's done. No more talking about it, so she can put it behind her."

"You're probably right." Kurt's voice was heavy with defeat.

* * *

March 2, 1969

Dear Diary,

Mom got up in the middle of the night. I peeked through the crack in my door and watched her walk through the living room and into the kitchen. I slipped out of my room and hid behind the kitchen door. Mom moved like she was in a dream. She picked up the coffee pot, then put it back and took a glass and the whiskey bottle from the cupboard instead. I've never seen her drink big swigs of whiskey straight like that. Her hand over her mouth covered up the coughs as she stared out the window. I could tell she was crying from the way her shoulders shook. I thought of going to her, telling her I was sorry, asking her forgiveness.

Suddenly the floor creaked as Dad walked past my hiding place and into the kitchen. He sniffed. Had he been crying too? He walked up behind Mom and pulled her into his arms. She pushed her face into his chest. I can't remember the last time I'd seen my parents hug.

They had a whispered argument about going to the police. Mom blamed Dad for what happened, that it was all his fault because he let me continue racing. I wanted to scream that it wasn't their fault. It was mine for being so stupid. I just wanted to have a boyfriend like the other girls. He made me feel special, grown-up, and it was exciting to keep our secret. Now I know he tricked me so I would let him have sex with me. But the poems sounded so true, and it was all so romantic.

I'm glad they decided not to go to the police. I want to just forget it ever happened. Sometimes I wake up in the middle of the night in a cold sweat from a nightmare where I've confronted him with a gun in my hand. I can never pull the trigger. What's wrong with me that even after everything he did— the sex, the baby, the mean things he said at the end—I still can't hate him enough?

When I look in a mirror I feel a blackness pulling at me. I'm afraid that if I give in, I won't find my way back out. That's when I hang on to the one good thing I learned from Ian. After every practice, he'd ask us to name one mistake we'd made. It might have been taking a gate wrong or missing it entirely, or catching an edge, losing the line leading to a fall. If you couldn't come up with something, he'd make you go back out and push your limits until you did mess up. You don't learn from being perfect and you don't win when playing it safe, was his philosophy. Well, Ian, I didn't play it safe with you and here's what I've learned. The only person I can trust is me and if I make bad decisions, then at least, from now on, they'll be my fault.

Angie

* * *

The coach never came back to the town. He was promoted to full-time team coach and moved directly to BC. And Angie locked the memories in a box and shoved it to the back of her mind, convinced that if she didn't think about it, then it never happened.

CHAPTER NINETEEN - 1969

Creative Defiance

Walking the halls of her school, students tormented Angie with sordid gestures and accusations. Then, Liz Chevalier started showing, and the principal made her drop out of school for being pregnant. The tormenters moved their attention to protesting Liz's removal. And Angie became invisible again. Liz married the father of her child in a quiet ceremony, and the crowd moved on.

Feeling some kinship for Liz's plight, Angie decided to visit her one day after school. Maybe Angie could offer to bring schoolwork to her so Liz could keep up her studies and write her exams. She found Liz slumped at the kitchen table of the house the company had provided to the newly-married couple. Plates littered with the remains of meals covered the table.

"What do you want?" Liz fixed her with a dull gaze, strands of lank hair hanging over her face. "Come to gloat?"

"No, Liz. I came to see, um, how are you?" Angie choked on the stench of spoiling food and cigarette smoke. *Could this have been me? No, Ian would have come around.* She squared her shoulders. "I think it's wrong that they kicked you out of school. You can still study and write the exams. I can help you." Her words came out in a rush.

Liz laughed. "That's why you're here? I should have known, little miss smarty suck up." She drew on her cigarette. "I'm happy to be out of there. And I sure as hell wouldn't want your help." She blew out a violent stream of smoke. "You think you're better than me, but I didn't destroy a family fucking around with a married man! Get out of my house, you little whore!"

Angie stumbled backward out the door and staggered down the street, Liz's words roaring in her head. *Am I really as bad as Liz says?* It had become clear to her that Ian had no intention of following through on all those beautiful promises. She'd been a stupid little girl ever to believe a man twice her age with a family of his own would ever leave it all for her. Where would she be now if she hadn't lost the baby? Probably with relatives in Germany, waiting to give birth so it could be given away, just like what Wendy Barnett's mother did to her last year. Or maybe in a home for unwed mothers.

"Get a grip, Angie. It was a mistake. It's over. You'll never be stupid enough to trust a man again." Angie gave herself a vigorous shake, like a dog shedding its coat of water. "Lock the memories away and move on." Angie lifted her head and walked home.

* * *

One day in May, the guidance teacher brought light back into Angie's life when he handed her a pamphlet for Europa

Kolleg. "This came in the mail today." His smile didn't cover the sympathy in his eyes. "It's a summer program in Germany." He pushed the page across the table to her. "I thought since you probably can't work this summer…" He cleared his throat. "I know you speak German. Anyway, here you go."

Angie had spent the rest of the day rehearsing the arguments to convince her parents to let her go. That night at supper, she barely began her pitch when her mother pulled the pamphlet from her hands.

"Wait, Mom. Let me finish." *Please don't tear it up*, she prayed in her mind.

"It's in Kassel," said her mother.

"Such a pretty little city," said her dad. "She'll learn good German there. How long is the course?"

Angie was reminded of watching a tennis match as she followed her parents' conversation.

"A month. Looks like she stays with a family. She'll be supervised, stay out of trouble."

Angie squirmed under her mother's harsh stare. *Will she ever believe what happened with Ian wasn't my fault?*

"When does it start?"

Angie grabbed the conversational ball. "It starts in early July. And…um…I thought maybe I could visit Tante Liesbeth in East Germany afterward. I'd love to see Ursula. Maybe I could drop in on Oma and Opa Langer in Wiesbaden before coming home?"

"It would look good on her university application," said her mother.

"And she can't work this summer with her leg still healing," her father added.

Angie held her breath. When the silence grew beyond her endurance, she broke in. "So, I can go?"

Her parents exchanged a look, then nodded.

Angie leaped out of her chair and threw her arms around her father. "Thanks, Dad." She felt her mother's body stiffen under her embrace. "Thanks, Mom." *She wants me to be away as much as I want to escape.* The thought gave Angie an untethered feeling like a balloon drifting on the wind. *Will my mother ever forgive me for the shame?*

Two days after completing grade eleven, Angie kissed her parents goodbye and caught the Greyhound bus at the junction where the Pusamakwa road met Highway 17. Fourteen hours later, she stepped into Toronto International Airport.

* * *

Angie had just lugged her suitcase from the third floor to the foyer of the Baumgartners' home when her cousin Monika pulled into the long, circular driveway and stopped at the front door.

Monika emerged from the VW bug, eyes travelling across the stone façade of the two-and-a-half storey home. "Wow! This place is amazing!" The girls embraced.

"My room was up there." Angie pointed to one of the dormers on the third floor. "I had my own bathroom, small study, and bedroom."

"You really got lucky with your family placement," said Monika.

"I know. And it's only twenty minutes from the Kolleg, one bus, and a streetcar, and I'm there. It's made my month here so easy."

"Angelika, don't leave your cousin standing out there. Bring her in," called an elderly woman from the doorway. The string of pearls around her neck glowed in the sunlight.

Angie grabbed Monika's hand and led her up the stairs. "Come on. Frau and Herr Baumgartner are very nice. They treated me like their granddaughter. He's a retired professor from the University, and she retired from her medical practice a few years ago."

"*Guten Tag,* Frau Baumgartner," Monika said as she shook the woman's hand.

"Come in, come in. You have time for something to eat before you start your journey, *neh*?" The woman moved elegantly through the marble-floored foyer and down an oak-panelled hallway. "I've asked Hilda to set up a light snack for us in the west verandah." A low table was set with cheese boards and plates of delicatessen meats. Dark rye bread and golden crusty buns peeked from their snowy napkin nest in a woven basket. Tiny crystal bowls of olives, pickles, tomatoes, and slices of hard-boiled eggs lent their brightness to the table. "Sit, girls. I will go help Hilda with the drinks." Frau Baumgartner disappeared into the house with a swish of her royal blue full-skirted dress.

Monika stood, gaping at the gardens and broad lawn surrounding the screened-in room. "I've never seen such wealth! And only the two of them live here?"

"Monika, please don't start you socialist rant, not here. These nice people have dedicated their lives to helping their community." Angie's gaze held a glimmer of pleading.

"Ah, there you are," a deep voice boomed behind them. "Paul Baumgartner."

Monika shook the tall, lanky man's hand. His navy blue sports coat and khaki pants draped his athletic build. The multitude of wrinkles on his face gave away his age.

"Please, sit." He gestured to the armchairs arranged around the table. "Ah, here come the drinks," he added as Frau Baumgartner returned carrying a silver tray holding a jug of lemonade, Fanta bottles, and a thermos jug of coffee.

"Please begin." Frau Baumgartner picked up the meat plate and passed it around while Angie passed the basket of bread and buns.

Soon, everyone had laden their plates.

"So, Monika, Angelika tells us that you will be starting University in September," said Herr Baumgartner. "What will you be studying?"

"Politics," Monika responded.

Angie held her breath, hoping her cousin wouldn't take Herr Baumgartner's conversational opening gambit as a signal to launch into her tirade about the need for a better distribution of wealth in Germany and its lack of engagement in accepting refugees from war-torn and despotic regimes.

"Very good to hear. We need our young people to take on leadership. Too many of our old guard don't understand the role we must play in supporting our global citizens.

We are too closed to refugees and immigrants, don't you think, Monika?"

"Paul, don't put the girl on the spot. She's our guest, not one of your students," said Frau Baumgartner.

Monika smiled at her hostess. "I don't mind." She turned toward the professor. "I agree. But I'm not interested in actually being a politician. I want to be part of the machinery behind the faces. That's where the power lies."

"Really? Tell me more." The professor and Monika became lost in their world of shared beliefs.

Angie put her hand on Monika's arm, but the conversation between the two didn't flag. "I'm sorry," she said to Frau Baumgartner. "My cousin is very passionate."

"*Ach*, don't worry." Frau Baumgartner smiled. "Let them talk. Paul misses the opportunities he gets to engage with young people. So, how long will you be visiting your family in the East? Will we see again before you fly back to Canada? We have so enjoyed your time with us."

An hour later, Angie hugged the Baumgartners, and the girls waved goodbye as their little car merged onto the residential street.

Angie sat in silence as Monika negotiated her way out of the neighbourhood and onto the main road.

"You're quiet."

"They are such kind people. I'm going to miss them." Angie brushed her cheeks with her hands.

Monika squeezed her cousin's leg. "How was the course? Your German vocabulary has certainly expanded."

Angie laughed. "It was great. We were in class every day from eight to one. A Canadian girl named Joanne was in my class. In the afternoon, we usually met up with one of the guys from Canada, his classmate Madeleine from Belgium, and two guys from Sweden. I spent the evenings doing homework, reading, and learning grammar."

Monika gave her a sidelong glance. "Sure. That's what you told your mother, but give me the real story."

Angie laughed. "Yeah, well, there were parties, nights at the disco, trips around the countryside, you know."

"Now you're talking. So you and one of the Swedes, maybe?"

"Actually, I got to know one of the teachers really well."

Monika's eyebrows climbed her forehead.

"He's a university student, so not much older, and we just clicked on the dance floor."

"And in his car, maybe?" Monika's voice had a teasing note.

Angie felt her cheeks redden.

"Really?" Monika chuckled. "So my perfect little cousin has a wild side."

"What do you mean? I'm far from perfect."

Monika drew her mouth tight. "Not according to Tante Marta. All we hear about is what a great student you are, the awards you win, and organizing and running charity runs and clothing drives. According to your mother, you're like a little Mother Theresa in your town."

Angie almost forgot to breathe. Her mother never told Angie she was proud of her, yet she painted this picture of a perfect daughter to her sisters. Was it to cover up Angie's failings? Or maybe having such an ideal daughter would show her family what a good mother she was.

"*Hallo!* Angelika!"

Monika's voice hit Angie's ear like an echo from a deep cave. "What? Oh, sorry." She adjusted herself in the seat. "Never mind about me. What's the plan for getting the stuff before we cross the border?"

Monika moved to the left turn lane and pulled the car into a large parking lot of the local Karstadt. "We'll load up here. Then it's about two and a half hours to Tante Liesbeth's in Merseburg, depending on how long it takes at the border. Papa suggested we use one of the rural crossing points, less officious."

The girls pushed their cart up and down the aisles of the department store, discussing and sometimes arguing over what should be taken. An hour later, Angie carried four laden bags to the car. Monika followed, dragging two large suitcases. "I don't understand why we need these. They're so flimsy. And besides, East Germans don't need suitcases. They aren't allowed to travel."

"Trust me." Angie opened the suitcases on the pavement beside the car, then directed Monika to hand her bars of soap, pounds of coffee, boxes of tea, and cans of fruit. "Now, take a few pairs of underwear and rub the crotch into the ground so they look used."

"You're kidding, right?" Monika curled her lip.

"Just do it. And then open the package of diapers and make a few look dirty, brown-stained."

Monika's brow drew into a frown, but she did as she was told. Angie wrapped the packaged and canned items in towels and clean diapers and arranged them in the bottom of each suitcase. Next, she folded the jeans, baby clothes, socks, and clean underwear into the cases, throwing the dirty articles on the top. Angie placed the two suitcases in the trunk at the front of the car, then set her own suitcase on top. She wrapped the detergent boxes in sheets and pillowcases and stowed them on the floor behind the front seats. Finally, she threw Monika's overnight case in the back seat and placed a pound of coffee, a box of tea, and several packs of cigarettes in each of two brown paper bags.

"What are those for?" Monika asked.

"Border tax," Angie said. "Put one on the back seat and leave this one on the stuff in the trunk."

Monika tilted her head at Angie. "How did you learn to do this?"

Angie smiled. "Remember I told you the Baumgartners did a lot to help their community? They buy contraband like our stuff and take it to the East, never on a regular schedule and never to the same place. They know many people in Kassel with family in the East, so the Baumgartners help. They started with their housekeeper Hilda's family, and it just grew."

"So Herr Baumgartner told you about this?"

Angie shook her head. "Better. I went with Herr Baumgartner twice, and he showed me how to do it. Most guards understand the game as long as there is something in it for them. And never go through Berlin. Too many *Stasi*." She flipped her hair back. "So you ready? Let's go."

Monika looked at her cousin, eyes wide, then put the car in gear and headed east.

At the border, a *Grenz-Trupper* directed them to the guardhouse to purchase their visitor visas. Monika worked in a grocery store for the summer, so she could only stay overnight. Angie had planned a four-day visit before travelling by train to her grandparents in Wiesbaden. She and her cousin Ursula planned to spend a day in East Berlin. Then Angie would cross through Check Point Charlie to West Berlin to catch a late-night train, and Ursula would return to Merseburg. When Monika and Angie returned to the car, the same *Grenz Trupper* held them back while two border guards searched their vehicle. Another guard stood by the guardhouse with a German shepherd on a leash at his side.

Angie gasped as one of the men set the paper bag to the side before removing her suitcase from the trunk. Opening the case, he moved the contents around, peering into interior side pockets. Monika nudged Angie and motioned with her chin toward the second man who had pulled the overnight bag from the backseat. They collectively held their breath as he prodded the bundles wrapped in sheets on the floor. Suddenly, paper crackled. Both men straightened. Holding the opened paper bags, they cast reproving looks at the girls.

"*Verboten!*" One guard brandished a pound of coffee as if raising a soccer trophy.

"These are contraband. You should know better," said the second man, his deep brown eyes piercing Monika.

Monika squeezed Angie's hand.

"We're sorry, sir," Angie spoke German with a made-up English accent. "We understand. We can't bring them in."

Monika nodded.

"Yes, these will stay here," said the first guard. "Now pack up your car and go."

The girls scrambled to throw the suitcase and travel bag into the vehicle. Monika sprayed gravel as she accelerated through the gate and into East Germany. Once out of sight of the border crossing, she slowed the car.

"My heart is still pounding. How could you stay so cool and calm?"

"Herr Baumgartner said that once they found the bags, they'd stop searching. He said you needed to be contrite so they could bluster before sending you on your way. I knew we would be fine."

CHAPTER TWENTY - 1969

Crossing the Line

According to her wristwatch, it had been three hours since Angie had presented her Canadian passport at Checkpoint Charlie on her way back into West Berlin. The border guard had flipped from page to page as if looking for something. In frustration, Angie reached over the counter to point out her visa. Two guards materialized out of thin air. They'd steered her through a labyrinth of hallways and shoved her into this room.

The chair creaked in protest as Angie pressed her back against the wooden slats. Her fingers traced the fine grooves scarring the tabletop. Could fingernails have made these? She fitted her nails into the grooves, then used her index finger to make a few marks of her own. The light from the naked bulb suspended over her head left the corners of the windowless room in deep shadow. Icy fingers scored her spine. She'd read about rooms like this in spy novels, but how could they think a sixteen-year-old could be a spy?

A female guard stood ramrod straight, hands behind her back, ready to defend the entrance to the room. *She doesn't look much older than me. Is she here to stop me from leaving or to make sure I don't do anything to hurt myself?* Reality crashed into Angie's chest. "It's okay. Everything will be okay," she murmured. Taking calming breaths felt like pushing against water.

"Why am I here?" Angie asked her guard in German.

The woman's stony stare didn't waver.

Angie dropped her head onto the table, cradling it with her arms. The vodka was inciting a war in her gut.

Crisp footsteps echoed down the hallway beyond the door. Angie jolted upright. The female guard—rigid and unsmiling—still stood by the door. Angie pushed her chair back. "I'm out of here."

"Stay," the guard hissed.

"I know my rights. You can't hold me here." She didn't fully gain her feet in the time it took for the guard to stride to Angie's side and press her hand onto her shoulder.

"Sit."

Angie felt the coldness of the woman's palm through her silky summer top. She flinched at the steel in the guard's stare. She sat.

"It'll go easier for you if you cooperate," the guard whispered. She returned to her station.

Moments later, the door burst open. A broad figure blocked the light from the open doorway. The man marched to the table and settled himself on the chair across from Angie while the guard closed the door and returned to her post against the wall. Angie pushed her chair backward to avoid the man's ice-blue eyes glittering crystal-like in the light. His voice reverberated from the concrete walls as he fired his questions. Their interchange was all in German. Name. Nationality. Birthdate. Birthplace.

Angie's pulse thrummed in her ears, but she kept her voice demure.

The man checked her passport with each response.

Suddenly, Angie lunged across the table. "Give me my passport!"

The man shoved her. She fell backward onto the floor, the wind whooshing out of her lungs. The man stared from his seat while she struggled for breath. "Get back to your place."

Angie remained where she was, gasping like a fish in the bottom of a boat, concrete coldness seeping into her spine.

"So weak." The man's voice dripped with disdain. "All bravado until they are caught. Then they cower like a little child." He stood. "Get up!"

When he moved toward her, Angie pulled herself to her feet. "Don't touch me!"

"You're drunk!"

She yanked her chair upright and flopped onto it. "Isn't that the way you want your citizens—too drunk to notice the hell they're living in? You let them start drinking as teenagers so they learn early how to overcome their empty bellies."

The man ignored her outburst, firing the same questions at her again.

"Why are you asking me the same thing? It's all right in front of you in my passport."

The man glared at her over the top of his glasses. "Then tell me, why are you trying to leave the Fatherland? You have everything you need here—education, comradeship, shelter, food. Why would you give that up for the corruption in the West?"

"I'm from Canada." Angie's anger took over her voice. "This isn't my Fatherland. It isn't even a country. It's an armed forced-labour camp." Angie leaned forward. "Education, yes, but only in a field decided on by the state, not the individual."

Earlier that day, Angie and Ursula had been sitting in an outdoor cafe in Alexanderplatz in East Berlin, when Ursula confided her disappointment about the coming school year. The state was forcing her into biology and anatomy courses in high school to prepare for a nursing career, while she wanted to study maths and computers.

Angie's eyes snapped with outrage at her interrogator. "Apartments with no hot water where wind and rain blow through the cracks in the walls. Neighbours who report neighbours in exchange for ration coupons. And don't even get me started about food."

The man sneered. "Ah, that's right. You're the one that tried to incite your fellow citizens against the state at the carrot wagon."

Angie's eyes widened.

The man leaned forward, his eyes piercing her. "We have excellent communication for, what did you call it, a labour camp?"

Yesterday's scene flashed through Angie's mind. Tante Liesbeth had sent Angie and Ursula to the shops. On the way, they'd come across twenty people lined up behind a wagon on the side of the road. Ursula had joined the end of the queue.

"Why are we stopping here?" Angie asked.

"To buy what the farmer is selling." Ursula explained that in East Germany, when you came across a line, you joined it because it meant there was something special to buy.

When Angie asked the person in front of them what they were selling, the woman shrugged. Moving up the line, Angie asked others the same question until she saw people walking away gripping a bunch of six fresh carrots. "He's selling carrots," she yelled down the line.

"My three-year-old son has never tasted a fresh carrot," Angie heard one woman say.

As she walked back down the line to rejoin Ursula, Angie noticed the lacy carrot tops fluttering in the breeze in the farm field beside the lineup. "People, look there." Angie pointed. "Carrots! Why do you have to stand in line for your measly ration?"

"But those carrots are for export," explained the old man next to her. "If we don't export them, our economy will suffer."

"And when our economy suffers, we suffer," added an older woman, her brow drawn into a frown.

"People, you're suffering now. This isn't 'Work by the People for the People' like those stupid signs say." Angie's voice was hot with emotion as she referred to the bright red billboards sporting communist slogans throughout the countryside.

Many of the older people turned away, muttering.

"You don't have to put up with this."

A light ignited in the eyes of a few of the younger people.

"Follow me." A sharp poke in the middle of her back brought Angie to an abrupt stop.

The crowd turned away.

"Come with me." The young man clad in an army-green uniform used his billy club to shepherd her toward a rusty, khaki-coloured jeep. Angie hadn't heard the vehicle arrive. She looked back to see Ursula's crumpled expression. "I'll go tell my mother," Ursula mouthed before running toward the apartment complex. *Oma and Onkel Herman would be proud*, Angie thought.

A cough from the female guard brought Angie back to her present situation. "All I did was show how your government abuses the people."

The interrogator shook his head. "You're lucky all you got was a warning yesterday, thanks to your aunt's intervention. And now you repay her by leaving?"

Angie sighed. "I'm leaving because my visa, which you can see in my passport, expires today, and my Oma and Opa in Wiesbaden are expecting me."

"*Ja*, everybody who sits here has an Oma and Opa somewhere waiting for them. What is their telephone number? Maybe I'll let them know you won't be coming." He stood, his mouth bent into a sneer. "Never mind, they'll hear soon enough about your failed escape." His nose wrinkled as if he'd smelled something rotten, then he turned and stalked out.

Angie had barely brought down her breathing and heart rate when a paunchy grey-haired man with colourful medals and ribbons hanging from his uniformed chest took the chair opposite her. He began with the same questions about her identity, but his manner was much milder. Almost like a grandfather. Still, she began to fidget under his scrutiny as his eyes moved back and forth between her and her passport photo. "Why so nervous? You've done a perfect job learning everything in this passport."

"I didn't have to learn it. It's *my* passport."

"That's what they all say." He raised his eyebrows. "Then tell me why the picture doesn't look like you."

"The passport is three years old. I was thirteen there. Teenagers change a lot."

Angie's hopes rose as the man's silence extended. Suddenly, he slammed his nightstick on the table, barely missing her hands. Angie jumped, hitting her knees on the underside of the table. A macabre grin revealed yellowing teeth. "You traitors are all the same." Then he turned on his heel and walked out.

"No, wait. Please. I'm telling the truth." Angie pounded her fists on the door until the guard guided her back to her chair. "Hey, I want to make a phone call!"

Maybe she could call Edgar? What would she say if his wife answered the phone? Edgar was the young teacher Angie had told Monika about. Tall, blue-eyed, and able to match Angie's dance steps toe to toe, Edgar was enticing. He and Angie had become an item by the time he drove her home that first night. He'd been an eager partner after his initial wide-eyed expression when Angie reached for him while they drove through the dark streets, The coach had taught her well. And what did it matter now? According to her mother she was a bad girl, so she might as well act like one. She knew how to navigate a relationship with a married man, and getting the question of sex out of the way early made the rest of their time together less complicated. But, realistically, what could Edgar do for her from Kassel?

Exhausted, Angie dropped her head back onto her forearms on the table. She should have heeded Herr Baumgartner's advice and avoided crossing in Berlin. Would she ever see her parents again? She scrubbed hot tears from her eyes. Stories of dissenters sent to salt mines in Siberia assaulted her.

"Why don't you believe me!" She screamed into the dark corners of the room. Her shoulders began to shake. Angie had never felt so alone in her life.

"*Psst.*" Barely above a whisper, the sound dropped between her gulps for air.

"What?"

"I'm not allowed to talk, so keep crying."

When Angie continued to stare in silence, her young jailer made waving motions with her hand. Angie resumed her sobbing sounds.

"You speak perfect German," the guard whispered under the muffling effect of Angie's sobs.

"So? My parents moved to Canada, but I've spoken German all my life. And I've been studying in Kassel for a month."

The guard motioned for her to keep crying and continued, "But, if you are Canadian, why can't you speak English?"

Angie threw up her hands, saying through clenched teeth, "Of course I can speak English. But if I did, nobody would understand me."

"Exactly," whispered the guard.

Angie frowned.

The guard resumed her stony stare as the door opened, and yet another uniformed person stepped in, a woman this time.

"*Name.*"

Angie shook her head.

"*Geburtsdatum.*"

Angie shrugged her shoulders. "I don't understand," she said in English.

"*Geburtsort.*"

"I don't know what you're asking."

"*Notfallkontakt.*"

"Note what? I'm not saying another word." Angie sat back in her chair, arms across her pounding heart, lips forced together. It took all her courage to still her shaking legs until the woman left. The guard threw Angie a wink.

"*Danke,*" Angie said to her new ally.

"You're welcome," said the guard in English.

Angie's jaw dropped.

The guard held her finger to her lips and donned her stern mask as the door opened. Two people strode in—Angie's first interrogator, accompanied by a new woman, tight body clad in a drab brown suit, her brown hair drawn into a knot at the back of her head. What was this about? Angie studied the new person. Strength of spirit sparked from the woman's hazel eyes behind round wire-framed glasses. Her smooth complexion gave away her youth. The interrogator sat on the only vacant chair, then motioned to the woman to begin.

"My name is Ilse Schuppenhauer, and I'm here to assess your language facility," the woman said in English.

Angie stared. The woman's English was accented by her German heritage and marked by British vowel sounds, but she spoke with ease and confidence.

"Never tell them your name. She's not your friend." The man said in German. "Get on with it."

Ilse's cheeks were pink as she resumed in English. "Please tell me about yourself."

"What do you want to know?"

"Why don't we start with describing your town, what you like to do for recreation?"

Five minutes into Angie's response, the man held up his hand. "*Halt.*"

Angie turned to the English speaker. "But I'm not finished."

"He doesn't need to hear more. It is evident you are an English speaker."

"So, what now?"

The man strode out. Angie's heart sank. "I have a…" She didn't finish her sentence in the face of the hard stares from both young women still in the room.

"It's okay, as you Americans say," said the English tester. "You are free to leave. We will be taking you to the border crossing."

Angie's didn't bother to correct the woman. Her knees trembled with relief as she walked through the door between her two escorts. The border officer stamped her passport and passed it across the counter. As she prepared to walk through the gate, the English-speaking woman touched her briefly on the forearm. "Some advice?"

Angie struggled to stop herself from running to freedom.

"Don't come back soon. And only come back if you can keep your opinions to yourself."

The young guard stepped forward. "And get your passport picture updated." She gave Angie a slight push forward.

Angie smiled. "Thanks. Hey, do they know you speak English?"

The guard shrugged her shoulders, her lips curling into a smile that seemed to say much more.

Angie vomited in the garbage container on the West Berlin side of the barrier.

CHAPTER TWENTY-ONE - 1970

Choices

The idea first came to Angie after reading the construction update in the weekly *Echo*. The mining company was paying for the project that would fill the remaining gap in the array of services every town needed.

The next day, after school Angie took the exit at the roundabout toward the recently paved two-lane highway out of town. She opened the throttle and popped a wheelie. The Honda 90 had become her freedom machine from the day her father had brought it home in the spring. Learning to drive had been easy here with no traffic lights, just yield signs. *We yield a lot here.* Control of their homes to the company who owned and maintained them, few career opportunities for women, no tolerance of individuality.

Angie was done yielding to the small-minded bullies and her mother's overriding pressure to conform. "A girl riding a motorcycle? What will people think?" No concern for her daughter's safety. "What will people think if I let you walk around showing off your bum in tight bell-bottoms?" Or "Take off that lipstick. It will confirm that you are a loose girl. People will think I'm not doing a good job as your mother." Angie vowed she was going to find a place where she could stand proud of who she was as a person and not be vilified for one "mistake."

Curling out of the curve, Angie brought her bike upright and pulled onto the shoulder. Construction tape flapped against the densely packed, thin-trunked evergreens demarcating the proposed four-hundred-foot frontage for the new service. Heavy machines sat poised like dinosaurs, ready to play shot put with the granite boulders. Satisfied that it was really happening, Angie kicked up a stream of gravel, turned, and sped for home. The project was to be completed by the end of August, which fit her timeline perfectly.

That evening, Angie and her father attended the movie night at the rec centre. Mrs. Savoie had started a classic movie night once a month as part of an ongoing art and film appreciation program. Angie's mother said movies were a waste of time, but Angie and her father never missed a showing. Tonight's offering was the Swedish film, *The Emigrants*. Afterward, father and daughter sat across from each other in a red vinyl booth of Audrey's Diner.

Angie fiddled with the in-booth music juke box while her father ordered their usual coffee and apple pie. Her heart warmed at the sight of the fluorescent light sliding down the slope of his aquiline nose, recognizing it as her own every time she looked in the mirror. Decades of hard labour underground had permanently curved her father's shoulders, and Angie owned some of the deep wrinkles that forever etched his forehead. How many more would she add in the coming weeks?

"What you thinking?" The touch of his cool fingers broke into Angie's thoughts.

She stared blankly into her father's eyes before improvising. "Did the movie bring up memories of when you and Mom immigrated?"

"The Nilssons came a century before we did." Her father's gaze drifted as if he was watching his own memories. "But it's hard to start over with nothing in a strange culture, no matter what century you live in."

The waitress placed their pies and coffees in front of them. "Any word from the university yet, Angie?"

Angie pressed her back into the booth. "How do you know about that, Sue?"

"Trudi told me. She cleans houses on snob hill, and she heard Mrs. Brooks talking to Mrs. Barnett on the phone about your application. Something about a special early scholarship?"

"But how did Mrs. Brooks know?"

"Your mom plays bridge with those ladies, doesn't she?"

Angie nodded. It was one of her mother's proudest accomplishments to be the only miner's wife to play bridge with the big bosses' wives.

Sue raised her eyebrows. "Well?"

Angie gave a wry smile. That's how her town worked. "Not yet." Her thoughts floated through the rising scent of coffee. In March, the guidance teacher had again lit a light at the end of her tunnel when he shared a scholarship opportunity with her. Four of Ontario's smaller universities were offering high-achieving grade twelve students entry into first year without completing grade thirteen. All her teachers had provided glowing references. She'd aced the English and math entry exams and scored over ninety percent on both the German and French tests, her chosen majors.

"Imagine, university." Sue sighed. "The best I can hope for my Ronnie is a company job."

Angie covered her snort with a cough. *The best she can hope for Ronnie is that he stays out of jail. Must be nice to have a mother who sees the best in her child.*

"Just stay away from the boys," Sue continued. "You don't want to end up like half the girls in this town." She cast a glance to the ceiling. "'Course, they do have that pill now."

Her father cleared his throat.

"Oh, sorry." Sue threw him an apologetic smile and moved on.

"I'm so proud of you." Angie's father smiled at her. "And so is your mother."

"I'm surprised Mom even agreed to let me apply since it means I'll be moving away. She's been even stricter since the coach—you know. Like she thinks it was my fault."

Her father reached across the table and grabbed her hands. "She doesn't think that! She loves you. It was hard for both of us to see you hurt."

Angie sighed. "I'd like to think so, but…" She'd lived through too many report cards where her mother's first question was who had the most As or the highest average. There were times when Angie had been tempted to lie and claim her marks were the highest just so she wouldn't have to hear, *If you aren't the best, the first, or the only one, you're nothing*. Angie leaned across the table. "It feels like nothing I do is good enough."

"She wants you to be the best you can be."

"No, Dad, she sees me as an extension of herself. She wants me to be the best that *she* could have been."

Her father winced.

Angie jabbed her spoon into the sugar bowl, then tapped it against the lip of the cup to knock every grain into her coffee. "And I always disappoint her." She hung her head to hide the tears gathering in the corners of her eyes.

"You might not know this, but your mother had a chance to go to university before the war." Her father splayed his fingers along the edge of the table. " As one of the oldest of eleven children, she was needed at home. When the war came, she ended up working as a shop girl."

Angie's spoon stopped in midair. "I didn't know." She shifted in the booth. "I'm sorry the war squelched her dreams, but that's not a reason for her to smother me. All my life, I've been afraid that if I wasn't the best, then she wouldn't love me anymore."

Angie leaned across the table to keep her voice low. "Up until I started high school I could go anywhere, do anything. She was fine with me biking all over the countryside, hanging out with Peter Schmidt, playing monopoly for hours in his basement. Then bang, I turned fifteen and I couldn't even go to a movie." Angie couldn't stop talking. "Peter was two years older than me. We could have been doing all kinds of stuff." She flung her hands in the air above the table. "Why was it okay for us to be unsupervised? Because he was German? Because I wasn't in high school? What was so magical about changing schools that she had to slam down the gates of hell—no boyfriends, no dances, no mini-skirts or jeans." Angie gave an ugly laugh. "She never questioned the extra practices with the coach. Because he was an adult?" Angie was panting.

Her father sat with his back pressed into the booth. His expression reminded her of what a bug might look like after impacting the windshield of a speeding car.

Angie's breathing slowed.

He took a shaky breath. "Feel better?"

She nodded. "Sorry."

"It's your mother's way to protect you from making the same mistakes she made."

"So I'm her do-over?" Angie searched her father's face. "What mistakes? She always does the right thing."

Her father puffed out his cheeks. It felt like an eternity before he answered. "That's her story to tell."

The cutlery and dishes rattled as Angie hit her fist on the table. "Damn it, Dad. Why does everyone say that?"

Diners at a nearby table stared at them.

Her father gave Angie a hard glare.

"I'm sorry, Dad. I shouldn't have done that. It's just so frustrating."

Several minutes of silence reigned as her father sipped his coffee and Angie played her fork through her pie.

"Tim Niedermeir was a good friend that she let you see. He seemed such a nice young man," her father spoke softly. "I haven't seen him in church lately."

"His parents sent him to live with his aunt in Orillia where he's undergoing 'correction therapy.'" Angie made air quotations with her fingers.

Her father's brow furrowed. "Correction therapy?"

"Yeah. He told them he's gay, so they sent him to a program to get straight."

"Oh." Her father ran his hand through his brush cut.

Angie went back to stirring her coffee. "It seems you and Mom fight a lot about me. I appreciate you taking my side, but I feel like I'm wrecking your marriage."

Her father shook his head. "Your mother's and my relationship is not your responsibility. We'll work things out. We always do." His eyes seemed to plead. "Sometimes I regret that I didn't get more involved with the decisions she made in raising you."

"You were perfect, Dad." She forced a smile. "Besides, if my plan works, I'll be out of here soon."

Angie's father reached across the table and squeezed her hands. "You need to spread your wings, *Schatzi,* and find your place. If it doesn't happen this year, then next year for sure after you finish high school the universities will be lining up to have you." He forced a grin.

They clinked their forks together and dug into their pie.

"I'm going to miss this."

"Me, too." Angie felt her voice strangle around the words.

On her second visit to the site, pine, spruce, and fir trees littered the area, looking like a giant had plucked them up, roots and all, so his children could play pick-up sticks. She walked the perimeter of the cleared site. What had families been doing when they lost someone over the past thirty years? Finding a place in another town? She doubted that it was legal to bury them in the backyard.

Two weeks later, the trees were gone, and the ground had been graded level. Orange stakes mapped out one broad laneway up the middle, with pathways branching right and left at regular intervals. It didn't overlook a lake, and there weren't any hundred-year-old leafy oak trees shading the grounds like the ones she'd seen in the south, but it did have a granite boulder the size of a VW Bug glistening with grey-green lichen in the northwest corner. The screech of a blue jay pulled Angie out of her reverie. It was twilight—time to hop on the bike and get home.

A few days before the Grand Opening, Angie hid her bike in the bush beside the new parking lot and clambered onto the corner boulder. This would be a lovely spot, a mix of sun and shade, quiet, away from the main path. Or perhaps right in the centre would be a better spot? Her mother would see it as fitting, especially if her daughter was the first one buried here.

Angie flicked an unopened envelope against her hand. The blue-and-gold university coat of arms glinted from the top left corner. Her mother's agreement had been limited to applications to Laurentian because she could live with her Uncle Herman and Aunt Karin in Sudbury, and Waterloo Lutheran because her godparents, Peter and Elisabeth Erb, could keep an eye on her from Kitchener. Angie ran her finger under the sealed flap. Her eyes scanned the single page. Her heart sank.

> *Thank you for your application to the Grade Twelve Special Program at Laurentian*

> *University. We regret to advise you that although you are an excellent candidate, the faculty of our Translation Program have determined that due to the complexity of the curriculum, they will only consider successful completion of grade thirteen as a minimum entry requirement. We hope that you will consider reapplying next year . . .*

And blah, blah, blah. They hadn't even considered that she had spoken both languages all her life or that she completed the advanced German program at Europa Kolleg in Germany. Angie balled the letter and threw it into the bush beside her, scaring the rabbit hovering at the edge of the clearing.

Damn! One choice eliminated. "Come on, Angie! Don't be such a baby." She scrubbed her palms across her cheeks in frustration. The white-throated sparrow's call from the pine behind her sounded like, "University or first one in here, here, here" in her head. The bird was right. University meant freedom and a future. Being here on this site brought peace. Both meant escape. Both would be a first that would make her mother proud. She still had a few days to make a decision. Angie pulled her bike from the bushes and headed home.

That evening, Angie's father was unusually quiet during supper, and his forehead sported wrinkles like the folds on an accordion. She knew something was up when he joined her in walking the dog.

"Street or bush?" she asked as they walked out of the driveway.

"Bush." He turned toward the walkway between two houses that allowed pedestrians access from one street to the next without going around the block. Entering the forest beyond the recreation centre, they followed the trail through the pines used by hikers in summer and snowmobilers in winter. They walked side by side on the packed earth while Robbie sniffed the edges of the pathway ahead of them. Her father's pace slowed. "The coach." He cleared his throat. "The men were talking after shift..." Angie's father stopped and turned to face her. "The coach is dead."

Angie caught her breath. The bird song faded.

"Angie?" Her father touched her arm.

Angie felt short of breath.

"It's okay to cry." Her father's eyes shone in the gathering twilight. "I know you cared for him, even though he hurt you."

"How?" she asked.

"He was found in his car at the end of a deserted mountain road."

"Shot? Stabbed?" Angie's voice was hard.

Her father grimaced. "He died of an aneurysm. His brain exploded."

Angie bit her lip.

"There were signs that he'd been with someone, that when he...they believe the person just left him there."

"Signs?" Angie's voice shook. "You mean he was screwing a woman who just left him there when he croaked on her?"

Angie's father blanched, then pulled her into his arms. "It's over. You can put it behind you now."

Angie pushed back. "Dad, I'm okay." Tears of joy, of sadness—Angie didn't know which—streamed down her cheeks while her mouth curled into a grin. "So many times I thought about how I would hurt him back. I fantasized about going to BC and waiting for him in the dark outside his house, blowing his brains out, but this— I couldn't have scripted it any better." Angie loved her dad, but she knew he could never understand that the memories, the maelstrom of conflicting emotions, would never disappear. Only knowing the coach wouldn't be hurting anyone else ever again made it easier to go forward.

Angie and her father retraced their steps. As they walked down the driveway, she turned to her dad. "Can you please tell Mom? I can't talk to her about it."

"Sure." He kissed her on the forehead.

Angie and her father found her mother sobbing at the kitchen table, a litter of envelopes scattered in front of her.

Angie's father held her mother by the shoulders. "Marta, what's wrong?"

Her mother kept repeating, "How can it be? She was so young."

Angie picked up a flimsy blue airmail letter. "Dad?"

He pulled her mother into his arms. "Has something happened to someone in the family?"

Her mom's whole body shook against his chest.

Angie scanned the letter. "It's from Tante Liesbeth." She struggled to make out her aunt's gothic writing. "Dad, I think Rolf's daughter, Mandy, was hit by a car and killed." She held the page up to her father.

"She was only three years old," Marta wailed. "Her poor mother."

Angie left her parents in the kitchen and flopped onto her bed, arms folded behind her head as she stared at the ceiling. Rolf was only a couple of years older than her. She remembered the uproar a few years ago when Tante Liesbeth had written that he'd fathered a child. Now that baby girl was dead, and Angie's mother was inconsolable. And that baby was across the ocean, a child her mother had never met. Angie had been so focused on finding an escape that would make her mother proud by being the first that she'd never considered the impact her choice would have. But she had to get out, one way or another.

Laurentian had already turned her down. What if Waterloo Lutheran did, too? It would be easy, she'd thought. Just drive the motorcycle, full speed, into a rock-cut along the highway. People would think it was an accident. Lately, she'd begun to worry about how her father would feel, but until today, she'd never considered that her mother would be anything but proud. Her daughter would be the first person buried in the town's cemetery. Would she even have the courage to do it now?

A soft tap on her bedroom door. "*Schatzi*? You awake?"

"Come in, Dad. How's Mom?"

"Sleeping. Here, this came for you today. It was on the table." He handed her a large white envelope. "I'm going to bed."

"Thanks for today." She paused. "Dad, why are you staring at me?"

"Something has changed." He smiled. "You look lighter." He kissed her on the forehead. "Goodnight." He closed the door behind him.

Angie snapped on the bedside lamp. Taking a deep breath, she slowly raised her head and forced herself to look deeply into the mirror on her dresser. A smile spread across her face. There it was, a small flicker of the old light was back in her eyes.

Sitting back on the bed, the envelope her father had given her crackled beneath her butt. The purple-and-gold logo shone in the dim light. She opened it. Her eyes scanned the letter while her fingers fluttered along the edges of the stack of additional pages. Angie dropped off to sleep, clutching the papers to her chest. In her heart, she'd known she could never follow through on her other choice, and now she wouldn't have to. Everything was going to be okay.

Angie was up early the following day, rummaging through the back of the garage before going to school.

"There you are!"

Angie jumped at her father's exclamation.

"What are you doing?" Concern clouded his eyes.

"Is Mom okay?"

Her father nodded. "She's writing a letter to Rolf and his family right now and muttering swear words at the East German government for not allowing overseas phone calls to their citizens."

Angie turned back to the wall of deck planks. "Do you know where my skis are?" The blue, red, and white Rossignol emblem caught her eye. "Oh, never mind." She pulled the skis clear of the other lumber and leaned them against the front corner of the garage.

"Angie." Her father blocked her movements. "What's going on?"

"Waterloo Lutheran accepted me! I start summer school in July and go into first year in September." She grinned. Was that a flash of relief on her father's face before the joy for her success lit his eyes? "I bet I can get a job teaching skiing on the weekends at Chicopee in Kitchener or maybe at Blue Mountain." She could already feel the wind in her face, hear the rhythmic shushing of her skis on the snow, taste the snowflakes melting on her tongue.

* * *

June 20, 1970

Dear Diary,

I'm going to University!

I haven't written to you for a while. After all the stuff with Ian, my mind has been wrapped in a dark shadow and I haven't felt like putting things into words. But today, it's like the sun is shining in my head again. I can't believe I actually thought it would be a good idea to kill myself just to make my mother proud that I would be the first person buried in our new cemetery.

I leave in a week. Dad will drive me to White River to catch the train to Toronto where I'll switch trains to Waterloo. Classes start on Thursday, July 2. It seems weird to start in the middle of the week but I guess they want to fit in the six weeks of summer school and still have part of the summer left. I'm taking French 101 and German 100. Feels a bit like cheating, but they're both required courses to get into my French and German translation program. If I get a B average or better, I will be accepted into first year in September. If I get As in both, I will get a scholarship that pays my tuition for the year. The best part is, the two courses don't cost me anything and they even pay my residence fee for the summer, so I don't have to use any of the money I've saved up.

Mom's really happy. Not sure if that's because she has something to brag about since I'm the first one in Pusamakwa to do this, or she's just relieved that I'll be gone and she won't have to keep monitoring my every move.

I'm going to have a roommate, which is a little scary since I've never shared a room. I hope we get to be friends. I can be just Canadian, and she'll be smart and a serious student like me since she got into the program. Classes are from eight in the morning until noon so if we are friends, we'll have time in the afternoons and evenings to maybe go to a movie or go shopping or do whatever university students do when they aren't doing homework or studying.

I can't wait to start.

Angie

CHAPTER TWENTY-TWO - 1970

Mini-skirts, Jeans, and Rouladen

Angie dropped her battered blue suitcase on the sidewalk and pulled the crumpled paper from her pocket. Her eyes moved from the address on the page to the prominent black numbers beside the green wooden door of the house in front of her. "86 Bleecker Street," she confirmed to herself under her breath. "This is it." She took a few deep breaths. "Here goes." She hefted her suitcase, straightened her back, and, with her head up, started up the cracked concrete path.

Suddenly, the door opened. Two girls exited, chatting as they descended the wooden porch stairs. Angie dropped her suitcase on the patch of worn grass beside the path and was moving out of the way when the girl with flaming red hair stopped in front of her. "Hi."

"Hi." Angie forced herself to keep her head up. She'd never seen such bright green eyes. "Um, is this French House?"

Both girls nodded. The redhead's companion smiled and extended her hand. "I'm Jenny. Welcome, or um, *bienvenue*." She turned to her friend. "Are we supposed to speak French outside the house or just inside?"

The redhead reached across Jenny. "I'm Laura. And the rule is we speak French in the house."

"I'm Angie."

"Come on. We'll show you to your room. You're with Mary."

Angie reached for her suitcase, but Jenny was already swinging it onto the porch, letting it bounce against each tread as she went. "Is this all you have?" Her soft brown eyes were wide.

"I'm in room five." Angie turned her head from Laura to Jenny. "And no, I have a trunk back at the Women's Res."

"Yup, that's Mary's room. Let's get this stuff upstairs. Then we can go get your trunk." Laura led the way through the door.

Angie took her suitcase from Jenny and followed Laura through a darkly paneled foyer and up an ancient staircase that creaked with every step. Jenny kept up a running commentary as they progressed. "You can leave your coat and boots in the foyer. Everyone has a hook and cubby. To the left is the common room or, as we call it, the *salon*. And to the right is Françoise's suite."

Angie threw a look of confusion over her shoulder at Jenny.

"Françoise is our live-in tutor. She's a grad student from Paris."

Angie's head was spinning. What was a grad student? And what did a tutor do? She didn't want to appear stupid, so she decided to figure it out later.

"The hall beside the stairs takes you to our kitchen. It has a big table that fits all of us, and we have a sunroom off the back of the house."

At the top of the stairs, six doors opened onto a narrow hallway. Three were numbered 1, 2, and 3, and the doors at each end were labeled '*Salle de bain.*' "Debra and Karen, Cheryl and Dina, Toni and Barb." Jenny rhymed off the names as she pointed to each door. "They all lived here last year. As the newbies, we get the attic rooms." The door facing them had a picture of a person on a staircase. Laura opened it and began mounting another narrower and steeper staircase.

As Angie dragged the suitcase up the treads, Jenny pushed from behind. Would her trunk even fit up these stairs?

"Don't worry, if your trunk doesn't fit, you can empty it here and carry your stuff up. There's a storage space in the basement beside the laundry room where you can store it. That's what I did."

It was as if Jenny had read her mind.

"Thanks." Angie smiled gratefully.

The four girls shared the two rooms with slanted ceilings under the eaves at the top of the house. Their bathroom had two toilet rooms with tiny sinks on one side of the landing and two shower stalls on the other. It was much tighter than the Women's Residence rooms where she'd spent six weeks in the summer, but this was much quainter. And to Angie, it felt like freedom.

It turned out that Angie's trunk did fit up the stairs, thanks to Jenny and Laura pushing from behind while Angie tugged it up each stair. It sat perfectly beside her bed as a night table. Once she'd unpacked, she decided to explore the house. Laura and Jenny had gone to Follwell's Convenience Store at the corner. Jenny informed her that her new roommate, Mary, was probably in the library.

Whoever had provided the décor for the *salon* must have thought plastering the walls with posters depicting Parisian street scenes would inspire the students living there. The Victorian mansion, located on a tree-lined street adjacent to the university campus, was the university's French immersion experiment. There was only one rule: speak French while in the house. There were no restrictions concerning male visitors as long as you were considerate of the housemates, and there was no curfew. Everyone had a key to the front door, so there was no fear of being locked out. During her summer stay in the Women's Residence, Angie had been locked out several times, written up for male visitors after hours, and for openly consuming alcohol in the hallways. No wonder Miss Parker, the middle-aged spinster Matron, or warden as Angie thought of her, of the Women's Residence had directed Angie to campus housing. She'd suggested Angie might be better suited to the remaining vacancy in French House.

Angie met Françoise in the sunroom during her exploration. While smoking her *gauloise* and blowing the smoke out of the screen door, Françoise explained that as part of her Master's thesis on second language acquisition for her home university, the Sorbonne, she would be living in the house for the year. She would assist the girls with their French studies and teach language labs and seminar groups for the university. Françoise was thrilled to hear Angie's comfort in French and suggested she could help her challenge some of the first and second-year language and grammar courses. Angie welcomed any advice or assistance that would reduce her time, and therefore her costs, in completing her degree.

* * *

"Come in," Angie called in response to an exuberant rap at the door.

"Ready for supper?" Jenny peeked around the door. "Wow! This looks homey." She took in Angie's purple and gold crocheted bed cover. "Those sweaters are gorgeous." She fingered the yarn as Angie put them into drawers.

"Thanks."

"Did you make them?"

"Some. And my mom."

"Will you make me one? Is it expensive?"

Angie hesitated. She'd never made anything for someone other than herself. "Sure," she said.

Laura appeared behind Jenny. "Thought we'd show you to the dining hall." Both girls had changed from shorts into mini-skirts, reminding Angie of her summer wardrobe that she'd dropped into the Salvation Army bin before returning to Pusamakwa. Her mother would never have let her return to university if she'd seen the mini-skirts and jeans Angie had purchased with her savings.

"Thanks, but I know where it is already. Let's go!"

"We can wait out here while you change," said Laura. "Hey, how do you know your way around campus already?"

Angie's smile turned down at the corners. "All my clothes are like this." She gestured at her baggy cotton pants and collared blouse. "My mom doesn't allow me to wear mini-skirts or jeans." She took a breath. "And I know the campus because I attended summer school here."

"You're one of those Grade 12 Special Scholarship students!" Jenny's eyes lit up. Turning to Laura, she added, "She must be brilliant."

"Wait here." A few moments later, Laura returned with a blue mini-skirt and an orange, yellow, and green striped top. "Put this on." She thrust the outfit at Angie. "Tomorrow, we've got to get you some new clothes."

"Thanks, but I couldn't…"

"Well, you can't go around dressed like that. How did you ever survive summer school?" Laura pulled Jenny out of the room and closed the door. "We'll wait out here."

Over supper, Angie told her new friends about how she'd "survived summer school" with her temporary wardrobe. Now that she was in school, Angie needed her money for books and meals not covered by her scholarship, so she'd have to make do with what she had. By the end of supper, the girls had devised a plan where they would advance Angie money so she could buy some new clothes, and she'd knit them sweaters.

* * *

September 10, 1970

Dear Diary,

I'm living in French House but it feels more like living in heaven. My room-mate Mary is from Stratford, Ontario. She worked as an au pair in Paris last year. She's super studious and spends every spare moment in the library and goes home every weekend to work in the family store.

I've made friends with two other first year students in the house, Laura and Jenny. Yesterday they went clothes shopping with me. I bought a plain black mini skirt to go with the sweaters and tops I already have. Laura talked me into a blue and green flowered mini dress that flares over my hips. I feel like I'm wearing wings cause the gauzy sleeves widen like bells over my wrists. And, with my long hair hanging over my shoulders, I kind of look like a hippie. They picked out bell-bottom jeans that hug my butt and squeeze my waist so tight I can barely move or breathe, but they do look cool. We bought a pattern and the yarn, and I already started knitting their sweaters to pay them back for the clothes.

Last night I wore my new dress to the frosh week pub night on campus. I was terrified.

Jenny and I stood around talking to other girls while guys kept asking Laura to dance. Then a cute guy asked me to dance and before I knew it, they called last dance and it was after midnight. As we were leaving, a few guys asked us to meet them this weekend at a bar called "the Loo" in downtown where all the WLU students hang out.

I feel so free being with people my age who don't know my background, who seem to like me for who I am. I can start over, and not worry that someone isn't going to like me. Sometimes when I listen to Jenny, Laura, and the other girls talking about guys and managing physical relationships, I feel like a toddler learning the rules all over again. I seem to have jumped right over a part of growing up where you make decisions and limits about how far you are comfortable going with the strength to walk away if the guy doesn't like it.

The best part is that I got A+ in both my summer courses. Quelle surprise, considering I've spoken both languages all my life. Free tuition means I have money for books, food, and residence without having to find a part-time job, and any money I make teaching skiing will help for next year.

Time to get some sleep. Orientation to classes starts at 8:30 tomorrow morning.

Angie

* * *

The housemates came together every Sunday for a home-cooked, family-style supper throughout the academic year. Everyone chipped in ten dollars and took turns preparing the meal.

Haunted by the events of her disastrous thirteenth birthday sleepover, Angie froze when it came to her turn. What could she prepare that they wouldn't laugh at or refuse to eat? Barb had made roast beef, cooked medium rare and juicy, unlike the well-done dry ones Angie's mother had taught her to cook. The skin on Debra's roast pork had crackled. Karen prepared something Angie had never eaten before—shepherd's pie—a layer of minced beef, another of peas and carrots, and a topping of mashed potatoes. When Toni made lasagne from her Italian mother's recipe, Angie considered making something German. Still, the world loved Italian foods, while you rarely saw lineups in front of a German restaurant. The week leading to her turn, Angie scarcely slept, and when she did close her eyes, curled lips and sympathetic glances on the faces of her housemates tortured her dreams. Midweek, she called her godmother, Elisabeth Erb, in Kitchener.

" Make *rouladen*," Elisabeth said.

"What if they don't like them?"

" What's not to like?" Elisabeth chuckled. "Every culture rolls foods around other ingredients. Ukrainian pierogis, Chinese dumplings, Italian cannelloni, every culture has cabbage rolls. The British put pastry around meat."

"Maybe I should just move out."

Silence.

Angie sighed. "Okay, but where do I get *rouladen* meat? Mom had to get it from the German butcher in Port Arthur."

"*Ach* Angelika, you live in the most German city in Canada. I'll give you the name of the best butcher at the farmers' market. He's cheaper than the stores."

That Saturday morning in early October, Angie stepped into the Kitchener Market hall and was instantly transported. Mennonite *Plattdeutsch*, Bavarian German, *Hochdeutsch*, and dialects Angie had never heard filled the air as the vendors called customers to their wares. The cinnamon and almond aromas drew her feet toward the bakers. Her stomach growled at the savoury scents of grilling sausages, transporting her back to her father's barbecue. She soaked up the atmosphere, wandering among the stands until she found the butcher Elisabeth had recommended. With the *rouladen* meat banging against her leg in her carrier bag, she followed her nose to the earthy smells of the fresh vegetable vendors.

On Sunday evening, the nine housemates and Françoise took their usual seats around the pine harvest table that dominated the kitchen. Debbie poured the wine.

"Oh, real wine glasses. Where'd they come from?" Karen examined her glass.

"I asked my mother if she had extra wine glasses when I was home this weekend. She thrust a cardboard box into my hands." Barb changed her voice to imitate her mother's. "Here, take these. I don't know how many there are here, but you and your friends are welcome to them." Barb simulated a sniffing sound.

"I asked her if she was sure because the box was taped shut."

Barb pulled her face into presumably her mother's grimace. "I'm sure. They're from your Aunt Mona. You've seen her house. The woman has no taste." She humphed. "Besides, I don't understand how the university can expect you to drink wine from water glasses."

Everyone exploded into laughter.

"To Barb's mother!" Said Debra. Everyone clinked their glasses while echoing Debra's toast.

"Hey, Angie, you're killing us. The aroma is making my mouth water," said Cheryl.

"I'm starving."

"Smells amazing."

Angie stirred the gravy, swallowing repeatedly to quiet her nerves. All day, she'd felt like she would vomit with fear.

"We want food! We want food!" The girls began to chant, banging their cutlery on the table.

Angie turned from the stove to face everyone. The tradition dictated that the cook explain the dish and why they had chosen it for the occasion before serving.

"*Silence, tout le monde! Elle est prête!*" Laura called.

The room hushed. All eyes were on Angie. She gripped the handle on the oven door behind her to stop her from running out of the room. With a deep inhale of breath, she began. "This meal is called *rouladen*. It's from Germany. You roll bacon, onion, mustard, and pickle inside a slice of beef. It's usually served with *Rotkohl*, red cabbage, and *Kartoffelklösse*, which are potato dumplings, but I've made mashed potatoes instead of the dumplings."

"Sounds delicious."

"Can't wait to try it."

"So why did you make this for us?" Debra prompted.

"*Rouladen* is a special Sunday meal or for a family celebration. You guys have become my family, and I wanted to celebrate that." Angie's eyes glistened. *Don't make a fool of yourself. Don't cry.*

The room stayed quiet. Then Jenny said, "I'm starving. Let's eat."

Everyone lined up for Angie to fill their plates at the stove.

Toni caught Jenny's attention across the table. She cast meaningful looks from Jenny's eyes to the meat roll on her plate swimming in rich brown gravy. Toni mouthed the word poop. Jenny smothered a giggle. Toni covered a snort with a hand across her mouth. Mary intercepted the interaction. "What's so funny?" She whispered to Jenny.

Jenny spoke from behind her hand. "What do these remind you…" She coughed to disguise the guffaw bubbling from her throat.

"These are delicious," Laura declared. "What?" Her brow wrinkled at the tittering around the table. "They are. Have you tried them?"

Angie felt herself shrinking lower in her chair. She wanted to run from the table and hide in her room. Then she looked up to find Debra staring hard at her. Debra's expression seemed to say, *Run now, and you'll be isolating yourself forever. Standing up and embracing it makes you one of them.* Debra was a couple of years older and had seen a lot of life before coming to university.

Angie cleared her throat. "I know. They look like poop, don't they?" She laughed at the shocked expressions. "But I assure you, they taste great." She stabbed a chunk with her fork, lifted it in the air, and called. "*Guten Appetit!*" And popped the morsel in her mouth. Her new friends followed suit, and the kitchen echoed with the chorus of "*Guten Appetit!*"

CHAPTER TWENTY-THREE - 1971

Just an Ordinary Girl

Angie sat on the narrow wooden bench, watching her teammates congratulating each other.

Debbie tapped her on the shoulder, commenting, "Nice game!" and Sue said, "Great job on the mound." Angie smiled.

The team dissipated quickly into the small crowd of supporters sitting on the grassy hillside that formed a natural amphitheatre for the ball field. Some kissed boyfriends or husbands who flung their arms around them and led them up the hill. Others caught young children running toward them, arms wide and yelling, "Mummy!" Car doors opened and closed to a chorus of calls.

"Coming to the hotel?"

"Yup, see you there."

"Not tonight. Gotta get the baby to bed."

"See you Thursday."

The lowering sun reflected golden off the last of the dust drifting to its resting place on the field. Bending over, Angie was shoving her baseball glove and running shoes into her gym bag when a new voice crested over her head.

"You pitched a great game."

Angie sat up, almost banging her head against the Levi-clothed crotch of the man with the deep voice who stood in front of her.

He jumped backward. "Whoa! Watch it!"

Angie glared at him. "Serves you right. You shouldn't stand so close." Her voice petered out as she met eyes as dark as moss. "Um, thanks." She rose, threw her bag over her shoulder, and walked away.

"Too bad you have a tell." The voice called from behind her. "That's why they were hitting you in the last innings."

Angie turned and started up the hill. "I don't have a tell," she called back over her shoulder,

Rapid footsteps caught up to her. "Yes, you do. You're a really good pitcher." He hesitated.

"For a girl?" Angie kept walking.

The man rushed to stand in front of her, forcing her to stop. His eyes were only a few inches above Angie's. "That's not what I was going to say." He brushed his hand backward through his deep brown hair.

Angie smothered a smile. His wiry hair looked just like those cartoon characters after they'd been electrocuted.

"Why are you so prickly? I was only trying to offer some friendly advice." He offered his hand. "I'm Rick."

Angie was tempted to move past him and keep walking, but she was intrigued by the sincere, almost vulnerable quirk to the corners of his mouth. She shook his hand. "Angie."

"Can we start over?"

Angie softened her shoulders.

"I'm new here. I mean, I've been here before, visiting my aunt and uncle, but I didn't grow up here or anything. I'm sorry, I'm rambling." He exhaled loudly. "Anyway, I got the feeling you might be new, too?"

Angie shook her head. "Why would you think that?"

"Everybody seemed polite, but I noticed no one invited you to the bar." His brow furrowed.

"That's just the way it is for me here. And, no, I'm not new. I moved here when I was eleven." Angie stepped around Rick and headed up the hill.

He followed her. "Then they're just mean?" He pointed in the direction of where the crowd had been. "Do you want to go somewhere for a beer? Or a Coke if you're not old enough."

"I'm old enough. What is it you want?"

"To talk to you. Get to know you."

I want to have sex with you,. Angie finished his comment in her head.

"My uncle got me a job at the mine for the summer. I screwed up last year, partied my way through a whole year of university, so my parents won't support me until I pay them back."

Last thing I need is a party boy.

He raised his hands palms up, then shrugged. "I don't know anyone here and could use a friend. Please, can we start over? "

He looks like a contrite puppy who's just been caught tearing a hole in the sofa, and he is cute. Having a friend would be nice. He'd be good practice for my new approach, sticking to

263

limits. Angie cleared her throat. "Sure, why not? Let's go to the hotel for a beer."

"Yes!" His eyes narrowed. "We don't have to go the hotel; I mean, there's the diner if you want."

"The hotel. I'm sure." Angie's voice shook. *Was it with conviction or uncertainty? Not important.* She was done with slinking away from her peers. It was time to bring the new Angie out in Pusamakwa.

Rick led Angie to his blue 1966 Pontiac Laurentian and they drove up Ohsweken Drive, halfway around the traffic circle, and into the Pusamakwa Motor Inn parking lot.

Rick held the door for Angie to enter ahead of him. She forced her way through the smoky haze, the fugue of stale beer catching in her throat. Rick bumped into her while she stood just inside the dingy room, assessing the best strategy for seating. The table for two in the corner screamed intimacy. The last two vacant stools at the bar were between her father's friend, Mr. Steiner, a regular, and Liz Chevalier, who was chatting up some guy in a suit. No, for more reasons than Angie wanted to enumerate. *What's Liz doing here? Her baby isn't even a year old. And the guy has to be a salesman staying at the hotel.* They were the only men who wore suits in town except at church on Sundays or for a funeral, and Angie hadn't heard of any deaths in the past few days.

"Hey, Angie. Come on over." Debbie beckoned with her arm from the long table, crowded with some of her teammates and their partners.

Debbie was already adding two chairs to the end of their table. *Damn. Too late to decline. Hey, that's Adam from the ski team with her.* Like most of the guys in town, Adam had gone to work at the mine. At least he finished high school, unlike most who were lured by the good money once they finished Grade ten. *Good for Debbie. Adam was a kind, gentle guy.* Angie turned to catch Rick's eye, hoping he'd suggest they go elsewhere.

"Your boyfriend's welcome to join us, too," Debbie added.

Rick shrugged and pressed Angie forward with his hand on her back.

Angie's mouth twitched into a watery smile as she settled on one of the vacant chairs. "Um, he's not my—"

Rick's hand shot past her and shook Debbie and Adam's hands. "I'm Rick," he called, then waved to everyone down the table before settling beside Angie.

Debbie leaned on her elbows. "You new in town, Rick?"

"Yeah. Just here for the summer. I'm staying with my aunt and uncle. You might know them, the Hudsons?"

Adam pushed two glasses of draft in front of them. "I work in accounting with Budd. Nice people." He turned to Angie. "Helluva game you pitched there. Get rid of that tell, and we'll wipe Marathon off the map at the tournament."

Rick threw Angie a triumphant look. "We'll get rid of it."

Angie opened her mouth, but the denial died on her lips as Adam continued his conversation with Rick. "You a university student?"

"Yeah, Waterloo. Hopefully they'll take me back in September."

"Waterloo!" Debbie grinned. "That's where you are, right Angie?"

"Well, I *am* in Waterloo but not at…"

Debbie's attention turned to join a conversation further down the table.

"Never mind." Angie finished in a whisper.

Rick held up his glass. "Cheers."

Angie clinked it with hers. Their eyes met across the rims. "You must be at WLU."

Angie nodded.

They drifted into a world of their own, talking and sipping and collecting information from each other. Angie learned Rick was an Air Force brat, so his family had moved to a new base every few years. He'd lived in Ontario, BC, Nova Scotia, and northern Alberta before his father had been stationed in Wiesbaden, Germany. When his father was posted to Kenya, his parents enrolled Rick and his younger sister in boarding school in England, where Rick finished high school. His father was now retired, but his parents had enjoyed Kenya so much that his dad had signed on as a teacher with CUSO for three years. Angie relaxed as they shared stories about Germany. Soon, she found herself swapping anecdotes about Austria, France, and Switzerland, where Rick and his family had vacationed, and where she had skied.

"You've travelled a lot," Rick commented.

"You mean for a miner's kid? Or an immigrant kid?" Angie tilted her head to check for signs of derision or disbelief in Rick's expression.

Rick sat back, hands up in a gesture of surrender. "No, none of that. You have to admit, though, that there probably aren't a lot of kids here in Pusamakwa whose parents have taken them to Europe."

"Oh, her parents didn't take her."

Angie's shoulders went rigid. That voice was like nails on a chalkboard to her. She turned slowly. Sharon, red hair bouncing against her shoulders like always, grinned down at her. "Long-time no see, Angie."

Ralph waved at her from behind Sharon's shoulder. "Hi, Angie. You look great."

Sharon turned to glare at him. "Go sit with Pierre." She gestured to the end of the table where Pierre Morrisette stood, arm raised. Pierre and Ralph had been close friends in high school, bonding over their keen interest in technology and photography. Ralph looked back at Sharon.

"Go on. I'll join you in a minute." Sharon's voice dripped with a tone generally reserved for encouraging a child or a puppy.

Sharon and Ralph? She hadn't seen that coming.

Adam stood. Sharon settled in his chair, pushing her back into it and wiggling her butt so her breasts wobbled. "Angie travelled all on her own, just with her skis…and her coach, of course." Her teeth glistened through the smile she directed at Angie, even though her comment was meant for Rick. Angie's skin stung as the yellow sparks from Sharon's eyes impaled her.

Rick raised his eyebrows at Angie.

"Watch yourself, Rick." Sharon's lip curled. "Our sweet Angie has a dark side."

Angie swallowed a gasp. She felt her weight involuntarily transfer to her feet. *If you run now, you'll never stop running.* Her weight settled back into the chair. She gripped the table's edge and turned her narrowed gaze directly into

Sharon's eyes. "I feel sorry for you, Sharon. So insecure you can only feel good when you tear others down. We're not twelve anymore. I'm past you."

Angie stood and walked to the door with a measured stride. The door slammed shut behind her on a bar room that had suddenly become quieter.

Angie leaned against the building's brick wall outside in the light dusk. Her heart hammered, and she was panting. "Yes!" She raised her arms above her head revelling in the sensation of adrenaline flooding her body like when she'd crossed the finish line at the end of a race.

The door cracked open, and Rick stepped outside, carefully approaching Angie. "That was…something." He placed a gentle hand on her shoulder. "Slow down. Breathe in through your nose and out through your mouth."

Angie followed his directions until the adrenaline flood ebbed. Rick remained beside her, staring into the slowly gathering twilight. He glanced at his watch. "It's eleven o'clock. Does it ever get dark here in the summer?"

"Yeah, about half an hour from now. It'll start to get light again around three."

"Amazing!"

Angie laughed. "But not so great in the winter when it doesn't get light until around ten and is dark by three-thirty." She pushed herself away from the wall. "I better get home."

"Come on. I'll take you."

Angie shook her head. "No, thanks. My mom will already be pissed cause I didn't tell her I was going anywhere after the game. I don't need the complication of explaining a guy in a car."

"See you at the game on Thursday?" Rick asked.

"Maybe we can meet half an hour early, and you can show me that tell?" She raised her eyebrows.

Rick's grin glowed in the fading light. "Absolutely."

* * *

December 20, 1971

Dear Diary,

I'm writing this on the train north. Dad is picking me up at White River.

You won't believe this, but I have a boyfriend! His name is Rick, he's four years older than me, and he studies computer programming at the University of Waterloo. We met last summer in Pusamakwa, of all places. His uncle, Budd Hudson, got him a job at the mine, and we met at my first softball game in May. I wasn't very friendly to him at first and walked out on our first sort of date when we went to the hotel for a beer after the game. I was trying to be a normal girl, getting to know an ordinary boy when Sharon showed up. She's with Ralph! I wanted to tell him to run, but actually, he's perfect for her. He's happy to have someone direct his life as long as he can take photos and tinker with technology. Sharon started sending some hints to Rick about the coach and me, and I wanted to run out of the room. It took all my courage, but I stood up to the bitch. I loved the way her eyes almost fell out of her head. After that, the team treated me as a real teammate. Wish I'd done that years ago.

Adam (he and Debbie got together, by the way) invited Rick to join the men's team, so we spent a lot of time at the ball field together in the summer. Rick proved to me I had a tell by predicting where my pitch was going. Apparently, I was dropping the corner of my mouth to the side where I was aiming and tilting my head up or down for high or low pitches. Once I mastered keeping my expression flat in my wind up, I became even more challenging to hit. After a few weeks, he asked me out to a movie.

We talked so much all summer, in the bar, over coffee at the diner, in his car when we watched the bears scavenging at the dump. I finally told Rick about racing in Europe so he'd understand why I'd been to so many countries, but he never asked about Sharon's comments. I told him about my ski accident, and he was sympathetic. While he seemed slightly impressed that I raced for Canada, he mostly got very excited talking about how we could take ski holidays out west and to

Europe and how he always pictured having a family that skied together. That scared me, but he only brought it up once, so I pushed it out of my mind. What if I couldn't have babies? He says his favourite scent is the freshness of falling snow in the woods, and his favourite sound is the chatter and laughter reverberating off wooden beams in a chalet. Makes me feel we're perfect for each other.

I was shaking when I introduced Rick to my parents. Dad was friendly, and they were soon talking about fishing, sailing, barbecuing, which they both love, and cars. Mom quizzed him on his family and his achievements. She softened when she heard about him being a Queen Scout, but when he revealed he'd failed a year of university because he partied too much, her mouth tightened again. Rick won her over when he described his plan to pay back his parents for the year and that he would return to university in the fall.

I feel comfortable being with someone who understands what it's like to experience different countries. I don't have to feel like I'm walking a tightrope between two cultures. And he's used to accented English.

The summer flew by. We went fishing and sailing with my dad, and my parents invited him to go camping with us on three weekends.

He slept in the tent while I stayed with my parents in the new camper trailer. My mother made sure we didn't get much time on our own.

We did a lot of kissing and touching all summer, but I didn't let him go any further until we got back to university, and he respected that. I like Rick, and I didn't want to wreck things by rushing it. I wanted to keep us all about doing things together, not about finding chances to have sex. I think he could tell how nervous I was the first time we did it, so he was slow and gentle. Although it wasn't my first time, somehow, it felt like it. Can a man tell you're not a virgin? He never mentioned anything. With Ian, I always escaped into my mind. With Edgar, it was just something to get out of the way, and we only did it three times. But with Rick, I am starting to understand what Ian meant when he said it's what people do when they love each other, even if he didn't feel that way about me. Rick and I are having fun both in and out of bed. I wonder if this might be love.

Our university life is packed with movies, football games, dances, pubs, and sleeping together on the weekends. During the week, we only see each other every Wednesday evening when I walk from French House to

Rick's room in the Student Village at U of W. We work on our assignments for a few hours, then have a beer and snacks and make love on his single bed before he drives me back home. I've pushed everything about Ian so far back in my mind that I don't want to bring it out to tell Rick. I'm afraid of what he'll think of me, and it isn't relevant to our life together. Besides, he hasn't told me much about his past girlfriends.

I'm going to miss Rick over Christmas. His dad has arranged for him to hitch a ride on a forces flight. It sounds so cool; my boyfriend is hitching a ride with the Canadian Air Force to Africa. Rick says it's twelve hours of hell in an open hold with wooden benches and a few thin pads on the floor to stretch out on.

When he gets back, we'll start skiing together. We both have weekend jobs at the ski school at Horseshoe Valley. Can't wait.

Angie

CHAPTER TWENTY-FOUR 1972

Home for Christmas

Angie stowed her suitcase, ski boot bag, poles, and two shopping bags brimming with brightly wrapped gifts alongside Rick's baggage in the trunk of his car.

"One of the first things I'm buying when I have some money is a ski rack," Rick muttered as he guided Angie's skis beside his own through the middle of the car's interior. Orange dawn painted the sky as he steered the loaded vehicle out of the parking lot beside French House and onto University Avenue.

"So glad we're doing this." Rick squeezed Angie's hand.

"Me too." She squeezed back. "I was so excited about another summer together. That stupid strike! Why couldn't they have stopped work in the winter?" With the union on strike, the mine in Pusamakwa had been closed from April to mid-August. Rick's parents had returned from Africa in March, so he lived with them in their new house in Barrie and worked at a tire factory for the summer. Angie went home. She took a full-time job in the meat department of the Hudson's Bay Store in Pusamakwa during the week. From five o'clock to midnight every Friday and Saturday, she worked at the hotel reception desk and switchboard. "I missed you so much!"

"At least our parents finally met each other." Rick wore a crooked smile, his face reflecting ambiguity concerning the success of the meeting.

Angie's parents had driven her back to Waterloo in late August for her final year of university and to visit Peter and Elisabeth, Angie's God-parents, in Kitchener. When Rick's parents heard of their plans, they invited the Langer family to visit them on their way past Barrie.

"I'm still not sure if they actually liked each other, but they were polite and friendly, so..." Rick exhaled loudly.

Angie felt her brow wrinkle. "Yeah." Their mothers had behaved like two prickly mama bears trying to determine if the other would be ally or foe.

Angie turned back to Rick. "Won't you miss your parents at Christmas?"

"They did offer me a ticket to Barbados with them," Rick paused.

"Really? You're giving up Barbados for Pusamakwa?"

Rick laughed. "I'm giving up Barbados because I'd rather be with you wherever you are. And I am looking forward to talking to your dad."

"What do you want to talk to him about?"

Rick gave a slight cough. "Um, nothing special. He's such a level-headed, interesting guy. Now, sit back and get some sleep. I'll take us through Toronto, and you can take over in Parry Sound." She gave him a grateful smile. He knew she was nervous driving on the multi-lane highways.

Angie leaned back and closed her eyes. She didn't think she could sleep, but relaxing and humming along to the radio was nice. She felt for Gilbert O'Sullivan singing about being alone again, naturally— something she didn't plan on being ever again. Mac Davis's warning not to get hooked on him came too late. She was definitely hooked on Rick.

Angie drove from Parry Sound through Sudbury onto Highway 17 while Rick snored softly beside her. From Blind River to Sault St. Marie, they spent the afternoon planning the next two weeks. Skiing, of course. When Angie told Debbie that she and Rick were coming up for Christmas, she was surprised at Debbie's excitement. "We can use your help with the ski hill." The Pusamakwa Ski Club still operated solely with volunteers. Since Adam and Debbie were the only ones from the ski team still living in town, they'd unofficially taken over the management for the past few years.

Angie looked forward to being in her element, and as long as she avoided the chalet basement, the old memories would remain locked in the box on the back shelf of her mind.

As they continued west from the Sault, the air thickened with perfectly shaped snowflakes that Angie had loved catching on her tongue as a child. By Batchawana Bay, the full force of Lake Superior winter gales buffeted the car from side to side. The road ahead disappeared behind a curtain of snow.

"I can't tell where I am on the road," said Rick, his face pressed forward over the steering wheel, eyes squinting through the blinding snow.

Angie pulled on her tuque and tied her hood over the top. She rolled down her window and stuck her head out into the blizzard. "I can see the snow bank. I'll tell you if you're getting too close or far away. Use the yellow signs that tell you when there's a curve ahead."

"Maybe we should pull over."

"No! My dad told me that's the biggest mistake you can make. We could get stuck or hit from behind."

"But you must be freezing out there."

"I'm okay. This might clear up once we get away from the lake. If it's still bad, we'll stay in Wawa."

It was almost midnight when Angie and Rick pulled off the highway and into Wawa. The weather hadn't cleared, and the OPP had closed the highway.

Angie called her parents from the gas station pay phone to explain the situation.

"We're just glad you're safe," said her dad.

"Thanks to your daughter, Mr. Langer," Rick called. He was leaning over Angie's shoulder to listen in on the conversation. "She ensured we stayed on the road with her head hanging out of the window for hours."

Angie felt her face heat in the glow of Rick's compliment. "We're staying here until the highway opens." She said. "The OPP say probably by sometime in the morning."

"Okay, stay safe," said her dad. Angie heard her father's voice float away from the phone. "Marta, they're staying in Wawa until the highway opens."

"Tell her we'll pay for her room," Angie's mother's voice came from the background. "And for Rick's room, too. Tell her I don't want my daughter—"

Her father's voice came back on the line, so Angie didn't hear the rest of what her mother had to say.

"Dad, can you please call the Hudsons and fill them in?"

"Sure. Call us when you are leaving."

"I will. See you tomorrow." Angie hung up and rolled her eyes.

"Everything okay?" asked Rick.

Angie nodded. "Yup. Just my mom being her usual self. More concerned about my reputation than my safety."

Rick raised his eyebrows. "Don't you think you're exaggerating a little?"

"You tell me. She insisted my parents would pay for *both* our rooms."

Rick grimaced.

Angie squinted through the snow at the motel across from the station. "Come on." They plowed their way through knee-deep drifts.

At the sound of Angie and Rick stomping snow off their boots inside the motel entry, the night clerk staggered through an open doorway between the office and what appeared to be a living room behind him. Johnny Carson's voice, followed by a laugh track, blared over the clerk's shoulder.

"Help you?" The clerk rubbed his eyes.

"We need a room," said Rick.

Angie elbowed him. "Two," she whispered.

The clerk looked from Rick to Angie and back to Rick. Angie pushed her snow-sodden hair behind her ears and straightened her clothes under his scrutinizing gaze.

"We don't have any left."

"What do you mean? You have to have rooms. We're stuck here. We can pay." Angie's voice rose several notes with every statement.

"You and everybody else, kid." The clerk smacked his lips against his toothless gums.

Rick put a hand on Angie's arm. "Can you direct us to another hotel?"

The man behind the desk stroked the stubble on his chin. "The hotel above the bar is full. Marg just took the last couple into her B&B, putting them on cots in her basement. You could try the cop shop. They might have a suggestion."

"The cop shop?" Rick's forehead wrinkled.

"He means the police station. It's a northern thing." Angie flipped up her hood and headed toward the door.

"Thanks, man," Rick called as he followed Angie out.

"Just don't stay in your car. People die that way." The door closed on the clerk's final words.

Angie and Rick pressed through the wind and snow back to the gas station and into their car.

"What did he mean by that? People die?" Rick asked.

Angie shook back her hood, dumping snow into the backseat. "Another northern thing. You get cold, run the engine, the car fills with carbon monoxide, and the next day, the cops find both you and the woman, who is not your wife, pants-less and dead in the car."

Rick's mouth dropped open.

"Or you don't turn on the car and freeze to death in minus forty degrees. Same result."

"You're serious. People do that?"

Angie nodded. "Sure, at least a few times each winter. You can hardly go to the only hotel in town when everybody knows everybody, and they all love to talk." She settled into the seat. "Let's go back to the cop shop and see if they have any ideas."

* * *

Angie pulled the car up against the snowbank in front of her parents' bungalow. Jumping out, she clambered over the snow mountain clogging the front of the driveway, forcing her legs through the thigh-deep snow, hands moving like she was treading water. Rick caught up with her as she flung her arms around her father, who was clearing the back stoop.

"Your mother's inside making lunch." Her dad gave her a gentle shove toward the back door.

Rick shook Angie's father's hand. "Good to see you, Mr. Langer."

"Come here, son." Kurt hugged Rick.

The men slapped each other on the back as Rick stepped out of the embrace. "Do you have another shovel?" he asked, looking toward the open garage door. "Hey," his eyes narrowed. "You got a snow blower?"

"Yeah. Can't shovel like I used to with this bum leg." Angie's father cleared his throat. "It's been working like a charm, but, well, let's just say I miscalculated how much gas I had left." He chuckled. "And I can't get to the gas station." He motioned to the snow.

"No problem. Grab the can, and we can go right now."

"Thanks. Marta's making lunch, so let's get inside first. This snow isn't going anywhere."

The two couples settled around the kitchen table. Rick breathed in the steaming aroma of homemade beef and vegetable soup and fresh bread. "My mouth's watering, Mrs. Langer. Angie, can you cook like this?"

"Of course she can," Angie's mother's voice had a sharp edge. "I taught her. I'm a good mother."

Rick's eyebrows shot up his forehead.

Angie threw Rick a smirk. "Mom's surprised," Angie laced the word with sarcasm, "there weren't any rooms available in Wawa."

"Everything *was* full, Mrs. Langer. Cops said we were the last ones to make it through." Rick dipped his bread in the soup and popped the soggy mass into his mouth. "This soup is delicious. Yeah, so the cops let us stay in their lounge room at the station." He stretched his back. "Not the most comfortable, but at least we were warm and safe."

"Humph." Angie's mother's expression remained doubtful.

"So you two must be pretty tired," said Angie's dad. "Probably a good idea to have a nap this afternoon."

"Dinner's at six, and the candlelight service is at nine," said Angie's mother. "Maybe you better get going, Rick. Your aunt and uncle are going to be anxious to see you."

"Right, can I use your phone? I'll call and let them know I'm here and get over to their place as soon as we take care of your driveway."

"Oh, don't worry about the driveway," said Angie's father.

Rick stood. "No, no, Mr. Langer. I'll call, then we can get the gas. While you blow the light stuff, I'll break down the mound that the snow plow left across the front."

Angie accompanied Rick to the phone in the living room.

CHAPTER TWENTY-FIVE - 1972

From Heaven to Hell

Christmas Eve dinner passed without incident.

"Let's open our gifts before we go to church." Marta shepherded Angie and Rick to the living room once they'd finished washing the dishes. *This is strange*, Angie thought. *We always open our gifts after church.* Excitement glittered in Marta's eyes as she handed each of them a soft-sided, shapeless bundle encased in red Christmas paper.

Angie's mom had knitted Rick a dark green sweater, the complex pattern of cables evoking a forest of tightly packed trees. Angie's sweater was in a creamy Aran shade with delicate cables embracing the light. *Was there a message behind these sweaters? But dark green is Rick's favourite colour. Stop it, Angie. You're overthinking.*

"This is beautiful, Mrs. Langer." Rick pulled the sweater over his head, then wrapped his arms around Marta. "Come on, Angie, let's see yours. I'm wearing this to church tonight."

Marta preened with joy. Her handiwork would be on display this evening for all to see.

The two couples trudged along the snowy streets joining a growing procession of churchgoers.

"This is magical, but why is everyone walking?" Rick asked.

"It's too cold to leave the car unplugged." Angie's dad explained. "Nothing more frustrating than coming out of church to a dead frozen car."

Angie still missed the community *Réveillon* dinner after Christmas Eve midnight mass in the church basement in Beauprè-sur-lac—the *tourtières* and *bûches de Noël*; the glowing faces and warm embraces as everyone called *Joyeux Noël* at midnight. While the Christmas Eve candlelight service at St. Paul's United church in Pusamakwa—the interior of the church bathed solely in candlelight, walking down the central aisle as part of the choir, carrying a candle, every voice filling the air with "Once in Royal David's City"—couldn't replace her French-Canadian memories, Angie still looked forward to the service just as much.

Christmas Day, Rick and Angie met Debbie and Adam at the ski club for a refresher course on opening and closing the hill.

Angie let her skis float through the fresh powder along the unpacked side of the main hill, hitting her edges hard at the groomed crest above the mogul field.

"Whoa!" Rick sprayed snow over her skis to avoid colliding with her. "You okay?" Angie never stopped suddenly like that. She was known to rant at skiers who would pull up unexpectedly, creating an obstacle for those coming up behind them.

"Look!" Angie stood, arms wide, poles dangling from her wrist straps. "That's heaven."

Rick side-slipped until their skis formed four parallel lines across the slope. His eyes followed her gaze over the snow-mounded roofs of the town site in the valley and across to the hills rising on the other side. Small beetle-like forms glided on a snow-free square of ice-covered lake in the middle of the town.

"Have you ever seen a bluer sky?" Angie planted her poles and jumped to point her skis straight down the hill without waiting for a response. "Follow me," she called. "Stay close and watch for those evergreen ladies draped in elegant white gowns. They'll knock you over and bury you in snow if you get too close." Then she charged downhill, bobbing and weaving like a boxer over moguls and around the snow-laden evergreens.

Rick steered his skis into Angie's track, keeping her bouncing red pompom in sight to help him anticipate the terrain ahead. Pulling beside her at the bottom of the hill, he panted, "That's a wild ride." He leaned over and wrapped his arms around her. "You're beautiful. I love you," he whispered into the soft folds of her tuque.

Angie held her breath. *Had he really said that?* She'd stopped herself a few times from spontaneously blurting those three words, wanting him to be the first to say them. And now, she gaped soundlessly like a fish out of water.

"Hey, you two. Save that for later. You're here to work," Adam teased, skidding to a stop. "Still crazy, eh, kiddo," he said to Angie. Turning to Rick, he added. "Good job, man. She's always been a tough one to keep up with."

Rick transferred his weight back over his skis and winked at her before turning his attention to Adam. Angie leaned down, pretending to adjust the buckle on her boot.

"Thanks." Rick grinned. "She's worth it."

He's smiling. He must not have seen my reaction. Thank God. But what was that? Why couldn't I say it? She straightened up.

Adam laughed. "I believe she's blushing."

"It's just the cold." Angie turned her skis toward the tow shack. "So you two gonna stand around talking all day, or can we get to work?"

Debbie joined them in the chalet at the end of the day.

"You look radiant," Angie said. "But you sure you're not due 'til March?"

Debbie grinned. "I know, eh, but the doc says March and he assures me there's only one baby in here." She caressed her hand over her pregnant belly.

"Thanks so much for helping out over the holidays, guys. The place is a handful for two of us, but with Debbie out of commission…"

"No problem." Rick grinned. "We don't exactly have a heavy social calendar."

"In that case, you've got to come to our place on New Year's Eve. We're just having a few friends over."

Angie's mouth wobbled into a smile. Debbie's invitation seemed genuinely warm and sincere. "Let me check with—"

"Sounds great!" Rick interrupted Angie.

Adam laughed. "Things a little tense at the in-laws?"

"Come on, Adam, take it easy on them. And no, Angie, Sharon won't be there." Debbie grabbed Angie by the arm and manoeuvred her away from the guys. "Looks serious with you and Rick."

When Angie didn't say anything, Debbie added. "Don't worry, your secret's safe with me." She squeezed Angie's arm. "I'm happy for you."

Boxing Day, the Langers joined Rick and the Hudsons for a pleasant afternoon visit and dinner. Then, Rick and Angie embraced their daily routine of skiing. The stars still pricked the sky when he picked her up every morning at seven. The aroma of breakfast greeted him as he kicked off his boots. Angie's mom prepared bacon and fried eggs, porridge, or sausage and fried egg sandwiches so they could hit the hill full and warm and ready to work. They opened the slopes just as the sun peaked over the valley at ten each morning and closed it in twilight at four each afternoon.

Angie's favourite job was pulling the packer up and down the trails behind the snowmobile to keep the base solid and ice-free. They snuck off to find privacy and make love in the shelter of a snow-laden evergreen bough a few times. Some evenings Rick joined the Langers for dinner; a few times, Angie joined the Hudsons, and twice Angie and Rick ate out at the diner. The two weeks flew by, and Angie was starting to breathe easily. Maybe she would get away without fighting with her mother.

On the last day of the visit, Angie's ears tingled with the electricity in the air as she walked through the door after skiing. Her father was still at work. Rick was going home to shower and would return for supper in an hour. It was just Angie and her mother in the house, something that hadn't happened much during the visit, partly due to Angie's engineering.

"Hi, Mom."

Her mother sat in her usual spot on the couch, but the TV wasn't on, and she wasn't holding yarn or needles.

"I'm going to grab a shower before supper. The spaghetti smells great, by the way." Angie hated the placating note in her voice.

"Sit, little girl!"

Angie cringed. Her mother knew how to diminish her in two words. She perched on the edge of her father's chair.

"What is this?" Her mother threw the pink plastic holder on the coffee table.

Angie felt her eyes would pop out of her head. She swallowed hard.

"Well? Answer me!"

Angie unclenched her jaw. "What were you doing snooping in my stuff?"

Her mother stood, leaning toward her daughter. "Answer me!"

"They're my birth control pills, but you know that." Angie's lips pulled so far back that she felt the air cool her teeth.

"Slut!" her mother screamed. Her hand raised as she moved forward.

Angie wanted to run like a scared rabbit, but she was cornered. Her mother's blazing eyes ignited Angie's courage. "Stop, Mom! If you hit me, it will be the last time you see me. I'm not your little girl anymore. I'm my own person, and I make my own decisions." Angie's heart roared in her ears.

Her mother froze. The two stared at each other in a silence only broken by the clock's ticking. Angie counted twenty tick-tocks when her mother sagged into herself and dropped to the chair across from her.

"All I want is a good life for you." Her voice trembled. "A faithful, loving husband, a career until you have children. Men don't marry girls who give it away before marriage." Her tone hardened. "And those," she pointed at the case where it remained on the coffee table, "they say: 'I'm easy.'"

"No, Mom, those say making love with someone you love is natural, and they say I am responsible enough not to get pregnant until I'm ready." Angie scooped the case from the table and turned toward her room. "You know what digging around in your daughter's drawer says? 'I don't trust you. I don't think you're smart enough to care for yourself.'" Angie took a deep breath. "Stay out of my stuff, Mom. You brought me up right, but this isn't the 1940s."

Just as Angie reached her room, her mother said, "Rick asked your father for permission to marry you." Angie's body went rigid, her hand on the doorknob. By the time she turned around, her mother was in the kitchen. *What? Why would her mother tell her that when it refuted her argument?*

Angie hid in her room, waiting for Rick to arrive. When her father came home, her mother greeted him in the kitchen with angry whispers.

"She's a smart girl, Marta, and he's a nice boy. They'll be fine." Her father's words filtered to Angie as he spoke to his wife from the living room.

"You always take her side." Lids slammed on pots.

The doorbell rang. Angie kissed her father on the cheek and murmured, "Thanks," in his ear before rushing to meet Rick at the back door.

"You're late," Marta muttered in Rick's direction. "Dinner's ready. I hope the spaghetti isn't stuck together from waiting in the pot."

Rick gave Angie a quizzical look as they settled at the table. She shook her head.

"This spaghetti is perfectly spiced, Mrs. Langer."

Angie's mother humphed.

Rick and Angie's father made a few forays into conversations, then gave up, leaving a symphony of spaghetti slurping and the clinking of forks twirling noodles on spoons to fill the air. After supper, Angie's mother claimed a headache and retreated to her room. Rick and Angie did the dishes, then abandoned her father in front of the TV and headed to the bar.

When Angie told Rick about the birth control pills scene, he was sympathetic and tried to reassure her that her mother would be fine in the morning. *He doesn't know my mother*, Angie thought. She didn't mention the part about Rick asking her father's permission to marry her. *Was that what he was referring to when he said he wanted to talk to my dad at the beginning of our trip? I told Rick I loved him the day after he told me, and we say it all the time to each other now. What if he intended to ask me over the holidays? I think I hope he didn't change his mind.*

CHAPTER TWENTY-SIX -1973

Belonging to Herself

Lounging against two brown corduroy cushions on the orange shag carpet, Angie let her eyes wander around the common room. Her knitting rested in her lap. This close-knit community had brought Angie peace. Barb's eyes sparkled now but a few months into their first year, Angie had found her housemate sobbing in the kitchen. Barb's mother had been sending her appetite depressant pills disguised as vitamins. Her mother defended her actions saying Barb was already too chubby and she didn't want her to gain more weight while away from home. "I've never been thin enough or graceful enough for my mother," Barb had moaned.

"That's horrible!" Angie had put her arm around Barb. "I was never smart or perfect enough for my mother. You're beautiful and kind and funny. Never mind her. We love you just the way you are."

When Laura was getting ready for a date with her boyfriend one evening, she suddenly broke into tears. Jenny called Angie because Laura was inconsolable. It turned out Laura loved him, but he was pressuring her to have sex. Laura confessed that she'd had an abortion when she was sixteen. The guy had pressured her then as well, but when she told him she was pregnant, he'd disappeared. After Laura cancelled the date, the three girls spent the evening sharing their experiences. It was like a tight knot suddenly unravelled from around her chest when Angie told Jenny and Laura about the coach. Jenny spoke barely above a whisper as she revealed that she hadn't seen her grandfather since she was six. Her mother caught him with his hand up Jenny's skirt, pulling on her underpants at a family function.

Today, surrounded by the friends she'd lived with, studied with, laughed and cried with over the past three years, Angie's emotions tumbled from exhilaration to panic. *I've done it! University degree in hand, the world is my oyster, and the sky's the limit. But where do I start?*

"I think it should be green, 'cause it matches your eyes."

Angie tore her attention from the Toulouse-Lautrec print of *Aristide Bruant, dans son cabaret,* picked up the sleeve for the sweater she was knitting, and tuned into the conversation unfolding around her.

"Yeah. And it goes with your hair."

Jenny and Mary were right, green was the perfect colour for Laura's wedding. Maybe Laura had the right idea. Getting married would mean Angie wouldn't have to face the next step on her own. Rick had finally popped the question at Easter and he *was* still waiting for her answer. But wasn't the expected path—marriage, teaching, having children, relying on a husband—the easy way out? Easy had never been Angie's approach to life. Heck, she'd even taken Russian 101 as her third language instead of Spanish like most of her housemates.

Laura's cheeks were flushed with the attention. "When do you leave for Tanzania, Debra?" she asked.

Debra pulled her hands through her dark, short cropped curls. "Orientation starts next week in Toronto, and we fly to Tanzania on May fifth." She was going to work in an orphanage near Mount Kilimanjaro.

"You must be so excited."

"Aren't you scared?"

Debra's eyes shone. "I'm very excited and a little scared, but I'm going to be living my dream. It doesn't get any better than that."

Debra didn't need a man to define who she was. *If she can do it, maybe so can I*, Angie thought. *I have friends now.*

"You taking the offer to teachers' college, Angie?"

Laura, Jenny, and Mary would all be starting at the college in Toronto in September.

Angie's fingers moved automatically through the stitches. "I'm not sure that 'teacher' is who I am or want to be at this point in my life."

"But you're a natural. You taught me French grammar when no one else could," protested Jenny.

"The kids in ski school adored you," Mary added. "And what about those elementary school kids that you directed in *You're a Good Man, Charlie Brown*? They thought you were cool."

Angie felt the heat rise up her neck. "Come on." She pulled on her ponytail. "A part of me loves teaching and working with kids. But I can't help wondering if there aren't other alternatives to explore, other experiences out there. Maybe the diplomatic corps?" As she took in the "here she goes again" expressions on her friends' faces, she held back voicing her ambivalence between having supposedly unlimited opportunities and the societal and familial pressures to maintain the traditional path. Teacher would make her mother happy. She sighed. "I probably will accept it. After all, what else can you do with a BA in French and German these days?"

This was greeted with nods of agreement.

"Teachers make good money."

"There are lots of jobs for French teachers."

"You can always teach part-time once your kids are in school."

The corners of Angie's mouth pulled into a wry smile. "Once my kids are in school? I have to find a man first, don't you think?"

Laura and Jenny exchanged glances.

"We thought...I mean," Jenny stuttered.

"Didn't Rick...?" asked Laura.

Angie laughed. "Yes, he did."

"And?" asked Jenny.

"I haven't answered yet." *But I'll probably say yes*, she added to herself. Rick was a good guy. He'd just landed a great job as a computer analyst in Toronto. Once they were away from university, Angie was sure he'd stop drinking so much.

"This is a scary time." Debra looked around the room. "We've belonged to our parents all our lives. It's okay to take some time, belong to ourselves first, before we leap into another big commitment."

Debra leaned over and whispered to Angie, "You're going to be okay, you know."

Hot tears pricked the backs of Angie's eyes. Angie admired Debra's courage and respected her conviction to remain true to herself and her goals. Her reassurance meant a great deal, but what did she mean about belonging to yourself?

Angie fingered her pocket where the single page of airmail paper had resided since this morning. Had her mother used airmail paper to signify the distance between their convictions? Angie gave herself a mental shake. *Your reading too much into this, she probably just didn't have any other paper around.* What wasn't ambiguous were the words written on the single, flimsy page.

Dear Angelika

My heart started living the day you were born. If you marry Rick, my heart will die on your wedding day and you will never see me again.

Your mother

The message was an iron fist around Angie's heart. Was she prepared to draw the line at letting her mother think she could pick her husband through emotional blackmail? After all, Angie was prepared to fulfill her mother's dreams for her—teacher and marriage. Her mother would come around, wouldn't she? She'd try calling her father this evening, but her mind wouldn't let her ignore her mother's history of refusing to back down.

"Come on, everyone. We all know Angie marches to her own drum." Debra broke through Angie's thoughts. Everyone was looking at her.

"My mom says she'll disown me if I marry Rick." She pulled the letter from her pocket, then covered her face with her hands.

All the air whooshed out of the room. Then everyone spoke at once.

"She wouldn't do that. You're the centre of your mom's life."

"She bluffing."

"Just talk to her. Ask her why she doesn't like Rick?"

"What does your dad say?"

Angie raised her head. "I'm going to call my dad after supper. But my Mom's really stubborn. It's not in her to back down."

Debra put up her hand to silence the next outbursts. "Angie, you know we're all here for you. Maybe talk this through with Rick, too. In the end, you have to make the decision that will work for your life, not your mother's."

Angie nodded. She looked around the room at the concerned gazes. "Thanks. Can we talk about something else now?"

Debra forced a brighter tone. "So let's talk about our last *souper en famille*."

Angie blurted, "I'll make *rouladen*."

"Absolutely you will," said Cheryl. "But will you make your famous Black Forest cake?"

Angie felt the pressure in her chest lighten. Baking had become one of her best stress-management strategies. During exams, it wouldn't be uncommon to find her in the kitchen muttering French verb conjugations while she whipped up a batch of *Amerikaners*—thick, iced, butter cookies—or a Black Forest cake at two in the morning. "Sure."

"The tall one, right?" said Mary.

Angie joined everyone in laughter at the memory of her first cake. Instead of slicing the layers, she'd piled three whole round chocolate cakes one on top of the other and put cherries and whipped cream between each layer. They'd needed dinner plates to accommodate the slices.

"Of course," Angie said, smiling to herself with pride at how much she'd grown from the scared girl who would have withdrawn from this teasing.

Appearing to listen as the conversation buzzed around her, Angie tried to permanently etch her friends' faces in her mind. But, just like the images of her family in Germany, she knew that these, too, would fade over time, no matter how frequently she brought them to the forefront of her mind. No matter how hard you tried, it seemed that memory's carefully stored images became wrapped in time's nebulous fog until the edges blurred and the colours muted. This house and its residents had given her a sense of belonging she hadn't felt since her family had left Beaupré-sur-lac over ten years ago. They accepted her for who she is, not who she pretended to be to fit in. When she'd felt she couldn't be who her mother expected, she'd turned to the coach. But hadn't she just turned herself into who he wanted? Was she doing the same in considering Rick's proposal? But if she didn't marry him, wasn't she letting her mother win again?

The electric guitar opening of "I Am Woman" brought an abrupt halt to her thoughts. The salon erupted as eight young women joined Helen Reddy in declaring a woman's ability to overcome the cost of being born in her skin.

Soon, Angie would pack up and leave this phase of life behind her. There would be time enough to make decisions. For now, she needed to seize the moment. Angie took another sip of wine and returned to her knitting.

CHAPTER TWENTY-SEVEN - 2000

The Good Mother

Marta hummed "You Are My Sunshine" as she made the bed. Kurt would be back from his morning walk soon. In the kitchen, she poured herself a cup of coffee. "Blah!" She spat a mouthful of the brown liquid into the sink. Tapping the carafe with her index finger, she felt the glass. "Cold," she muttered. Her brow wrinkled. Kurt always made the coffee before he left so they could enjoy a fresh cup together when he got back. The ringing of the phone interrupted her confusion. Carafe in hand, she went into the living room and stared at the phone stand.

"Hello. Hello!" Marta yelled at the stand. *Why did no one answer? Wait. Wasn't there a piece that you had to pick up and put to your ear?* Marta set the carafe on the end table as she searched for the handset. She pulled the cushions off the couch, tore the covers off the bed, and checked in the bathtub.

"Stop!" She pressed her hands over her ears to dull the insistent ringing. Spying the coffee carafe, she touched the side of it and sighed. "It's cold. Now I have to make another pot."

As Marta opened the fridge to pull out the tin of ground coffee, the phone began ringing again. "How did this get here?" She took the handset from inside the fridge door and glanced at the clock on the wall. Angelika called at eight o'clock every morning, and it was ten minutes after eight. She hit the button on the phone. "So you remembered you have a mother."

"Good morning, Mom." Angelika's voice was cheerful. "I'm coming this afternoon, remember?"

Marta glanced at the calendar on the wall where "Angelika" appeared in every Wednesday block. So today must be Wednesday. "Of course. You think I don't know what day it is?"

"No, Mom." Angelika's tone tightened.

Marta frowned. "What's wrong? You sound upset."

"Just busy. I'll see you around four o'clock."

"*Ja, ja.* I have to go. Your father will be back soon. Can you believe he left without making the coffee this morning? And you keep saying I'm the one that's going crazy."

"Mom, wait!"

"What?"

"You know Dad's not out for a walk, right? You remember he's been gone for two years?"

Marta stood in the middle of the tiny living room that wasn't hers, filled with the furniture that was. Instead of her kitchen, there was only a short counter stuck in the corner with a small sink and the coffee maker. A half-fridge was pushed under the counter. Marta felt on the edge of sliding as the world faded away. She hated the coming state where she felt like the letters in her beloved crossword puzzles kept jumping from block to block.

"Mom, you there?" Angelika's voice pulled Marta back from the brink.

"Of course I know *that*." Marta's voice choked.

"Maybe we can have dinner at the Mennonite restaurant you like, then go visit Dad today?"

"What's the point of staring at a stone?" Marta hung up the phone. She sank into her favourite chair, the colonial-style rocker with crushed velvet orange and gold flowers, as the memories crashed over her head. Kurt gasping and clutching his chest. The paramedics and sirens. The doctor at the hospital shaking his head, his mouth moving with words she couldn't hear. Then, long, lonely days. Angelika took her to appointments for months where strangers quizzed her on the date, what she'd eaten for breakfast, when she saw her friends, where she lived. After endless tours of senior living homes, Marta had buckled under the pressure and sold the condo she and Kurt had moved to in Kitchener when Kurt retired. She had to admit it was easier not having to cook for herself. Secretly, Marta wished Angelika would invite her to move in with her, even though she knew that meant she'd probably never see her friends again. Marta couldn't remember precisely where Angelika lived, but she did recall Angelika complaining about a two-hour drive.

A soft knock at the door. "Marta? It's breakfast time."

Marta pushed herself up as the door opened.

"Good morning. You ready?"

Marta searched the shining blue eyes of the young woman standing in front of her.

"I'm Betty. I'm here to take you to the dining room."

Marta's brow cleared. "Yes. Betty. How's your little boy?"

"You remember!" Betty smiled. "He's much better, thanks. Just a stuffy nose now, so he's allowed back in daycare." She offered her elbow for Marta to hold as they walked down the hall. "This morning, we have a lady talking about her safari in Africa. Then, there's Wii Bowling in the Rec Room. After lunch, I'll help you get dressed up. Your daughter's coming today."

"Angelika's coming?"

"Yes. She comes every Wednesday."

Marta humphed. "That's news to me."

"She left me a phone message to confirm."

"Would it hurt her to call her mother? No, but she can leave messages for others."

"Now, Marta. I'm sure she's busy." Betty patted Marta's arm. "You're lucky to have such a wonderful daughter taking care of you."

"*Ja*. I was a good mother, you know."

"I bet you were," Betty said.

"To help her make friends with good girls, she went to Sunday school, sang in the church junior choir, and... what's that group where they wear blue uniforms?"

"Girl Guides?" Betty offered.

"Yes, that. I even became a helper so she wouldn't be scared when she started." Marta stopped and turned to Betty. "Angelika was a good little girl."

Betty made a sound of agreement and moved Marta further down the hall.

"When she was a teenager, there were no boyfriends, none of that rock and roll music in our house or those disgusting teen magazines. But I couldn't stop her from skiing. I told her father she should stop, but he took her side. Those two always teamed up against me." Marta stopped and turned to meet Betty's gaze. "If she'd listened to me...I tried to protect her like a good mother, but—"

"Well, it seems she has grown into a fine person."

"Yes, she's a big shot with a college." The smile drifted from Marta's face. "But no children."

"Here we are." Betty's tone was cheerful. "Let's get you settled for breakfast. Look, there's your friend Dorothy." Betty left the two women chatting over their toast.

* * *

Angie sat in the parking lot of Golden Meadows, listening to the ticking of the cooling car engine. She'd become more aware of her mother's befuddled memory in the months following her father's death. Her mother's doctor had suggested depression due to grief and prescribed antidepressants. But when Angie found her mother in her condo, delirious and dehydrated from an overdose of her diabetic medication, she recognized something more serious was wrong. Specialist assessments confirmed that Marta Langer had dementia, likely Alzheimer's given the family history, and needed twenty-four hour care.

Angie pushed herself out of her vehicle. Her abdominal muscles tensed as she entered the code and waited for the electronically controlled entrance to swing open. The receptionist told her that Marta was in her room. Angie signed in, then walked down the hallway labelled, "Daisy Lane, Memory Care Unit." The irony of the name never ceased bringing a sardonic twist to her mouth. She knocked softly on her mother's door before entering. "Hi, Mom!"

Her mother was in her chair, staring at the blank television. "Angelika!" Her face brightened.

Angie relaxed. *Off to a good start.*" "How are you, Mom? You look terrific." Angie's expression froze at the gauntness of her mother's face. *She looks like a scarecrow in her clothes.*

"Thank you. I'm getting company today."

Angie felt her smile slip. "You are? Who?"

Confusion clouded her mother's eyes momentarily, then her features cleared. "It doesn't matter. You're here now and just in time." She turned back to the television. "This thing is broken."

"Let's see. Where's the remote?"

"I don't have that."

Her mother's expression told Angie that she had no idea what a remote was.

Angie hated that vacant look. "Never mind. I'll find it later. Now, tell me, what have you been doing this week?" Every subject Angie introduced—the meals, the activities, the in-house church service—was like pulling maple taffy through snow, slow moving and sticky with misunderstandings and incorrect words.

Spying knitting needles poking out of the basket beside her mother's chair, Angie asked, "What are you knitting, Mom?" People had admired Angie's wardrobe of knitted sweaters, hats, and scarves. There wasn't anything her mother wouldn't make for her, even that mini dress of fine yarn where every row was a different shade of blue when she was sixteen.

Her mother pulled up a jumble of wool strands. "A sweater for Lena's granddaughter. She's crazy about cats." The muddle of grey, white, and pink was riddled with dropped stitches and jagged pulls. Marta held up the misshapen piece with a broad smile. "Nice kitty, *neh*?"

She'd be mortified if anyone saw this. "Beautiful," Angie forced. "Now, I need to go to the bathroom, then we'll get that TV working."

Angie reappeared moments later, waving the remote. "It was on the back of the toilet."

Her mother shrugged.

"See, Mom, you push this button to turn on the TV, and these arrows move you through the channels. You still watching *The Young and the Restless*?"

Her mother went to the TV and started poking at the side and bottom of the set. "Where are the buttons? I watch *The Edge of Night*."

"I don't think it's on anymore, but if you use this, it has all the buttons to go through the channels from your chair."

Her mother pushed the remote away. "I've never seen that before."

"Sure you have. It came with the TV. Remember, Dad used it when you two moved to the condo—"

Her mother's eyes narrowed. "Dad. Of course, you think about your father. But do you ever take the time to think about me, visit me?"

Angie felt a fist squeeze her throat. "Mom," she kept her voice low and soothing. "I'm here now."

"*Ja*. What would people think if the big boss didn't visit her mother? I know the truth." Her voice rose. "If your father were alive, you wouldn't stick him in this place. I know the wrong parent died that day."

Angie gasped. Her mother had put words to the painful truth that pricked Angie's heart at the most inopportune times—standing in line at the grocery store, sitting in a meeting, on a dinner date. *Keep calm. She doesn't know what she's saying.* Angie moved her chair closer to her mother. "I miss Dad too, but I'm glad you're here."

Her mother spoke so quietly Angie had to lean in to hear. "I could live with you, take care of you, be part of your life."

Angie grimaced. She'd thought of that. It would be the right and generous thing to do, but given how they'd been all their lives... "You'd be alone all day and many evenings because of my work. And you'd be far away from your bridge friends."

"They've forgotten about me. I never see them."

Two days ago, her mother's friend, Lena, had given Angie an earful over the phone about her dereliction of duty as a daughter. According to Lena, Angie's mother told everyone her daughter hadn't visited her in months. When Angie explained her weekly visits, Lena conceded that Marta couldn't follow their conversations, and they'd long ago given up playing bridge with her.

"Mom, we talked about this. You have a disease that makes you forgetful. Like Oma, Tante Klara, Tante Liesbeth. I don't know how to help you the way the people here do." Angie white-knuckled the chair arms.

Her mother's eyes shot nails. "What, all that education, and you can't help your mother? *Pah!*"

Angie's stomach clenched. *Was this the chance finally to be honest with her? Tell her that all her life, she couldn't breathe when she was around her? That she seemed to care more about what other people thought, what others might say, than how her daughter was feeling or how she could help her?*

Angie moved to the couch.

"I was a good mother. Who was up with you all night when you got a fever? Who taught you to speak? To walk? Who changed your dirty diapers?"

"Nobody said you weren't, but—"

Her mother held up her hand. "I'm not finished. I taught you to cook and clean, to knit and crochet, to obey your elders." She gave her daughter a pointed glare as she drew out the last words.

And then you wondered why I didn't stand up to the coach when he—

"I didn't want to be disappointed in my only child. It isn't my fault you turned out to be like this."

Pull back. She isn't processing a word I'm saying. What point am I trying to make? But Angie's jaw wouldn't unclench. "Like what, Mom? I went to university like you and Dad wanted. I became a teacher like you wanted." *Stop talking.* "I worked all day and studied at night and in the summers, earned a Master's degree. Now I'm the president of a college, and it's still not good enough for you." Angie's nails dug into her palms with anger—at her mother or herself? Either way, the damage was done.

Her mother's voice became menacingly controlled. "You're wrong. I was proud of everything you did. But where would you be if I didn't push you, expect the best from you?" Before Angie was able to formulate a response, her mother held up a silencing hand. "I know. You complained to your father that I was mean because I didn't let you run wild, do what you wanted. I'm your mother. That was my job."

Mother and daughter locked eyes across the coffee table.

"I didn't want you to repeat my mistakes. But you wouldn't listen. You knew everything better. Like Rick. You were too young, and he was too busy with his friends and his beer to take care of a wife."

Angie felt her eyes widen. "I didn't need anyone to take care of me." *Trust Mom to remember my failures.* Angie had never had the courage to tell her mother that Rick left after four miscarriages and the doctor's pronouncement that continuing to try to bear a child would likely lead to Angie's death. It took Angie years to stop wondering if her deficiency had been due somehow to the surgery in France that Ian had engineered after the ski accident.

"*Na ja,* and what kind of life do you have now? No husband. No children. Just a parade of men that come and go and a wall of degrees where your children's photos should be."

Angie felt gut-punched. She decided to not rise to the bait. "What mistakes? You never told me anything about your life before I was born."

Her mother crossed her arms, and stared into the distance.

Angie's vision shimmered with unshed tears. They'd never been able to talk to each other.

Her mother's eyes began to wander around the room.

Don't drift away now. Please stay. Tell me. She'd been talking about—"Marriage! Mom, was your mistake about a marriage?"

Angie's knee bounced as she watched her mother's inner struggle play across her face. *Stay quiet. Give her time.*

Her mother's eyes landed on the old wedding photo Angie had framed and placed beside the TV to help her remember her husband. Her expression softened. "Kurt was everything I could want in a man. He was gentle, kind, loving, and patient." She paused so long Angie feared she'd lost her to the past. Then, her mother's hands balled into fists. Her mouth tightened until her lips almost disappeared. "Not like Franz." She almost spat his name. "Filled with promises that we would run away together, then one day, pouf, he was gone and I was pregnant."

I knew there was more to her relationship with Franz. Angie leaned toward her mother. "Did Franz promise to marry you?"

Her mother's eyes rose to meet Angie's. "Franz was like every man, tells you he loves you, says he will marry you so you give in, then he takes off." She gave a triumphant laugh. "But his mother wasn't going to let her son get away with it. She paid my train fare to Hamburg and ordered him to meet me at the station and do the right thing for me and his coming child."

"So that's how you ended up in Hamburg?"

Her mother nodded. "He found a little apartment and I worked in a fish store." She smiled. "I thought I was in heaven for the first few months." Her face drooped, "But when I got bigger, he stopped rushing home after his performances, stayed out all night drinking, gambling, whoring."

Do I have a half-sibling somewhere? No, Mom would never have abandoned a child.

"When little Kristof fought for his life in hospital while the bombs shook the walls, his father never even came to see him. Three days after his birth, I buried my son and filed for divorce."

Her mother looked hollowed out. Her withered cheeks were wet.

"I'm sorry, Mom." Angie held back a sob.

"No more questions! Just sit there and be quiet."

Instead of reassuring, she'd pushed her mother to dredge up her pain, baited her to release the words that had been festering for years; the things between them they'd both known lurked under the surface but had an unspoken agreement not to touch.

Angie's soul felt diminished, as if her insides had been scrubbed formless with guilt. .

"I was a good mother, wasn't I? Say it. Say I was a good mother."

Angie recognized her own desire for affirmation in her mother's anxious expression. *What a pair they were, incapable of expressing words of approval to each other.* She let out a deep, calming breath. It made the sound that hot sauna stones make when you pour water on them. "You were the best mother to me that you could be, Mom."

Her mother sniffed. "That's right. I was the best. Now was that so hard?"

The two women huddled under their separate blankets of silence. Her mother's stare fixed on the kitchenette as she shifted into German. "Now, Liesbeth, go feed the ducks while I make coffee. Then we'll have some marble cake."

A glance at her mother's vacant eyes told Angie the curtain had fallen. She refrained from pointing out that she was her daughter, not her mother's younger sister. "*Ja*, Marta." Angie left, closing the door behind her.

In the quiet of her car, Angie stared through the windshield at the falling snow. *All I ever wanted was for her to tell me she loved me just the way I was, and now I'm never going to hear those words.*

"Damn Alzheimer's!" Angie pounded the steering wheel and sobbed until her sides ached. She took a shuddering breath. *Let it go. You belong to yourself. Your successes and failures are all yours. Embrace them. You know who you are.*

Then, clarity dawned. Her mother's doctor had suggested keeping her near her friends as long as she could socialize with them. That situation had shifted. Maybe seeing her daughter more frequently could slow her descent into complete confusion. Angie reached for her phone and did a quick Internet search, then hit the call button. "Hello. Do you have any vacancies in your Memory Care Unit?" Several inquiries resulted in two appointments for Angie to visit facilities near her home. *I'll drop in for short visits on the way to or from work. I'll pick her up, and we'll make* rouladen *and bake* lebkuchen *cookies together. And we'll eat off those dark green depression-glass dishes from the cupboard, the ones Mom and Dad brought from Germany when they emigrated.*

Angie knew her plan wasn't perfect, but it would be good enough. And sometimes good enough is all that's needed.

Epilogue - 2003

Angie stood, hands on hips, and surveyed the garage. The late afternoon spring sun streamed through the open double doors and between the two cars parked in the driveway. She blew upward to lift the bangs off her sweaty forehead as she assessed the results of her work. A four-foot stack of flattened cardboard boxes sat to one side, ready for recycling. In the middle of the garage, a stack of black garbage bags waited to be taken to the landfill, and six full cardboard boxes were destined for donation. Not bad for a few hours work. Angie hadn't been able to bring herself to deal with the last of her parents' possessions when her mother died, but after a year of scooting around the piles of boxes and keeping her car outside through a full winter, she'd decided today was the day. Dragging the three plastic bins of stuff that she wasn't ready to part with across the concrete floor to the shelving unit at the back of the garage, a smaller bin caught her eye. "How did I miss you?"

Angie sat cross-legged on the floor beside the container, clicked back the handles, and lifted the lid. Her hand flew to her mouth. "Oh, my God! I thought she threw this stuff away decades ago." With shaking hands, Angie lifted out the first item. She gave the skier at the top a gentle wipe before setting the trophy on the floor beside her. One by one, she removed each of her skiing trophies and medals and spread them around her. She chuckled as she removed the knitted navy blue headband from its resting place around one of the trophies. She ran her fingers over the circle of white snowflakes, then pulled on the band and adjusted it to cover her ears.

Angie read her elementary school report cards, organized in chronological order under the skiing awards. From kindergarten to grade eight, every teacher remarked on Angie's commitment to learning, her messy handwriting, and her tendency to spend too much class time lost in a book. Angie laughed aloud. "At least I was consistent."

The blue, badge-laden sash from her years in Girl Guides was wrapped around the Gold Cord she'd earned at just thirteen. A lump in her throat made it hard to swallow as she gazed at the photo of her mother fixing the cord to her shoulder at the awards ceremony. Marta looked so proud. *That's probably the last time she was happy to be my mother.*

At the very bottom of the box, Angie recognized the blue notebook. *Journal* was written in bold black marker, surrounded by the words *Privé, Confidentiel, Ne lis pas!* in red. She wondered whether her mother had read her journal. She hoped not. Angie opened the book and began to read. There weren't many entries. Writing to an imaginary entity had never ignited Angie's enthusiasm. She'd preferred creating mysteries that her brilliant, popular, fictional character, Violette Regenbogen, always solved with the help of her two friends. Violette was everything Angie wasn't but wanted to be, and she certainly wasn't lonely or trusting enough to fall prey to a predator like the coach.

As Angie came to the entry where her parents had decided not to report the rape to the police, a loose page dropped into her lap. Her heart thudded in her ears. A remembered rummy scent filled her nostrils as her eyes drifted across the familiar handwriting. She couldn't stop her mind from repeating, from memory, the words that wavered in and out of focus.

Doe soft eyes, lips that show a faint inviting smile
All answered.
Remember,
And in remembering leave no regret.
For what has passed, though gone, was good.

Angie let out a low moan and doubled over. *How can his memory impale me after all these decades?* She began to rock silently, pushing images of the coach back into the box in her mind until she was strong enough to slam the lid. Gradually, the pounding in her ears quieted, and her breathing calmed. When she raised her head, her eyes were clear, and her hands had stopped shaking. She refolded the page and slid it into the journal. Glancing at the end of her last entry, she saw more familiar handwriting, her mother's Gothic script. So she had read the journal. Why did that not surprise her? And why did the knowledge not disturb her? She worked to decipher the swirls and humps of her mother's message written in German.

Dear Angelika,

I think maybe we didn't handle the situation with the coach very well. But we always loved you and were very proud of you. I know you didn't always think I was a good mother, but in this new land and so many differences between our generations, I did my best. I know I never told you I loved you, but that wasn't how I was brought up. My way to show love was by pushing you to be good and kind, to always do your best, and making you work for the things you wanted so you would grow up strong and independent. Sometimes that meant I had to be hard on you, punish you, so you would learn.

My biggest regret was banning you from my life for a year. I wish I would have been there to see my daughter get married. I'm glad you found it in your heart to accept me back into your life. I hope you will remember me with kindness and love.

Mit Liebe, Deine Mutter

Angie felt the hard lump in her chest release into her mother's words echoing through her mind. Rising slowly, Angie picked up a pen from the work bench.

July 10, 2003

Dear Mom,

After we left Beaupré-sur-lac, I was always haunted by the question: Where do I belong? It made me restless. As an adult, I was on a constant quest, for a better job, a higher degree, another man. I was always certain that something better was just outside my grasp. It was easy to blame you, your constraints and expectations, for making me into that person who could never bask in the sunlight because she was too busy reaching for the next shiny star. I know now that was unfair. You and Dad did the best you could even though you had different outlooks on how you should raise me. I'm sorry I was the cause of so much friction between you. The year we were apart was very hard. When I think back, that year was when I started to understand that whether we agreed or not, I needed you in my life.

The way my life has gone, the good and the bad, is a result of my choices, and I have learned to stop blaming you. Thanks to you I can keep my nose to the grindstone and capitalize on opportunities, and thanks to Dad I remember to look up and take in the beauty and wonder around me along the way. I truly have ended up being a blend of you both, and have made a place in the world where I belong to myself. I think I've turned out alright. I'm not a mother but I am a grandmother. I'm a wife, a lover, an English-Canadian with German blood and a French-Canadian with a German heart.

I love you, Mom.

Angelika

Angie laid the book into the bottom of the bin, handling it like a valuable heirloom.

"Wow, babe! This looks terrific." Paul's stocky frame was silhouetted by the sun as he stood in the open doorway.

Angie finished putting the rest of her life's memorabilia into the bin as her new husband walked across the garage.

He took her hand and pulled her to her feet. "What's in there?" He peered over her shoulder.

"Just some of my old childhood stuff." Angie clicked the lid in place and carried the bin to the storage shelf.

Paul helped her hoist the three larger bins in place, then turned and pulled her into his embrace. He brushed her hair back from her face. "This must have been tough. You okay?"

Angie's mouth moved into a broad smile as she gave a deep sigh. "Yeah, I feel great, actually."

Leaning back, Paul's eyes raked across her face, stopping when they connected with hers. His expression narrowed.

"What" asked Angie.

"You look different…lighter…peaceful maybe?" He smiled. "I like the headband."

Angie pulled the band backward through her hair. "I hated wearing hats when I skied so my mom gave me this pattern to try. It was the first thing I made knitting in a continuous circle on four needles. My mom showed me how to change colours to make the snowflake pattern as I knitted." She ran the band through her hands as if examining it for errors. "I'd have to keep ripping back rows because of mistakes. When I got frustrated, my mom would tell me to put it aside. Miraculously, the next day when I'd pick it back up, I couldn't find the mistake." Angie gave a little laugh. "It took me a while to realize that Mom was fixing the mistakes after I was in bed."

"Well, I think it's perfect. You should wear it next winter." He headed toward the door. "Do you want me to make lasagne for the family dinner tomorrow?" Paul's son and daughter, their spouses and children descended on their home once a month for Sunday dinner. It was a tradition Angie had initiated. With all her relatives living in Germany, it was an experience she'd never had but one she'd always longed for growing up.

"No, I got the meat for *rouladen.*"

"Great! The kids love those." He kissed her neck. "And your famous Black Forest mountain cake?"

"Sure." She laughed.

AUTHOR AFTERWORD - LEGACY

My Oma was a knitter. When she was six, her mother moved my Oma's tiny fingers through the motions of inserting the right needle under a stitch on the left needle, pulling through a loop of yarn, and slipping the new stitch over to the right.

When Oma married, she spent every evening knitting by the wood stove under the light of a lantern Opa had hung above her chair. Her right foot rocked the cradle. Over twenty years, bridging the Great War and its aftermath, she and Opa worried for the future in socialist Germany to the rhythm of the clicking of her needles while their eleven children slept upstairs. On each of her daughters' eighth birthdays—Oma thought six was too young—she put needles in the girl's hands and moved her fingers the way her mother had taught her. The child would then join her mother and sisters in front of the stove, knitting hats, mitts, scarves, socks, and sweaters for the family. My mother was one of those daughters.

Once everyone was asleep, Oma would pick up a child's work, correct mistakes, and add a few rows. Her heart glowed watching the secret smile when the daughter found her work had grown overnight. No daughter ever shared with her sisters what had happened, choosing to believe she was so special that her mother had gifted this progress to her alone. The reward for completing a project was a coveted free evening.

Oma taught her girls to carry different colours of wool behind the stitches, so every scrap could be worked into different coloured stripes. When sweaters wore out, they were unravelled and made into socks. When money was tight, the older girls would stay home from school for several days and produce sweaters that Oma could sell to the rich people in the large houses on the hill.

Even when the cradle was finally empty, Oma's right foot continued to move in time with her needles. When Alzheimer's robbed her of her memories, the muscles in her fingers continued to knit with a mind of their own. Every July 14, I squeeze my hands into the rough, grey mittens with the red thumbs that Oma gifted me when I was twelve, while memories of the family reunion celebrating her eightieth birthday flood me.

My mother brought her knitting skills with her when my parents immigrated to Canada. She knitted hats, mitts, scarves, socks, and sweaters for our family, as well as dresses, skirts, and Barbie doll clothes for me, her only child. Even without a baby in a cradle, her right foot moved in rhythm with the clicking of her needles. Mornings were for cleaning, baking, and laundry. Every afternoon, she knitted while watching her soap operas. Every evening after supper, she knitted, only putting down her needles at ten o'clock to watch the CBC newscast before bed. Except for Saturday.

All work stopped when *Hockey Night in Canada* started. When they'd arrived in Canada, my mother had heard you had to watch hockey to be a real Canadian. After one game, she became a lifelong Toronto Maple Leafs fan.

On my tenth birthday—she thought eight was too young—she put needles in my hands and moved my fingers the way her mother had taught her.

When we had all we needed, she knitted for the church Christmas bazaar and the hospital auxiliary. Soon, she began taking orders from friends and neighbours—twenty-five dollars plus the cost of materials for an adult sweater, fifteen for a child's, ten dollars for a baby sweater, hat, and booties. The *Sifton Products/Mary Maxim* mail order catalogue became her supplier since the shops in the isolated northern communities where we lived didn't carry yarn. And I became her clerk, completing the order form and cheques because my mother felt her written language skills were inadequate. From her chair in the living room, my mother knitted multi-coloured patterned sweaters for the cost of my father's trip to Germany to attend his father's funeral. She knitted twisting cable and honeycomb patterns to realize her dreams—wall-to-wall carpeting for our nine-hundred-square-foot home, new dining room furniture, and a colour television.

Alzheimer's erased my mother's ability to read, but her fingers continued to knit with a mind of their own. When I cleared out her condominium after her death, I found certificates from Guardian Angels recognizing her contribution of one thousand hats for premature babies. She'd kept the thank-you letters from the nursing home where she'd donated dozens of knitted lap robes for people in wheelchairs. Every February, on my birthday, I pull on the four-coloured, Nordic-patterned sweater, the last one she made for me, and I murmur a thankful prayer to my mother's spirit.

I am a knitter. My mother's knitting needles are my tools. My right foot moves to the rhythm of my needles even though I've never had a child to rock in the cradle.

I knit hats, mitts, scarves, socks, and sweaters, for my step-children and step-grandchildren using the cable, honeycomb, and multicolour-pattern knitting I learned from my mother. Weekdays are for working, but winter evenings and weekends are for knitting or crocheting while sitting on my sofa watching television. When my family members have what they need, I knit for the homeless and women's shelters in my community. The hospital auxiliary gift shop sells my stuffed mini unicorns, teddy bears, angels, and giraffes to raise money for diagnostic equipment.

An infinite variety of yarn is readily available in box stores and wholesalers within an hour's drive from my home. Sometimes, I visit the small yarn store on the main street of our village for specialty yarns. But mostly, I order online from *Mary Maxim*. After all, she's been part of my family for decades.

I especially enjoy knitting during football games. The complex plays drawn on the screen by the commentators are like carrying different colours of yarn to create an image on a sweater. The frequent breaks in play of the game allow me to concentrate on a complicated pattern, and I can rely on the endless replays to show me what I may have missed while glancing down at my work.

My daughter-in-law is a knitter. She knits dishcloths and hair scrunchies, neck warmers and toques. Together, we sell our wares at Christmas bazaars, autumn harvest celebrations, and farmers' markets, depositing our earnings into her baby daughter's education fund.

I hope, one day, I will put needles into the hands of my granddaughter and perhaps my grandson, and move their fingers the way my mother taught me. I think ten would be a perfect age. I'll start with knit and purl and teach them more complex stitches when they express interest. They'll make a scarf to begin.

When Alzheimer's comes, I hope my fingers will remember how to knit with a mind of their own.

I come from generations of hard workers aspiring to live an honest life. Our family property in Germany was confiscated after the wars. Our heirlooms were looted by the Russians. But the art of knitting for family and community will be our legacy as long as we put the needles in the hands of our children.

ACKNOWLEDGEMENTS

I wrote this book to shed light on the universal struggles of the immigrant experience. It takes unfathomable courage to leave behind everything you love and know, and start over in an entirely different world, especially when you are uncertain of your welcome. Angelika's story is drawn from events in my own life. Names have been changed and details have been adjusted to serve the flow of the story.

I would like to thank my parents, who brought me up knowing my German family and culture. The stories of their childhood and the challenges they faced as immigrants to Canada in the 1950s live in the chapters and scenes within the book. Without their love and support through all our differences, I wouldn't have grown into the person I am today.

Writing is a solitary pursuit that requires many partners on the journey to a final manuscript.

Thank you to my editor, Maggie Morris (The Indy Editor), and my beta readers Connie Bryce, Susan Doornbos, Nicole Woods, and Maralyn Quinton. Without your keen eyes, deep insights, and inconvenient questions,

I would not have had the courage to plunge fully into the dark holes.

Thank you to my fellow writers at the Niagara Branch of the Canadian Authors Association and the CommuterLit Writing Circle who freely offered critiques to bring clarity to the narrative, and texture to the characters.

Thank you to the team at FriesenPress for their professional advice and management of the details, small and large, along the publication path to ensure the final product is worthy of sharing with the world.

And finally, thank you to Ron Whitman, my singer/songwriter husband, my biggest supporter, and my partner as we nourish and grow our individual artistic sides in retirement.

Printed in the USA
CPSIA information can be obtained
at www.ICGtesting.com
LVHW041747050724
784732LV00002B/31

9 781038 312228